Keeping Katerina

Keeping Katerina

The Victorians Book 1

Simone Beaudelaire

Acknowledgments

I would like to thank my dedicated team of beta readers without whose help this story would not be what it is. Thank you, Guy, Sandra, Leslie, Reed, Jill, Shirley, and Sue.

This book is dedicated to all survivors of child abuse.

Chapter 1

"ou want me to do what?" Christopher Bennett gawked aghast at his mother.

Julia returned his gaze levelly. "It's not so much to ask, son. She's a lovely girl, and I want to introduce you to her."

Christopher rolled his eyes heavenward in disgust. As he counted slowly in his mind, trying not to snap at her, his gaze lingering on his surroundings.

Billows of eye-stinging smoke poured from several chimneys atop the multi-story brick building—the cotton mill where Christopher worked. Even from the street, the hiss of steam boilers and the clank of machinery reverberated loudly. The streets around the factory, filthy with ash, and the tenement slums on either side sat forlornly under a blanket of garbage and soot.

The chill, humid air clung to the mother and son, moistening their skin with musty dew. A breeze picked up, sending the cold straight through Christopher's coat, which he had flung hastily over his shoulders and left unfastened.

He shuddered. When the wind passed the tenement, it picked up a vile aroma of human waste and unwashed bodies. *What a terrible place to live, so close to the factories, but for thousands of the poor of London, there's no choice. Thank the Lord none of them works for us. Every time I prepare the salaries for our workers, I remember that, but for our generous salaries, they might end up living here. It's worth what we give up in profits.*

A small and skinny child sat on the step across the road, dressed only in a thin nightgown despite the biting January cold, playing with some unidentifiable piece of trash.

The scene did nothing to soothe Christopher's temper, and his voice, when he spoke, sounded harsher than he'd intended. "Mother, I'm much too young for you to play matchmaker with me. I'm nowhere near being ready to get married."

"What a shame," Julia Bennett said, sweeping a strand of fiery hair away from her forehead and tucking it back under her bonnet. "You're twenty-four, just the age your father was when we got married. Please, son. I'm not asking you to marry her, just to let me introduce you."

"Why?" Christopher insisted.

* * *

This time Julia had to take a moment to consider her words. *I hate being here. While I approve of how my husband and son run this factory, I despise the heat and noise and filth of the place, not to mention its squalid surroundings. Tenements like this one are a breeding ground for cholera.* She shuddered in disgust. *Why the devil am I here?*

She knew the answer, though she didn't want to explain everything yet. *How can I explain to my son that an everyday visit with friends naturally led to a turn at the harpsichord, which then revealed what the long, lace sleeves had hidden?* She shook her head. It wasn't the first time she had encountered such heartbreaking marks on the poor girl, and Julia longed to take her away and keep her safe.

Alas, Katerina is my friend, not my daughter, and I have no right to interfere, but there is another way to wrest her from the care of that monster. It was an impulsive plan, fraught with potential disaster, but here she was anyway.

Christopher regarded her expectantly.

What to tell him? Something true... but not the whole truth. Not yet. "Why introduce you to her? Because she's not very popular, and there's no reason for it. I want everyone to see there's nothing wrong with her. Meeting a handsome and popular young man will help with that."

"Why do you care?" he asked.

She gave him a disapproving look, condemning his sarcasm, but answered, nonetheless. "She's my friend."

His eyes narrowed in suspicion. "How old is this woman?"

Julia threw up her hands in a gesture that recalled her less than genteel upbringing. "Don't look at me like that," she exclaimed.

The child across the street glanced sharply at them.

Julia lowered her voice. "Katerina is not a dowager. She's nineteen, I believe, and quite pretty. Please, son, can't you do this one thing for me? Just meet her?"

* * *

I suppose I cannot refuse. Once Mother digs her heels in, there's no moving her. Since she's decided I need to meet her friend, she will not let me hear the end of it until I do. Better to get it over with quickly. "Oh, all right then," he agreed sourly. "I suppose you can perform the introductions tonight. I'll meet her, but if she's some kind of pariah..."

"Oh no," his mother said quickly, making another of her famously unrestrained gestures, "just a bit shy, a bit of a wallflower. Nothing more."

"Katerina what?"

"Valentino," Julia replied. Her eyes bored into him, but he had no recollection of any such name.

"Italian?" Christopher asked, feigning interest.

"Her parents came from Italy," she explained. "Katerina, as far as I know, has lived in England her whole life. She looks rather Italian, but her manners and speech are very English."

"I see," Christopher replied. Inwardly he still recoiled at the thought of this obvious manipulation. "Fine. Tonight, at the ball, I'll allow you to introduce us, but that's all. Any further actions I take will be decided by me."

"I understand, son."

Christopher stalked back inside, slamming the heavy oak door.

* * *

Once he withdrew, Julia sagged with relief as she climbed into the waiting hansom cab. *If he meets Katerina, it will be a start. Something has to be done to help the poor girl I'm willing to give all my resources— even my firstborn son—to accomplish it. I only pray it will be enough.*

Chapter 2

"ᴮENNETT, glad you could make it." James Cary, one of Christopher's friends commented, extending a glass of brandy.

"Of course, of course, Cary. What did you expect? My mother wanted to talk to me." Christopher rolled his eyes, gratefully accepting the glass. He sank onto a high-backed sofa of carved wood with blue velvet upholstery; the best seat in the brick row house provided to Cary as vicar of a small, working-class neighborhood chapel.

A threadbare blue and black oriental rug on the floor and a mahogany table where he had arranged his prized collection of leaded glass bottles and decanters decorated his parlor. The rich burgundy and brown hues of the liquors inside the bottles gleamed dully in the fading light.

"About what?" came a voice from one of the armchairs beside the fireplace. Colin Butler, Viscount Gelroy, swallowed from his own glass, perhaps a little more deeply than was wise.

"A woman. What else?" Christopher replied, taking a more modest sip of his own.

"Did she finally hear about your opera singer?" Colin asked, smirking.

James grinned.

"No, not that one." Christopher grimaced. "You know," he drawled, "you two have gotten a great deal of conversation out of a single night that had more to do with wine than passion. It was eight months ago, and anyway, she was really not worth the trouble."

"Then who?" Colin asked.

Christopher rolled his eyes heavenward. "Mother wants to introduce me to her young friend. I fear she's matchmaking."

"Oh, Lord. Who?" James asked, raising his glass to his lips.

"Miss—or should I say Signorina—Katerina Valentino."

Colin stared open-mouthed at Christopher's words, and James choked on his brandy.

"What?" he demanded. "Is she hideous?"

"No," Colin said cautiously, "she's... powerfully timid."

"Boring, really," Cary added. "I tried dancing with her once. Felt badly she was standing alone. I don't think I saw her eyes once during the entire waltz, and if she said a word, I didn't hear it."

That didn't sound promising. Christopher flung himself backwards against the upholstery and glanced out the window, taking in the details of his surroundings, as was his habit.

In the brilliant crimson light of the sunset, the red bricks of the row house across the narrow cobblestone street seemed to glow, the light diffused by the particles of soot that always hung in the air. *In a city whose population has been swelling and is predicted to reach nearly six million in the next decade or so—with nearly all homes warmed by coal— smog and pollution are inevitable.* The added soot from steam-powered factories only made it worse.

A strangely-scented draft seeped around the window, reminding Christopher that the vicarage also sat uncomfortably close to the Thames. The stench of the river could be overpowering at times and living near it was certainly no blessing. "Well, I told Mother I would meet her, so I will. If she's nothing, at least I can say I tried." Christopher sighed, taking another sip of his drink.

Cary snorted.

"So, gentlemen, what do we have to look at today? Something... intriguing?" he asked, changing the subject "That 'newly discovered' work by Byron?"

"I read it. It was an utter fraud." Cary dismissed it with a wave of his brandy glass. "I suspect a barrister-in-training. It reads like legal documentation. No, no. I have something we've never seen before."

"What is it?" Christopher asked, leaning forward.

"The poet is called... Browning."

"Elizabeth Barrett Browning?" Colin complained. "Her poetry is hardly worth our time. A lot of girly sonnets to be used on susceptible young women. I'm not trying to woo one of you."

"No, idiot," Cary rebuked his friend with a laugh, "her husband Robert. I've never read any of his works before, but the title is promising."

"And that is?" Colin pressed.

" 'Porphyria's Lover,' " James announced, lifting a folio from his side table and producing a crisp sheet of printed paper.

Christopher raised his eyebrows. "It does sound intriguing. Perhaps he'll be the next Shelley. Who's reading?"

"I'll read," Colin volunteered, grabbing the folio from James' hands. " 'The rain set early in tonight/ The sullen wind was soon awake,' " he began, and then continued reading.

As he progressed through the poem, Cary raised his eyebrows in pleasure as the young lady partially undressed and cuddled up to her lover. And then, the poem took an unexpected turn.

" 'I found/A thing to do, and all her hair/in one long yellow string I wound/three times her little throat around/And strangled her.' "

Cary's eyebrows snapped together, and Christopher had to tighten his jaw to prevent it from dropping open. *This is no lascivious love poem.*

Colin started at what he had just read but bravely continued to the end, as the murderer embraced the corpse of the woman who had once loved him. " 'And yet God has not said a word,' " he finished.

"Good Lord," Cary said at last, dark eyebrows rolling like a ship on the sea of his discomfort. "What the devil was that?"

"I don't know," Colin replied. "I've never heard anything like it. How... distasteful."

They both looked at Christopher. The subject matter appalled him, and yet... a new thought germinated, took root, and grew. "I think he was trying to make a point rather than a beautiful poem," Christopher said cautiously. "Social reform, you know? Speaking out against violence towards women. Certainly, things like this do happen."

"Are you defending it?" Colin's disbelief hung heavy in his voice. "It's terrible. It hardly rhymes. I'm going back to Tennyson. At least he's elegant. Besides, any girl stupid enough to trust such a madman deserves what she gets."

"Perhaps," Christopher said without thinking, his mind preoccupied with trying to understand what he felt—let alone thought—about all the new ideas the poem had generated.

"I think you've been talking to your mother too much," Cary said, breaking the tension with a laugh.

The teasing bark shook Christopher's mind back to the present.

"It's only a poem, Bennett," Cary added. "Don't read so much into it. As for me, I've had enough for one evening. Shall we go get some dinner at the club?"

"Yes, I think so," Christopher replied, shaking off the somber mood of the poem. "Colin?"

"Sorry, no money." The young nobleman shook off the offer with a shrug but hunger glowed fever-bright in his eyes.

"I'll pay for you," Christopher offered.

Colin swallowed. "Very well."

Setting aside their glasses and collecting their coats, they went out.

Chapter 3

 HAT *a tremendous crush. It will be difficult to find room to breathe, let alone dance, in this environment.* He took in the sweaty mass of rarified humanity and sighed. The heat already clenched him like a fist, despite the icy wind blowing outside. *I hate this. Oh, for a smaller, more intimate kind of entertainment: a few friends, a good meal, some interesting conversation. At least I could hear the music.*

Flickering gaslights in the room provided better illumination than candles, but the compressed carbide flames only added to the warmth. A bead of sweat dripped down his cheek.

Feet pounded on the polished wood floor of the ballroom as he picked his way around the edges, near the hand-painted wallpaper the hosts had commissioned. Christopher had seen some terrible wallpaper commissioned by those whose wealth exceeded their taste, but in this home, at least, an attractive pattern of what looked like the eyespots on peacock feathers embossed on a rich silver background embellished the walls from the polished wooden wainscoting to the ceiling. Christopher traced a silver oval with the tip of his finger, enjoying the texture.

It took Christopher fully half an hour to find his mother in the mass of milling, sweaty bodies. Had he been thinking more clearly, he would have found her sooner. Wisdom would have dictated he look near the open doors to the balcony, where blasts of wintry air lightened the sultry atmosphere. Julia Bennett stood with her back to the door, letting the wind ruffle her skirt.

A brown-haired woman beside her turned out to be one of her closest friends, Colin's mother Mrs. Turner. After her marriage to Viscount Gelroy when she was extraordinarily young, she had remarried, not another nobleman, but a soldier, tossing her title away like rubbish.

Christopher approached. Tonight, his mother wore a lovely dress in a shade of soft blue, which complemented her rich, fiery hair. She had just celebrated her fortieth birthday had a few silver streaks in the glowing mass, a few crow's feet around her eyes, but that made her no less lovely.

Standing with the matrons was a taller, younger woman. *This must be the one I'm supposed to meet. She certainly looks Italian, with her dark brown hair.* Her skin, a darker shade than Julia's, had a hint of warmth to its tone, which spoke of foreign shores and stronger sun. *She has quite a pretty face,* he noted. Her nose was a trifle on the bold side, but not unpleasantly so, and her teeth flashed white and straight.

He arrived at her side, and she met his eyes for a frozen moment. In that heartbeat of connection, Christopher discovered something extraordinary. *She's more than pretty. She's lovely. Something undefinable flared to life between them, riveting him to the spot.*

The young woman sucked in a breath and her gaze skated nervously away. Her retreat broke the spell, and Christopher turned, masking his startled reaction by feigning normalcy. "Good evening, Mother," he said, kissing her cheek. "Mrs. Turner." He reached out to clasp her hand.

"Good evening, Christopher." His friend's mother, who had always been more like an unofficial aunt, greeted him warmly. "How are you?"

"I'm well, thank you," he replied. "Your son sends his regrets."

"I'm sure." Disappointment tightened her face.

"Good evening, son," Julia said, turning the attention from Colin's hopeless mess to the present. "May I introduce you to a friend of mine?"

"Certainly, Mother." Christopher's gaze turned from Mrs. Turner to the lovely woman his mother wanted him to meet.

"This is Miss Katerina Valentino. Katerina, my son Christopher Bennett."

He took the delicate, long-fingered hand and lifted it to his lips, and then raised his eyes to hers. She met his gaze for another long, unguarded moment, and then a wave of nervousness visibly washed over her and she dropped her eyes to the floor.

As Colin said, powerfully timid. "Pleased to meet you, Miss Valentino. How do you like the party?"

She replied so softly he couldn't hear her.

"Katerina," his mother said gently, "It's very loud in here. You needn't screech but do raise your voice a little."

She took a deep breath. "It's... crowded. The hosts must be quite popular." Her voice had a delicate and well-modulated pitch, and the sound sent an agreeable shiver up Christopher's spine.

I could listen to this woman talk for hours, he thought, enjoying the sensation.

Wait, what? Get ahold of yourself, man. "Yes, they are," he said, returning to the mundane conversation.

"I was... glad to be invited," she commented idly, though the force of will required for her to utter the simple phrase made it seem more important than it was. She tugged on her hand.

Christopher blinked, suddenly realizing he'd forgotten to let go. Her fingers fell from his grip. "I am also glad you were invited," he said, trying to be charming.

A hint of color stained her cheeks.

So, she's susceptible to a compliment. Good.

She glanced up at him again, meeting his eyes briefly. "The violin is... out of tune."

Christopher listened. *What an astute comment.* "You're right. I suppose hiring the highest level of musicians isn't necessary in this din. Do you like music then, Miss Valentino?"

"Yes, very much." She raised her head at that, and he saw a hint of passion in her eyes.

"Do you play any instruments?" he asked, thankful to have stumbled upon a means of prolonging the conversation.

"The pianoforte," she replied.

"Well?" he pressed.

Her eyes met his. "Yes."

He raised his eyebrows. While most young ladies did learn to play the instrument, admitting right out that one played well—rather than well enough or some other self-deprecating comment—might be considered immodest. However, given how shy she was, she might be giving a modest assessment of her talent. *How interesting it would be to hear that hint of passion expressed in music. I hope she isn't too shy to play for me sometime.*

Wait, what? Why am I thinking of another meeting? This is a favor to Mother, nothing more. His internal argument distracted his attention, allowing his mouth to carry on flattering the girl without his full consent. "I would enjoy hearing it. I love music. Alas, I have no talent."

"He exaggerates," Julia interjected. "He sings rather well."

Christopher shrugged. "Perhaps." *Only in your mind, Mother. I sing like an amorous bullfrog.* "Well, Miss Valentino, would you care to dance?" Though the invitation escaped before he could consider its wisdom, he could feel no regret. The opportunity to touch Miss Valentino was not to be missed.

The young woman looked up at him again briefly and then nodded once, returning her gaze to the floor while her cheeks flamed.

"Very good." He extended his hand into her field of vision.

Hesitantly, she placed her palm in his and let him lead her onto the floor.

"My dear," he told her as the waltz began, "I have a singular problem making conversation with your hairline. If you're a musician, then I'm sure you have enough rhythm to take your eyes off your feet and look at me. Can you do that?"

She raised her face. This close to her, he could see the luscious curve of her lower lip. She had a mouth made for kissing. Her slender body fit perfectly in his arms; tall enough that their position aligned naturally with no need for him to stoop.

"Thank you for asking me to dance," she said softly. "I know your mother put you up to it."

Christopher inhaled in preparation to speak and the soft aroma of lilacs teased him. In the heart of icy winter, this woman smelled like spring. He answered her honestly. "Not at all. She put me up to meeting you. I asked you to dance because I wanted to."

That hint of color darkened her cheeks again. "Why on earth would you?"

"You're quite… pretty, you like music, and you're interesting. Why would I not?"

Her blush darkened further. "Never mind."

It appears her susceptibility to compliments is limited. "Right. So, let's talk about something."

She gave him a considering look but remained silent.

He cast about for a topic. "Since you like music so much, do you have any favorite composers?"

"Beethoven," she replied promptly. "I also like Chopin very much."

He acknowledged her comment with a brief nod. "Not surprising. Do you play other instruments besides pianoforte?"

"Harpsichord. I'm afraid I'm useless on the organ. Those foot pedals defeat me." A hint of a smile teased the corners of her mouth.

Christopher considered what playing the organ must be like. "No doubt. If I'm honest, I have to admit that despite years of lessons, I've never even managed the pianoforte. Do you also sing?"

"I sing well enough."

Now there's the common response. "Alto?" he pressed, not ready to abandon such a promising topic.

"Soprano."

Their progress had led them to the open balcony door and a waft of welcome coolness washed over the couple. "Hmmm. I would like to hear that as well."

"Why?" she asked, tilting her head and regarding him with confusion.

"You're Italian, and you're a soprano. Sounds like opera to me," he teased.

She grinned. "Nothing like that, I assure you."

At the sight of her shy smile, Christopher became even more entranced. *She's more than lovely. She's... glorious.* Between one heartbeat and the next, the vague thought of finding an opportunity to meet her again crystallized into a firm intention. *I'm far from finished with getting to know Miss Valentino.* He sighed internally. *Mother was right.*

The conversation died, and they continued to dance in silence, but not the uncomfortable kind of silence that speaks of a desire to get away from each other. Instead, they engaged in a wordless exchange of attraction.

Christopher studied the details of his dance partner... the curve of her ear, the smooth line of her jaw, the slender column of her throat, the softness of her shoulder where it disappeared into her gleaming white dress, the dip of the bodice where it created the tiniest hint of cleavage. He could see her bosom was small, but on her slender frame, it only looked proportional. In fact, she was rather more than slender, almost emaciated. Her body felt fragile in his arms. A surge of protectiveness welled up, and he squashed it down. *It won't do to become enamored so quickly.*

She shifted her fingers in his grip. The hand in his captured his attention; dainty, but strong, with long, slender fingers; the hand of a keyboard player. *What would it be like to have those lovely hands caress my body?*

Christopher shook himself. *What's wrong with you? This is no time for lewd speculations.* Forcing his mind into safer territory, he savored his dance with his unexpected companion.

The music ground to a halt with a long trill on the out-of-tune violin. Katerina winced.

"Thank you, my dear, for dancing with me," he said as he took her arm in his and led her back to his mother. "May I claim another, later this evening?"

She looked at him, startled.

"Oh, is your card full?" he asked.

"Heavens, no," she replied, as though the answer were obvious. "Don't you think you've fulfilled your duty to your mother?"

"Yes," he agreed easily. "She asked me to meet you. I did. Wanting to dance with you again has nothing to do with her."

Katerina blinked. "Are you... joking?"

"Not at all," he assured her. "Will you consider it, Miss Valentino?"

"I will," she replied.

"Consider it?" he pressed.

"Dance with you." Her cheeks flamed, but she met his eyes steadily.

He smiled at her. "By any chance, do you have the supper dance free?"

Her eyes widened. "Yes, if that's what you want."

"It is," he said, allowing a hint of intensity to filter into his voice. "Shall we plan on it?"

"Yes." Her smile turned shy and she looked away.

He accepted the retreat with easy confidence. *She doesn't trust me yet, but I'll show her she can.* "All right then, here's my mother, and I shall be back to claim you later." He kissed her hand again and headed out of the room.

The crowd thinned in the hallway, dropping the temperature significantly. Christopher sighed in relief. His eveningwear felt uncomfortably hot, and his sudden arousal further intensified the sweaty closeness.

"Blast," he muttered. The last thing he wanted was to be struck by a mad attraction. On the other hand, not exploring this feeling would be much more foolish. *Miss Valentino is delightful, and I want to know her. I will know her. There really is no help for it.*

Chapter 4

 OOD Lord, Bennett," Cary mocked as he opened the door and admitted Christopher into the familiar parlor. "Late again? For your next birthday, I'm buying you a pocket watch." This time he offered a glass of hot, spiced wine, perfect for a chilly evening.

"Sorry, Cary. I've been rather busy lately," Christopher replied, cradling the warm beverage in his icy hands as he took his customary seat on the sofa. He had lost his gloves somewhere and was freezing. "Father and I are making several improvements to the machines at the cotton mill."

Cary nodded. The Bennetts' mill was already one of the most progressive, with children under twelve and pregnant women forbidden to work there, comfortable wages, and safeguards on the equipment to minimize injuries. All this cut into profits, but for the Bennetts, good working conditions netted them the best employees. Not to mention, it felt good to ensure in some small measure the comfort of the working class.

"Where's Colin tonight?" Christopher asked. While he liked Cary well enough in a group, he was not as close a friend as Colin, whom Christopher had known since childhood.

"Meeting with a potential creditor," Cary replied grimly. "The tenant houses on his estate are falling into ruin. He's hoping to get a loan to improve the buildings so people will stay and work the land."

"I must say, the aristocracy's in trouble," Christopher commented.

"They are," Cary agreed. "Poor Colin. He's too stubborn to admit defeat."

"What choice does he have?" Christopher asked.

"None," Cary agreed, "but the land on his estate is so overworked, he'll never grow enough to earn a profit. As it is, he can barely pay his taxes, let alone the debts his ancestors incurred."

Both friends shook their heads at their friend's woes.

"So, what did you find to read tonight?" Christopher asked, changing the subject.

Cary grinned and swallowed his mouthful of wine. "Well, I recall you enjoyed the first Browning poem, so I found you another."

"Lovely," Christopher said sarcastically. "What's this one called?"

" 'My Last Duchess.' " Cary replied, waving his familiar folio.

"Good Lord, the nobility again? All right, let's hear it," Christopher urged.

So, Cary read it, and then he looked at his friend, puzzled. "What happened? I don't understand."

Christopher shook his head. "He killed his wife."

"How on earth do you know that?" Cary demanded.

Christopher crossed to his friend's spot on the armchair and indicated the line with one finger. "Right here. Look. 'I gave commands/Then all smiles stopped together.' "

Cary regarded the paper with lips drawn downward and eyebrows nearly meeting. Then he raised his head, his expression stony. "He killed her for *smiling* too much? That's just unrealistic. No one would do such a thing."

Again, uncomfortable awareness rose up in Christopher. "Do you really believe every woman who is abused has earned it with bad behavior?"

"Well, no, but for smiling?" Cary said incredulously. "And who's the old man telling this to?"

"To the representative of the woman he wants to marry. See the reference to a dowry?" Christopher pointed again.

"Good Lord." Cary shook his head. "I don't like this Browning fellow at all."

"Why?" Christopher demanded. "Because he wants us to think and not merely enjoy pretty words?" "There are women everywhere who are treated terribly. Remember the sister of that fellow we knew at Oxford?"

"Which one?" Cary demanded.

"Williams. Her husband beat her, remember? It was so bad she miscarried. Then Williams hunted him down and beat him."

Understanding dawned in Cary's expression. "You're right. He took his sister and fled to the continent."

Good Lord, man, you're a vicar. You *should be telling* me *these things.* "That's the one. Can you imagine someone hurting Nellie, Cary?"

At the mention of Cary's beloved teenaged sister, his jaw tightened. "Fine. You win. People shouldn't be treated this way."

"Right." Christopher dipped his chin in a curt nod.

Cary shook off the heavy topic. "So, would you like to go for some dinner tonight?"

Christopher shook his head. "I can't. I promised I would attend a musicale this evening."

"What?" Now instead of confused, Cary looked incredulous. "Not the one we talked about last week?"

"Yes."

"But you didn't want to go," he protested.

"Now I do," Christopher replied blandly.

"Why?" his friend demanded.

"There's someone I want to see," Christopher said, remaining deliberately vague.

"Not that one your mother arranged..." Cary rolled his eyes. "Oh, Lord, Bennett. You're going *on purpose* to see Katerina Valentino?"

"Yes," Christopher replied simply, but a hint of irritation spiked.

"Why?" Cary asked, and his tone had the air of asking why someone would hand over a whip and remove his shirt.

"She's intriguing," Christopher said, willing his molars not to grind.

"She hasn't got anything to say," Cary protested.

Christopher's mouth tightened. His eyes narrowed. "True she's not inclined to prattle, but when she does speak, she's articulate and intelligent."

Finally noticing Christopher's reaction, Cary softened his tone. "You got her to talk?"

"Yes."

"About what?" he demanded.

"Music." Christopher snapped, not giving an inch. *You never took a second to try, did you? You waited for her to speak and when she didn't, you dismissed her.*

"Oh."

"Yes. Hence the musicale." He raised one eyebrow, daring Cary to comment further.

Cary conceded with a wry twist of his lips. "Well, good luck to you then. I'll see you next week."

Christopher accepted the capitulation with a parting shot. "Yes. Try to find something more uplifting next time, would you?"

"I'll try." The men shook hands, but the gesture lacked any hint of friendliness.

Christopher left the townhouse and hailed a hansom cab to drive him across town. A hefty bay horse pulled the shiny, black-lacquered vehicle along on two oversized wheels, controlled by a driver seated high on the back, behind the passenger bench. Christopher climbed into the open-sided conveyance and tucked his hands under his legs, thinking longingly of his missing gloves.

Outside the cab, the shabby row houses gave way to a series of little shops: a tobacconist, a grocer, a milliner. He grinned at the sight of the wildly-feathered and brightly colored hats in the window. The shops flowed into another row of homes, this area much statelier than Cary's neighborhood. They pulled to a stop in front of the one on the farthest end of the street; the home of a wealthy, middle-class couple, where a trio would be entertaining a few select guests with harpsichord, voice, and flute.

He arrived a little late, and the music had already begun when he handed his greatcoat to a footman and slipped into the parlor. Walking softly so as not to disrupt the performance, he approached the seated guests. Several were ignoring the performers and conversing softly amongst themselves.

It only took him a moment to locate Katerina. She perched in a corner alone with empty seats on either side, her attention focused solely on the music. He slipped in beside her and placed his hand on the bare space between the top of her long glove and the arm of her pretty, flowered dress.

She started at the soft touch on her exposed skin and turned. Then, recognizing him, she smiled broadly.

He returned her smile. Her skin felt silky and warm.

"Good evening," he said in an undertone.

"Good evening," she whispered a reply.

"Is this seat taken?"

"Yes." Her eyes sparkled.

He raised his eyebrows.

"It's taken by you."

The joke made him smile even wider. "Ah. How's the music."

"Fine so far, although..." she hesitated.

"Although what?" he asked. *Take your hand off the girl, Bennett.* He released her reluctantly while she pondered her answer.

"It's nothing really," she prevaricated, her eyes skating away.

"Tell me," he pressed, wanting to know what she thought. At his insistence, she returned her gaze. The warmth of her brown eyes captured him.

"I don't think the contralto is really doing her best," Katerina murmured at last. "Perhaps because so few people are listening. The harpsichordist is excellent."

"And the flute?"

"Perhaps it's best if I don't say."

Christopher listened for a moment. "Agreed. Say nothing. It's a performance completely unworthy of note. Neither good nor bad."

She nodded, agreeing with his assessment, and the light in her eyes showed his observation meant a great deal to her. "Exactly. In some ways, a truly bad performance is better than a tepid one."

" 'So then because thou art lukewarm, and neither cold nor hot, I will spue thee out of my mouth,' " he quoted.

"Revelation 3:16," she said softly, "how apt."

He ran his hand down over her glove, to clasp hers gently. They listened to the ragged performance for several minutes before Katerina shuddered.

"Have you heard enough, Miss Valentino?" he asked.

Katerina wrinkled her nose. "Yes."

"Shall we step out?" he suggested. "I dislike interrupting performers."

That comment earned him a lovely smile.

They left the music room and traversed a corridor lined by a rug of cream and gold scrollwork, bordered in black. Christopher took Katerina's arm and placed it around his, laying his hand on top of hers, where it rested on his bicep.

"Well, Mr. Bennett," Katerina said softly once they were out of earshot, "I'm rather surprised to see you this evening."

He glanced at her, frowning. "Why would you be? I told you I would come."

"Yes, you did," she replied, her expression nervous but otherwise unreadable.

Why so shy, sweet girl? He patted her hand gently. "Did you think I would break my word?"

"I wouldn't hold it against you if you did."

She's more than shy. She simply accepts that no one could possibly want to spend time with her. Well, she's wrong. "That would have been unmannerly," he explained, trying for a neutral response. Confused, affectionate feelings welled up in him, and he continued, his voice growing intense. "Besides, I wanted to see you."

"You did? Why?" This time she spoke with unadorned disbelief.

"Why not?"

Katerina opened her mouth, her hand fluttering around her face. Then, she fell silent, her head dropping as though the carpet fascinated her.

He stopped walking and turned to face her. Removing his hand from hers, he tucked one knuckle under her chin and lifted gently. Sudden connection flared between them. *I honestly want to know you,* he thought, trying to send a wordless message directly to her heart. *To touch you. To kiss you.*

Her eyes widened.

His thumb touched her full lower lip.

She winced.

"What is it?"

She smiled ruefully. "Oh, it's nothing. I bit my lip earlier. It still stings a little."

He looked closer at the tiny red imprint with its bruised, purple outline. "Sorry."

"It's fine," Katerina replied, still smiling.

"Miss Valentino..." Christopher began.

"You don't have to," she interrupted.

"Have to what?" he asked.

"Call me that. I think... I think I would like to be your friend." Her teeth fell into the scab on her lip as she sucked air into her lungs.

Christopher could only blink in silent shock. "So, I should call you Katerina then?" he asked at last.

"Yes, please." Her cheeks turned pink, but her gaze remained steady. *She really does want this little intimacy. Good. So do I.* "My name is Christopher, you know," he pointed out.

"Yes, your mother told me. May I?" Her shy expression spoke volumes of insecurity.

"Certainly."

She smiled at him. Beamed, actually, her face lighting up like a star in the night. His hand still rested on her face, and she leaned her cheek against him.

Her warm, soft touch elicited words in complete comfort that should have evoked nerves. "What would you say, Katerina, if I asked you to accompany me on a drive one day?"

Her smile evaporated, and she lowered her head, shattering the electric connection. The light dawning between them blinked out with the effect of extinguishing a candle. "I can't. My father would never allow it. I'm sorry."

Christopher ran his thumb over her cheek. "Is he so very strict then? Why does he let you come to these events? Is he here?"

She swallowed. "Oh, no. He rarely leaves the house. I'm here because there are many women around. Actually," her voice dropped to a whisper, "he thinks I'm with your mother right now."

"Ah. Does he know she has a son?" Christopher asked, trying to recapture lightness, since the intoxicating connection had been broken.

"I've never mentioned it," she replied.

I wonder why not. How odd. "Katerina, don't you think it might be a good idea for you to broach the subject of a... male friend with your father at some point? Does he not want you to find a husband one day?"

"I think he does not want that," she replied. Something he couldn't quite name flashed across her face. "He wants me to remain with him, to run the household, you see. My future is of little interest to him. I'm sorry, Christopher."

How selfish of him... and how sad for her. "Don't be sorry. It's not your fault he's unreasonable. He cannot keep you prisoner forever. Even the strictest parents eventually let their children go. You'll be no different. Consider it, Katerina. It's usually best to be honest with people."

"He's my father. I know how to handle him best," she snapped.

Goodness. That hit a nerve. He backed off instantly. "Of course. You're quite right. So..." he released her face and wrapped her arm around his instead, leading her down the hallway again, "when will I see you next? Is there another public event where we might meet 'accidentally'?"

"Perhaps." She paused to think without breaking stride. "There is a ball next week. I've received an invitation, but I haven't decided whether to attend."

"I haven't heard of any," he replied. "What is it?"

"Well it's largely for diplomats, you see," Katerina explained, gesturing with one hand. "Lots of foreigners. I don't like it much because the music is poor, and the swirl of languages makes my head spin."

"How many languages do you speak?" he blurted, not sure where the asinine question had arisen from.

She blinked at the sudden change of topic. "Myself? Three. Can you guess?"

"English, Italian and... French?"

"Excellent guesses. You are correct." She rewarded him with a pretty smile.

She seemed willing to indulge his curiosity, so he continued questioning. "Are you fluent in Italian?"

"It's all I speak at home. I learned English from my nanny. Though both my parents had passable fluency, they preferred their native tongue at home."

So that was the source of the occasional exotic flavor he heard in her pronunciation. "Interesting."

"And you?"

"I speak French passably well, and a smattering of German, mostly vulgar words," he admitted with a playful glance her direction.

The admission made her smile again. "With German, even words that are not vulgar sound as though they are. It's a particularly difficult language to sing."

"I imagine," he replied. "I'm also rather good with Latin," he added immodestly.

"So, you're educated then?" she asked, and he could almost hear her pondering it.

"Naturally," he replied. "One of the great benefits of being upper middle class is that I can dabble in a life of leisure but not be corrupted by it because I have plenty of work to do as well."

"Very good. I think too much leisure isn't good for a man." It was almost unheard of for a woman to voice such an opinion, and Katerina seemed to be holding her breath waiting for his response.

"Likely not," he replied with an encouraging smile. "And you? How is your education?"

"Rather self-centered I'm afraid," she replied. "I've never been to school and stopped having a governess quite young, so I've taught myself things I want to know, like music, literature, religion, and so on."

"Religion?" Christopher leaped onto a new line of inquiry. "Are you Catholic?"

"Actually, no," Katerina explained. "My parents found it too difficult to be a Catholic resident of England, so they joined the Church of England before I was born."

"Interesting."

"You've said that several times," she pointed out.

"Well, Katerina, it's because you are," he told her gently. "I really do enjoy talking with you."

"Why?" The stark question revealed a world of self-doubt, as did her lip-twisting, dubious expression.

"Because you're so real," he explained. "You don't simper and giggle and try to guess what I want to hear. You just tell me what you think. I enjoy hearing it."

"Goodness." Her eyes widened. "And here I've been told men prefer a woman with no opinion. Sounds as though nearly the reverse is true."

"Well I can hardly speak for everyone," Christopher admitted, "but I prefer my friends to be who they are, so I can know them. Particularly a friend with such… potential." He allowed the intensity he felt to bleed into the words.

She glanced at him sharply.

He continued. "Perhaps, Katerina, you might prevail upon my mother to walk with you tomorrow. And perhaps I might prevail upon her to invite me?"

She met his eyes with an unguarded expression. "Yes, that would be very nice."

He continued. "As for the ball, do you think a non-diplomatic type such as myself would be unable to attend?"

"Very likely," she replied with a nod, though something of her expression suggested the turning of gears in her mind as she tried to understand where his non-sequitur was leading.

"And your father is certain not to be there?" he pressed.

"He has never once accepted that invitation in all the years I can remember," she replied.

"So, if you forgot your way and accidentally found yourself at a little dinner party with some friends of mine; men and women?" Christopher suggested.

"That might happen," she said with an impish grin. "Where?"

"It will be at the home of the Wilders, a couple who runs a small printing business here in London. Gordon Wilder was just finishing school the year I started, but we met several times and got to be friends. We've formed a little weekly poetry club, him and his wife, me, my friends James Cary and Colin Butler, and a few others."

Her expression turned suspicious at the thought of so many men meeting in a home.

Christopher hastened to explain. "It's a totally respectable group. No young lady who attended would need to fear for her reputation, and we have several who come regularly. Everyone takes turns ferreting out new works to share. We've hit on a writer who might... well please is the wrong word. It's terrible stuff, but it might just incite some interesting conversation."

Her nerves eased. "I would enjoy that. I do like poetry."

"It's not for the faint of heart," he warned, wondering how she would react to the Browning.

"I'm ready for anything."

Christopher grinned at her words. In another woman's mouth, they might have been seen as a flirtation, even an invitation, but Katerina's obvious innocence showed she meant the words literally; that she liked poetry and was willing to listen to it.

"Famous last words, Katerina. Now then, my dear, here we are at the balcony." Sure enough, the arched, wood-framed doors appeared before them. "What would you think if we... stepped outside on it?"

* * *

Her breath caught, and her heart sped up. "I scarcely know. I've never been... taken to the balcony before."

"Would you object?" he asked, and his expression looked suddenly vulnerable.

"I don't think so." She felt hesitant but could not disguise the note of curiosity in her voice. *I hope I don't sound too eager. It won't do for Christopher to think me a hussy.*

He swept her out the door. Far from the partial warmth of the drafty parlor, the chilly wind teased her through the thin fabric of her gown and disarranged her hair. Instantly freezing, Katerina suppressed a shiver as best she could.

A sliver of moon, like the clipping of a fingernail, peeped between the naked branches of the trees that rose from the garden below. She looked up at Christopher, wondering what was next.

"Do you know why men take women to the balcony, Katerina?" he asked her, and the intensity in his voice had bled to heat.

Can he really mean what he seems to be saying? Her heart began to beat faster. "Yes."

"And do you fancy trying it?"

She swallowed but did not speak.

Tell me how you want this done, love," he urged.

"What do you mean?" she whispered.

"I'm offering you a kiss. Do you dream of being kissed, Katerina?"

Oh, Lord, he does mean it, and he's such a handsome man, and so kind. What a magnificent opportunity. "Yes." *Oh, how I want this, and I do like Christopher so. He's perfect.*

"How?"

She didn't know how to answer the question. She didn't even know how to ask for clarification. She gazed into his eyes, silently begging him to explain.

"Do you want my hands on you?" he asked.

Her breath caught. "Yes."

"Where?"

"Around my waist." She mouthed rather than spoke the words. He embraced her, his arms wonderfully warm.

"Where would you like your hands to be?" he continued.

"Your…" her voice stopped. She took a deep breath, drawing in the scent of cologne and aroused man, and tried again. "Your neck."

"Do it then."

She looked at him for a long moment. Then, hesitantly, she slid her arms around him.

"There. Is that just right?" he asked.

"Yes."

* * *

Beneath her barely audible reply, Christopher could feel Katerina's heart pounding against his chest.

"Look up at me." Brown eyes met gray, and another of those unforgettable electric shocks rocketed through him. "Close your eyes, little one, and feel your first kiss."

Her lids dropped. He lowered his head and laid his lips gently on hers. It was a kiss straight out of a dream. Her innocent mouth felt like heaven. Her lips yielded softly, but he applied no pressure, just lingered against her mouth for a long moment. When he lifted his head. She opened her eyes.

"Was that nice?" he asked.

"Yes, very," she breathed, her voice suffused with pleasure.

"Would you like another?"

"Yes."

His mouth brushed hers again. When he released her lips, he kept his arms around her, sharing the warmth of his body. "Please let me talk to your father," he urged. "It's for the best. I think we're going to be seen together often. Wouldn't it be better for him to be consulted right from the first? We have nothing to hide. You're eligible. I'm eligible. I want to be your suitor, see if whatever this is between us stays powerful over time. Don't you want to, Katerina?"

Passion shattered in her eyes, revealing terror that streamed from her like a torrent. "I do. Believe me, I feel it too. I just… You mustn't try to talk to him. It would be terrible. Promise me." Suddenly she sounded panicky, nearly hysterical. "Promise, Christopher. Don't seek him out. Don't ask him to be my suitor. You can't imagine… no. You mustn't!" She wrenched herself out of his grip and fled into the house. A moment later, before he could even gather his wits, she appeared outside. Summoning a carriage, she disappeared into the night.

Startled, Christopher left the icy balcony and stepped into the welcome shelter of the house. From the music room, he could still hear the sounds of the bored contralto, the lively harpsichord, the passionless flute. The whole conversation had taken less than half an hour.

Still wondering what the hell had just happened, he slowly descended the stairs and summoned a hansom for himself, this one pulled by a shining black horse that pranced uncomfortably in the chilly air.

Instead of going to his bachelor apartment at the hotel, however, he headed to his parents' home. As the vehicle clattered through the slippery street, he relived the conversation and the kisses he had shared with Katerina.

Perhaps she became panicked because she allowed the liberty at our second meeting. It's very fast to be talking of suitors, and I certainly won't ask for her hand. Not yet. We've barely met, and I plan to take my time wooing her. As for that kiss, it was an impulsive move, and really too soon, but she was so sweet, so eager. Now I know one thing for certain. Katerina, despite her shyness, has passion hidden inside her, and that's an excellent quality for… someday.

He arrived at the home where he had spent his childhood. For all their wealth, the Bennetts lived modestly, in a middle-class neighborhood in a comfortable spacious home, which was in good repair, but in no way resembled the showy mansions in Mayfair.

He walked up to the front door and knocked.

An elderly servant answered. He was far too old to work, but Christopher's tender-hearted mother hadn't been willing to dismiss him. "Good evening, sir," he said in a quavering voice.

"Good evening, Tibbins," Christopher replied. "Are you well?"

"As well as can be expected," he answered. "The cold, you know? My knees dislike it."

"I'm sorry to hear it," Christopher said indulgently. "Is my mother in?"

"Yes. I believe she's in the parlor," the servant said. He took a step in that direction and then groaned as the tortured joint gave off a noisy pop.

"No need to show me the way," Christopher insisted. "Have a good evening. Rest your knees."

"Yes, sir."

Christopher hurried to the parlor, where, sure enough, his mother had curled up on a scarlet velvet settee near the fire, reading a novel. She looked up at the sound of his approach. "Hello, my love," she greeted him. "Out on such a cold evening?"

"Yes, Mother." He got straight to the point. "What's wrong with Katerina?"

She raised her eyebrows when he said her first name. "So, you've moved to that level already, have you?"

"Yes," he replied, crouching to meet Julia's eyes. "She asked me to be her friend."

Her jaw dropped. "Did she? I'm astonished. She must like you very much. She can scarcely bring herself to talk to most men."

"She seems to feel rather comfortable with me," he explained.

"And you?" she pressed, intensity radiating from her vivid green eyes.

"I enjoy her company," Christopher said. Then he returned tenaciously to the point. "What's wrong with her?"

"Nothing. What on earth do you mean?" She said it too fast, her voice uncertain.

"So, there is something." He sighed. "I want to court her. I asked her if I could talk to her father. She refused."

Though Julia's eyes widened at his admission, she replied in a calm, neutral voice. "She did? I'm not surprised."

"What am I not understanding here? She accepted my kiss." The words escaped before he could stop them, and heat bloomed along his cheekbones.

"Christopher!" Julia sat up straight on the chaise and glared at her son.

"What?" he demanded, crossing his arms over his chest and leaning against the door frame, a study in false nonchalance. "I kissed her. I didn't seduce her. I wouldn't do that." *I would never harm a lady, particularly not this lady.*

"Of course not," Julia agreed. She set her novel aside and stood, pacing in front of the fire, her agitation radiating farther than the heat of the dancing flames. "Listen, she's right. You mustn't talk to her father. If you do, you will cause her all kinds of problems."

"So, he really doesn't want her to have suitors?"

"He really doesn't," Julia concurred.

"But what about her future?" Christopher demanded.

She gave her head a little shake. "It doesn't concern him."

"What kind of father is he anyway?"

Julia gulped. "A terrible one."

It's unlike Mother to say unkind words about anyone, Christopher thought, startled by his mother's vehemence. "How?"

She looked away. "I'm not sure it's wise to tell you, protective as you are. I wanted you to meet her, to be entranced by her."

Christopher sighed at her stalling. "I did, and I think most likely I am, but how on earth can I move forward with this if it must be kept a secret from her father? He has authority over her."

"Yes. Damned shame."

Christopher gawked. He had never in his whole life heard his mother use strong language. "You have to tell me," he insisted.

"Her father..." Julia took a deep breath and swallowed again. Her anger seemed solid enough to choke her. "He beats her."

Silence. Long silence as Christopher attempted, without success, to force her words and his image of his lady friend to integrate. *She's sweet, gentle and quiet. Why would anyone beat her? Mother must be mistaken.*

No. Be honest, man. Mother is no fool. There's some reason she believes it. Finally, he managed to blurt, "Badly?"

Julia bit her lip and nodded, her eyes growing shiny in the dim firelight. "Terribly. You can't imagine. The bruises I've seen... they would break your heart, and it's escalating."

He... no. That can't be. But it would explain everything. Her terror. Her strange secretiveness. An image of Katerina floated in his mind. Wide brown eyes. Bold nose. Full, kissable mouth marred with... "She had a cut on her lip."

Julia closed her eyes. When she opened them, tears shimmered, and she rubbed her face. "You see? I've never known him to hit her face."

"She said she bit it," he argued, trying not to accept the evidence he'd seen with his own eyes. Thought had long since deserted him, and he only disagreed to try to prevent his feelings from overwhelming him.

"If she did, it was because she was in pain."

"Oh, God." Christopher could hardly stand to consider the sweet girl he was coming to care for being brutalized, and yet, with each moment, the evidence of his senses merged with his mother's words to paint a picture he'd never considered. *Here then is the real reason Mother pressed for this invitation.* Pushing up from the floor, he laid a hand on Julia's shoulder, arresting her restless movement. "What do you want me to do, Mother? Why was I supposed to be entranced by her?"

"I want you to rescue her," Julia said, her tone telling him that should be obvious.

"How?"

His mother's eyes bored into his. "Think, Christopher. Only one man's rights over a woman supersede the father's."

Again, his mind attempted to reject her words. "Mother, I've barely met her. You can't mean… you want me to marry her?"

"Yes." The word was simple but firm, and the parental demand in her expression left no room for argument.

A vision of all a marriage would entail flashed before him. Much of it looked appealing, however… "I'm not opposed to the idea, but not yet."

"Every day she stays in his care, the danger increases," Julia pointed out.

Christopher scrubbed at his forehead with the tips of his fingers. His mind buzzed pointlessly among snippets of thought and refused to settle on a single coherent idea. "Just how am I supposed to do this if I can't ask for her father's permission?"

She made a wry face at him. "You know how."

"Elope?" *The buzzing in his head grew into a roar, a pounding in his ears.*

"Yes."

What mother urges such a thing? "This is a very strange conversation," Christopher said, and then wanted to slap himself at the inane comment. *You're babbling. Pull it together, man.*

"I know," Julia concurred. "Think about it, Christopher. When women are abused, the abuser is responsible, but so is everyone who knows and does nothing. I'm her friend, but I have no legal right to separate her from her father. This was all I could do for her."

"Marriage is a big step, Mother," he reminded her, rubbing the middle of his forehead with one knuckle. His hammering pulse had succeeded in making his head throb. "I wanted one like you and Father have. How can I with someone I've just met?"

"I barely knew your father when we married," Julia replied. "What we have has developed over the years. If you make the commitment and the effort, in time, the rest will come."

Christopher shook his head. "It's too soon. I... I understand the problem, but I have my own future to think about too. I'm not going to rush headlong into an elopement with her, no matter how lovely she is."

"I hope you can live with the outcome of waiting," she said darkly.

Christopher took leave of his mother and returned to his apartment in a hotel across town, where he spent an unsettled night lost in painful contemplations, which eventually gave way to terrible dreams of an innocent, dark-eyed girl crying out for help. No one came to her aid, and finally, the pleas cut off and a disturbing silence fell.

Chapter 5

ATERINA walked up to the door of the unfamiliar home, her heart pounding. *I shouldn't be here. If Father ever finds out…* she shuddered and then winced. *It's going to be difficult to act normally this evening.* The pain was intense, and, silly vanity, she had tightened her laces more than usual, wanting to look pretty for Christopher.

This flirtation is a terrible idea. I should leave, but where will I go? Home? The thought made her shudder, but before she could come up with an alternate plan, a gentleman of about thirty years opened the door, ushering her into an entryway lit with softly glowing candles. Trapped, unwilling to flee directly under this stranger's eye, she allowed herself to cross the threshold. To the left, a door stood open, beckoning her.

"Good evening, Miss Valentino," the host said. "Bennett said to expect you. My name is Jack Wilder. Welcome to my home. If you would please step into the parlor."

She nodded and approached the salon where the guests chatted while drinking sherry. They perched on armchairs, chaises and sofas around a cheerfully crackling fireplace with an attractive brick hearth.

"Would you like a glass of wine?" Wilder asked, indicating a tray set on a small table near the door.

Between the pain and the tight lacing, she felt dizzy enough already, so she shook her head.

Christopher appeared seemingly out of nowhere and took her arm. "Good evening, Miss Valentino."

For a heartbeat, she forgot her misery as his handsome face captured her awareness, driving pain and fear back and causing a welling-up of warmth and pleasure in the vicinity of her heart. "Good evening."

"Am I still in your bad graces?" he asked sheepishly.

She bit her lip, remembering the sweet kiss... kisses she'd allowed him to press on her lips. *Allowed, bah. You encouraged him.* "You never were," she replied. Her cheeks burned but she met his eyes, trying to tell him without words that his ardor had not been the source of her retreat. *If only shyness were truly the problem.*

"Good to hear." He grinned and her heart turned over. "I missed walking with you."

"I was... unwell," she explained, deliberately being vague.

His eyes darkened. "Unwell, my dear? I'm sorry to hear it. Are you better now?"

"Somewhat." She changed the subject. "So what does one do at these parties? I admit to finding your description intriguing."

"Well," he led her to an unoccupied settee and perched her there, sitting beside her and clasping her hand. "First, we act as though this were a normal party, conversing, gossiping, drinking and all." He suddenly seemed to notice her empty hand. "You don't have a drink." He seemed about to request one for her.

She laid her free hand on top of his, arresting his attention, and said, "I don't feel like it tonight."

His eyes roved over her face, considering. At last, he replied, "Very well," and then returned to the explanation. "Shortly we'll have dinner, quite a good dinner I might add. It's not until after we eat that the dark events begin to take place." His eyes sparkled with mischief. "It's an orgy of words, my dear. Women have been known to swoon."

Katerina rolled her eyes, although as bad as she felt, it wouldn't take much to loosen her grip on consciousness.

"Come now," a rather tipsy gentleman shouted from a burgundy armchair in the corner, "I'm bored. Can't we start the reading before dinner for once?"

"Now, now, Mr. Reardon," a lovely woman who appeared to be about thirty approached the gentleman and patted his arm, "It's our custom to wait."

He continued to grouse. "But there's no new gossip this week. Nothing at all. The conversation is getting stale in here."

"That's your cravat, not the conversation," a much younger man with sandy hair and a naughty twinkle in his hazel eyes, teased the malcontent.

The drunk colored and subsided.

"Well, he's not wrong," another lady, this one a gorgeous blond with a petulant expression and a pouty lower lip, whined. "There's nothing new to talk about."

"Well, Miss Carlisle," the young man called to her, "come with me and we can create a scandal."

She giggled, "No thank you, Mr. Cary. I would really rather not."

Now it was the young man's turn to pout.

Katerina felt dizzier than ever trying to keep up with the swirling conversations. Though only composed of seven people, to her, the party felt like a crowd... a noisy one. The swish of fabric sounded unnaturally loud in her ears, as did the thuds of booted feet.

She glanced around the room, hoping to fix her eyes on something to steady herself. The hostess wore a puffy brown dress with wild yellow flowers on it. Katerina blinked and turned away. The vibrant green of the blonde's gown assaulted her eyes with its painful brightness. Even the fire seemed to stab at her. A smell of stale cigars hung in the air, which added to her nauseous dizziness.

In desperation, she turned to the back of the room, behind the seating area, and the most welcome sight greeted her. A battered-looking pianoforte sat in the corner.

"Do you think," she asked Christopher, looking intently at the softly gleaming black of the wood, "that anyone would mind if I played the piano for a while?" She indicated the instrument.

"Let me find out." He addressed the room, "My guest, Miss Valentino, has offered to alleviate your boredom with a turn on the pianoforte. Anyone interested?"

"Oh God, another debutante hammering on the piano," the drunk complained. "My dear, have a care. If you play badly, we'll be delighted to eviscerate you in effigy."

"If I play badly," she said softly, "I would deserve no less."

Her comment made everyone gawk.

"Try it." The young man called Cary urged, and several other guests murmured in agreement.

Katerina attempted to stand, but the pressure of the corset against the wounds on her back made the move too painful. "Help me," she whispered to Christopher.

He shot her a concerned glance but rose and extended a hand, lifting her to her feet. Tonight, she had left off gloves, and her bare, icy fingers met his again, this time creating a shock of awareness that left her momentarily even more breathless. Then she inhaled as deeply as she could inside her tight laces and made her slow way to the piano, sinking onto the bench.

"Do you need any sheet music, my dear?" the hostess asked.

"Not at the moment," she replied. "I have a few favorites memorized. Does everyone enjoy Beethoven?"

No one objected.

Katerina took another breath, intending it to be deep, but was unable to manage it within the restrictive boning, She blew on her fingers to warm them, looked a long moment at the keys as though communicating silently with them, and at last positioned her hands on the keyboard. She closed her eyes and began a series of minor arpeggios with her left hand while the right began to form the mournful chords of the famous "Moonlight Sonata."

Though her eyes remained closed, she hit every note exactly right. To create tension and drama, she varied the volume and occasionally drew out the tempo.

Piano can be a rather emotionless instrument, but Katerina knew just how to caress the keys and make them weep. Conversations died around the room, enveloping her in a silence that allowed her to retreat entirely inside herself. Her overwrought feelings poured into the piano keys, momentarily obliterating her awareness of her distress.

* * *

As the sprightly second movement drew to a close, Mrs. Wilder began to worry. The first and second movements were rather manageable for a player of moderate skill. The last was not. Both mournful and dreadfully fast, it was inevitable that a dilettante would hit several desperate wrong notes and the piece would end in disaster. She almost interrupted the performance at the end of the second movement to spare her young guest being torn apart by the less polite members of the group, but she hesitated a moment too long.

Katerina, without pause, launched into a rapid-fire delivery of perfectly-executed notes. She even felt comfortable enough, as she had done in the first movement, to alter the volume and tempo to create more drama.

Amusement gave way to astonishment. *I've heard the Moonlight Sonata played badly; I've even done it myself. I've never heard it played well outside of a concert hall.*

At last, with a lightning-fast scale that climbed the entire keyboard, the piece found its conclusion, and the musician let her fingers fall from the keys. Complete silence enveloped the room, and even the fire seemed to refrain from crackling, giving the performance a well-deserved ovation.

* * *

Though she could feel the eyes on her back like a physical touch, Katerina didn't turn. She sat still on the bench, breathing slowly as spots floated in front of her eyes. *I shouldn't have come. This was a mistake.*

After an eternity that probably lasted five seconds, thunderous applause distracted her from her misery.

"Bravo!" the drunk howled. "Amazing."

"Play another," the pouting girl urged.

"Miss Valentino," Cary called, "do you know the Sonata Pathetique?"

"I do," she said. "May I?" *Please say yes. I need this more than ever.*

"Oh, yes," several voices from around the room urged.

She nodded. Giving the group several seconds to fall silent, she drew inside herself. This piece had proved challenging to her, and she had learned it more recently. It would require a different level of concentration.

She positioned her fingers above the keys and brought them down hard, so the opening chords crashed like thunder. She felt rather than saw several guests jump. The dramatic chords gave way to a rapid run of notes, and then back to chords. Alternating between the two formed the theme of the piece, and for emphasis, she crashed the chords loudly but touched the scales with gentle fingers.

By the end of the second piece, Katerina had completely won over the crowd, and they called for more. She switched from Beethoven to Chopin, and then other composers. By concentrating entirely on her playing, she was able to hold off her impending faint.

Go away, black spots, she willed, pondering what to play next. *While it's not unusual for young ladies to pass out when laced tightly, the loosening of my corset will reveal more than a less than perfect waistline. No one can know. I have to remain conscious.*

"Dinner," a Cockney-voiced servant-girl called from the doorway.

The rustling of fabric accompanied the sound of several booted feet making their way toward the door. Katerina drew in another breath, hoping to calm herself, but her bruised side compressed against her corset, and her vision blurred. Her breath caught in a pained gasp.

Unable to rise from the bench, and in excruciating pain, Katerina waited another moment, hoping for the spasm of agony to pass. A warm hand closed on her bare arm, just above the elbow.

"What's wrong, love?" Christopher asked, "and don't say it's nothing. I can see you're hurting."

"I'm fine," she replied, but the choked sound of her voice gave away the lie.

"No, you're not," he replied. "Can you get up?"

She shook her head.

Christopher slid his fingers down her arm to her hand, taking hold of it gently. She tried to use him as leverage, but it wasn't enough. Her back had stiffened and resisted movement. He sighed and placed both his hands on her waist, lifting her to a standing position. She walked awkwardly out from behind the bench and swayed.

Christopher gripped her waist again, preventing her from falling. Standing face to face, she looked up into gray eyes filled with concern.

"What happened?" he asked tenderly, stroking a bead of sweat away from her forehead.

"Please, I don't want to talk about it," she begged.

"I'm sure you don't, but I'm afraid I must insist. Did he beat you?" he demanded, his voice dark.

Oh, Lord, he knows. She looked away. Tears stung the corners of her eyes and one escaped. Still supporting her with one arm around her waist, Christopher used his free hand to brush away the drop "Why?"

She had to think for several seconds before she could formulate a coherent answer to his question. "He heard a rumor. He often has friends over, though he rarely goes out himself. They tell him things."

"A rumor about what?" Christopher asked.

Tonight, he won't be satisfied with partial answers, it seems. "That I was seen with a man."

"Me?" Guilt twisted Christopher's face.

"Unless it was a lie, there is no other possibility," she replied with brutal honesty.

She watched his throat bob as he swallowed. "How badly are you injured?"

She shook her head. "It's bad."

Christopher's jaw clenched. "Is this why you didn't come walking with mother and me?"

"Yes."

"Do you want to leave?"

That's what a normal person would want, isn't it? To go home and rest? But that was the last thing Katerina wanted. "Where would I go? He's been drinking all day. If I can stay away until he's passed out, I might just make it through the evening unscathed, but if he finds me when he's drunk..." she swallowed. "I'm afraid." She choked again.

"Afraid of what?" Christopher asked, and the worry on his face touched a place so deep inside her wounded heart, she feared her own reaction to it.

The honest truth, one she'd never before voiced aloud, spilled from her lips. "I'm not sure I can survive much more." Another tear escaped, rolling down her cheek.

Christopher drew a breath as unsteady as her shaking legs. "Oh, love. I'm sorry. This is my fault, isn't it?"

Despite her own distress, she tried to comfort him. "No, not at all. There's always something, Christopher. If it weren't you, he would find another excuse. This... flirtation means the world to me. You can't imagine how lovely it is to be able to leave the house and have something to look forward to. At home... it's always the same."

"Flirtation? No, love. This is not a flirtation." His voice grew dark with passion and intensity, and the appealing silver of his eyes turned steely.

"What then?"

"It's a courtship, of course."

Her eyes widened.

"Did you really think my intentions towards you were anything other than honorable?" he demanded.

"I didn't think you had intentions at all," she replied honestly.

"I do."

Much was said in those simple words, and Katerina understood it at last. A courtship was intended to lead to a marriage. Marriage meant the authority of her father over her would end. She could trust her future to the care of a different, hopefully less brutal man. But she knew herself, how desperately damaged she was. *How could I be a proper wife?* She shook her head. "Don't court me, Christopher. I'm no good for you."

"Let me decide what's good for me," he replied.

"I'm broken," she reminded him.

"I'll fix you," he said, brushing his fingers over her cheek.

"You can't."

"I will. If you want to be fixed, it can be done." He lowered his head, kissing her gently.

The touch raised delicious, tingling warmth, just like before. Wanton pleasure streaked through her as his lips compressed hers. His power to arouse passion in her despite her anguish astonished her.

"I want you, Katerina," he said, releasing her mouth. "I want to court you. I like the attraction between us. Don't you like it?"

"Yes, of course. *I haven't liked anything so much in years. Maybe ever.*"

"Do you like being with me?"

"How could I not? You're...quite wonderful."

He seemed for a moment to be at war with himself. Then he said, "I would never suggest this under ordinary circumstances, but let me court you in secret. If I can't do this the right way, let me do the wrong thing the best I can. Spend time with me without telling him. Get to know me. I think there's a future here."

A future with Christopher? Is that even possible? How long until he tires of this game, until his protective instincts give way to annoyance? "To what end? We can never become engaged."

"I know. When we're ready, we'll simply have to elope."

When. Not if. "He'll be furious." She shivered in terror and then winced.

"And as you'd be my wife, he would have to keep his fury to himself because he would no longer have authority over you," Christopher pointed out.

Katerina considered the possibility. The image of life as Christopher's wife washed over her. No fear. No beatings. Just a good man who cared for her. It was too pretty a picture to be real. And of course, she would bring her damaged, cowardly self to the equation. *This is impossible.* Her voice when she spoke sounded harsh. "How can I in good conscience allow you to do this? You want me to be your... sweetheart, maybe even your wife someday, and I just want to be rescued."

He grinned, not the unreserved smile he normally gave her, but one with a hint of humor despite the darkness of the situation. "Rescuing the damsel and marrying her is a fine English tradition, love. What comes after is up to you. Do you want to spend the rest of your life destroyed by the terror of your youth?"

"Of course not."

"Then take the opportunity. We could do well together, you and I."

She looked into his eyes. *He's so sincere, so open, and I'm a morass of dark and fearful impulses, little more than an animal, running and hiding. How could I ever be a true wife to him?* "I don't think I'm able to trust."

One hand lifted to cup her cheek. "Of course not. Not yet. That takes time. Give yourself the time. Eventually, you'll see I won't harm you."

"You're taking a huge risk," she reminded him, leaning into his touch.

"I know. I'm willing."

"You make everything seem possible. How can I say no?"

"Don't." As persuasion, he kissed her again.

There had been not one kind touch in her life in the decade since her mother's death. Christopher's mouth on hers represented every embrace she had missed because her father loved alcohol and control more than he loved her. Unable to resist him, she lifted her aching arms and slid them around his neck, pulling him closer. His hands left her hip and face to encircle her waist. He squeezed her.

Katerina screamed in agony as his arms pressed the bruised flesh of her lower back. She felt a deep scab split open and a trickle of blood ran down her left buttock.

His grip eased instantly. "Oh God, what? What happened?"

"It hurts," she sobbed. The pain of her offended bruises, her own mortification and the dizziness of tight laces conspired to shatter her calm.

Christopher's jaw clenched. "Just how badly are you injured?" he asked again.

She couldn't answer. She was shaking too hard.

Carefully he lifted her, one arm under her knees, the other behind her shoulders, and carried her out of the parlor. He brought her to a retiring room down the hall. After ensuring their privacy with a deft turn of the key in the lock, he laid her gently, face down, on a black velvet chaise in the corner.

"What are you doing?" she demanded, her voice far from steady.

"I have to know, love," he replied.

"Please, Christopher," she begged. "I don't want you to see."

"I'm sure you don't." But that didn't stop him. He opened the fastenings of her dress. As always, when threatened, she froze, trying to become invisible. It didn't work. It never did. She longed to protest, but the ability had long since been beaten out of her, and so she submitted in humiliated silence.

He opened the back of her dress, pulling it down around her waist, turning to her laces. "Love, why on earth did you wear this thing if you're hurting?" he asked.

"Vanity." Her voice caught again. "I wanted to be pretty for you."

"You are pretty," he reassured her tenderly. "Don't hurt yourself on my account again. Promise me?"

She didn't respond. After several minutes of fumbling, the garment fell loose, allowing him to remove it. As her compressed rib cage expanded, the spots swimming in Katerina's vision dissipated. She became suddenly aware of just how compromising their position had become. Mostly naked from the waist up in the presence of a man she had met a mere two weeks ago. If anyone found them... the wedding would become inevitable.

She didn't realize that for Christopher, it already was.

* * *

Through the thin fabric of her linen chemise, he could already see something alarming. The skin of her back was uneven. The garment lay in ridges and furrows as though on newly plowed earth. Gently, he slid the fabric down... or tried to. It stuck to her in several places. His fingers began to tremble as he revealed her body.

Christopher had always adored a woman's back; from the broadest point at the shoulders, narrowing to the waist, flaring at the buttocks, a long line of smooth unblemished skin, perfect for kissing. Katerina's back resembled nothing he had seen before. She was marked from her shoulder blades down, as low as he could see with her dress and chemise tangled around her waist, with thick crossing scars. Some were clearly old; pale cords of ruined flesh. Others, though solid, bore the pink tone of newly-healed skin. Horror of horrors, some were fresh. Deep, terrible marks, cut open and scabbed, revealed a beating bordering on torture. Low on her back, where he had embraced her, blood dribbled from an open wound down her spine. Interspersed among the whip marks, deeper bruises resembled long straight lines, some livid purple, others fading to yellow.

"Oh my God," he said, nauseous with disgust and rage. "What did this?"

"He started with a horsewhip, but it broke."

"And then?" he asked, not sure he really wanted to know the answer.

"A walking stick."

Christopher squeezed his eyes shut for a moment, trying to come to terms with what he had learned. Then he opened them and resumed his scrutiny of her wounds.

One deeply bruised injury wrapped around her side. He gently rolled her, following the line past her ribs, between which the undernourished flesh sank deeply, and onto her belly. There the black and blue bruises lay so thickly that individual impact marks could not be distinguished. Bad as her back looked, the blows to her belly concerned him far more. *She could have been killed.* "How on earth could you play?" he asked, appalled.

"It was distracting," she replied in a soft, flat tone. "It helped."

"This can't go on," he insisted.

"Nothing can be done to stop it!"

Such despair. No one has ever tried to help her. She has never known safety for a day in her life. Resolve hardened in Christopher. "Can you try to trust me, love? I can make it all stop, for good."

"It's too soon," she choked out.

At least she understands what I'm implying. "I know. How often… does this happen?" *Even as he pronounced the words, he yearned to slap himself at their stupidity. As though the heavy scarring doesn't answer the question for you.*

"Often," she admitted. Her breath sucked into her lungs, drawing her flesh even more deeply between her ribs.

"Weekly?" he pressed.

"Yes."

Viciously forcing down his rage, Christopher strived to address the problem. "You were right to worry you might not survive another beating. This," he touched her belly gently, "could easily have resulted in fatal internal injuries. I won't have your death on my conscience."

"You didn't hit me," she pointed out, her eyes pleading for he knew not what.

"But I know what's happening," he replied. "If I don't take action, I'm just as responsible. Marry me, Katerina. Let me take you away from all this. Please?"

She bit her lower lip and winced as her teeth hit the sore spot he'd noticed the other day. "Is this a valid basis for marriage?"

"I have to do something," he insisted, gesturing with his hand.

She flinched away from the movement.

Dear Lord, what a mess. What can the right answer possibly be? Forming the question produced the answer. *No matter how rash, no matter the outcome, I cannot let her die. I* will not *let him kill her.* "As for the marriage, once you're safe, we can work on making it what we want it to be. Please, love, let me help you." He knelt beside her on the floor. He longed to embrace her but could find no place to put his hands that would not cause her agony, so he cupped her face instead. She hissed. Removing his hand, he found it thickly smeared with cosmetics. "What are you covering up?"

"Don't ask questions, Christopher," she begged.

He swallowed. "Fine. I can guess, but there is one thing I have to know."

"What is it?" She lowered her eyelids halfway, as though trying to block out the sight of his banked rage.

"In order to be able to protect you, our marriage has to be… consummated." His cheeks burned, but he forced himself to continue. "The easiest way to demonstrate that is…"

"A bloody sheet?" she interrupted.

"Yes. Is it… possible? Has his abuse ever gone in that direction?" He hated even asking the question, though he knew such things did happen. *Please, Lord, not that at least.*

"I'm not sure what you mean." She blinked, clearly struggling to focus. "I've always wondered where the blood came from."

A hint of tension left his shoulders. "Likely he didn't then. Good. I'll explain the rest later. We should go."

"Go where?" she asked weakly.

"First of all, I need to collect Cary," he explained. "His uncle is a bishop. If we can get him to agree, we can get the license tonight, have the wedding first thing in the morning. It can all be over by tomorrow afternoon."

"All right," she said.

"Yes?" He blinked in surprise. *She's not going to resist the suggestion? Really? Can it be that easy?*

"Yes. I don't want to die, Christopher."

He kissed her tenderly. "You won't. Not now. You've found a champion."

She smiled wanly. *Such a pretty smile.* At last, he noticed that in examining her injuries, he had also revealed her breasts. How lovely they were, small but sweetly rounded, with dusky brown nipples. He felt a jolt of desire mixing into his tender protectiveness.

Carefully he eased her chemise up over her body. He settled her dress into place, startled to note that it fit without the body shaping undergarment. *Vanity is a terrible thing.*

Her modesty restored, he continued, voicing his plan aloud as he made it. "In order to get Cary and his uncle on our side, we need to show them how bad things are. I doubt you're going to want them to see your bare back. If you wash your face, is what's underneath… convincing?"

"Probably," she replied.

With a deep breath, Christopher tucked away his wild imagination and channeled his fury into motivation. "All right. I'll be right back. You wash up." He kissed her once more, briefly, and left the room.

* * *

It took her several tries, but Katerina managed to hoist herself upright and make her way to the mirror. On a wooden commode below rested an ewer, creamy white and painted with pink roses. She washed the heavy powder away from her battered face, sparing herself a single glance in the mirror. *I look terrible. Christopher's going to be furious when he sees.*

Suddenly, Katerina felt ill. She was intentionally defying her father. If they failed, she was dead. She had to trust her future to her little-known champion, a man of two weeks' acquaintance. He seemed kind, but how could she trust him? How could she actually marry him and give him complete control for the rest of her life? *What if he changes after we're married?* She was subtly aware that the abuse a husband could inflict on a wife would be different from that of a father. *Just look at how Mama suffered all those years until she finally died of it.*

In Christopher's defense, *his* mother had been one of her closest friends for the last year. *There's no way such a good woman could have*

49

raised an evil son. Realistically, he should be trustworthy. But the terrified creature inside her shied away from trust. Injured and frightened, nausea at last overcame her, and she stumbled stiffly to the chamber pot, knelt painfully, and vomited.

That was where Christopher and Cary found her a few minutes later.

As the last of the spasms passed, her suitor placed his hands on her shoulders, supporting her.

Cary approached with a glass of cool water. She rinsed, spat and took a deep sip.

Christopher helped her to her feet, turning her to face them. Both men reacted to the sight of her face.

"My God," Cary said.

"Was that the whip?" Christopher indicated a deep bruise on her cheek.

"The stick."

The corners of his eyes tightened. "Are your teeth all right?"

"They seem to be."

He sighed heavily. "Thank God. Cary, do you think your uncle would agree to issue a license tonight? There's no time for the reading of banns."

"And it would undoubtedly prove fatal if we tried," Katerina added softly.

Cary stared at the injury in silence for another moment, and then visibly shook himself. "My uncle is a rabble-rouser. He loves social reform. I think he would be delighted. Let's go right now."

Katerina attempted to take a step, but the room shifted around her. Everything seemed to be moving. She swayed.

Christopher scooped her into his arms. Although the corset had hurt, not wearing it meant the fabric of her chemise chafed her raw flesh uncomfortably. Determined to enjoy the warmth of his arms, she tried to ignore the painful sensations, even when a couple more of her wounds reopened and started bleeding. They would heal, and by then she would be safe.

Safe... does such a place actually exist? How wonderful it would be to find it. It seemed Providence had decreed she had suffered enough and provided her an escape. *If this is wrong, I don't care. Anything is better than waiting for Father to succumb to a fit of rage and beat me to death, and the risk is constant.*

A cab already waited, drawn by a black and white horse, and Cary gave directions to the driver while Christopher settled inside with her on his lap. She winced again as her weight settled on her bottom. He hadn't seen it, but she had the worst, deepest bruises there. It was where he had started, full strength. The pain dragged a confusion of terrifying images into sharp awareness. A rain of stinging blows onto her buttocks and thighs. The wood of his desk felt cold and unyielding under her hands and cheek.

His strokes lost focus, raining at random onto her back, her shoulders. The thick scarring protected her somewhat.

As the memory of the cane flying toward her face bloomed in her memory, a deep shudder tugged at her wounds. Her movement brought her face close to Christopher's shoulder. The appealing scent of cologne and her favorite man broke through.

With luck, this will be the last beating I ever have to endure. Imagine, a life without fear. With Christopher willing to help, I'm determined to make it happen... I only hope I'm able.

The ride to the bishop's home took only a few minutes. They approached cautiously, uncertain of their reception, especially as Christopher still cradled Katerina in his arms. She leaned her cheek against his shoulder, drawing more strength from his touch and the scent of his skin.

Cary knocked.

The bishop himself, wearing a burgundy dressing gown, opened for them and took in the scene with an eyebrow quirked in curiosity. "James, what's happening?" he asked his nephew.

"Can we please come in?" the young vicar pleaded.

"Of course." He ushered them through the door and into a sitting room, where they all settled.

Though her focus remained shaky, Katerina noticed a luxurious oriental rug, a table with an ornate Bible on it, and some threadbare but comfortable furniture, which had obviously been heavily used for many years.

The bishop and Cary selected matching black upholstered armchairs, leaving Christopher the settee. He sank against the back. Katerina breathed slowly to avoid crying in pain. Then she slowly turned to regard the bishop. Through the veil of swimming black spots, she saw him looking askance at her, sprawled in Christopher's lap. Her face burned with embarrassment, but she couldn't move. Once again unconsciousness tempted her like a siren's song, promising blessed relief from her agony.

"All right, James," the bishop said in a dark, suspicious voice, "what's going on?"

"Perhaps Christopher should tell you," Cary indicated his friend.

"Well, Bennett, what the devil are you doing?" the bishop demanded.

"I need a favor of you, Right Reverent Cary. I need a license right away." He stroked Katerina's cheek in a soothing gesture. His touch helped anchor her to her senses.

"A marriage license?" The bishop's eyebrows shot nearly to his hairline, furrowing his forehead into deep lines.

"Yes," Christopher replied simply. Katerina could see his focus was on her and not the conversation. His warm, gray eyes gave her something to hold onto, pushing unconsciousness back once again.

"I see you're making rather free with the young lady."

Christopher glanced at the bishop and Katerina could see the older man's wry twisting of the lips. "I beg your pardon. She's injured." He cuddled her gently.

"Injured?" Doubt hung heavy in the bishop's voice.

She lowered her lids in shame.

"Her father has beaten her nearly to death," Christopher explained. "If I don't marry her immediately, I doubt he'll let her live another week."

In his arms, Katerina shuddered. *He's right, and yet I hate to hear the words aloud.*

"How can I know this is true?" The bishop asked, suspicion thick in his expression and tone. "Sounds like a clever ploy to circumvent his wishes. Has he forbidden you to court her?"

"He's not safe to approach. If you doubt me, just look at what he did to her face." Christopher waved one hand in the vicinity of her cheek.

She recoiled instinctively from the movement.

The bishop approached and regarded the livid bruise.

"He did that with a walking stick. He could have knocked all her teeth out."

Christopher's blunt, horrified assessment of the abuse struck Katerina as strange. *What's been normal my whole life is suddenly abhorrent.*

"I have seen bruises like this feigned before," the bishop pointed out. "A skillful application of cosmetics can easily imitate an injury."

Katerina's breath caught on what must have been the hundredth sob. *Please, Lord, let him listen.* She closed her eyes against the sting of tears.

Christopher growled with frustration.

"Please, Uncle. Listen to him," Cary urged. "Christopher would not be doing this if it weren't vital. Last week he was all for wooing her slowly. Tonight, he's frantic to marry her. Something terrible has happened. Besides, you've known him since we were at school together. You know he's not the sort to take advantage of an innocent woman."

"My dear," the bishop addressed Katerina directly, "you would be best served to listen to your father."

She shook her head, but speech had abandoned her. Her tingling lips refused to follow her mind's commands and her tongue felt useless as a board in her mouth.

"I promise you, I'm not trying to dupe anyone." Christopher's tone softened. "Katerina, I think we need to show him. I'm sorry, love. Will you let him see your back?"

She nodded numbly.

"All right, I'm going to set you on your feet. Don't worry, I won't let you fall. Just lean on me." He stood, still holding her close, and then lowered her to the floor, his arms under hers. She rested her head on his shoulder.

* * *

"Cary," Christopher started. *No. That's too formal.* After everything that had gone on this evening, their friendship had moved to a new level. "James. Can you... can you open the back of her dress?"

"What? Why?" the other young man asked, his entire face scrunched in consternation.

"Trust me. Please," Christopher urged.

He approached. "What in heaven's name is all over her dress?"

Christopher glanced over her shoulder. "Damnation!" *Quiet, fool. Cursing in front of the bishop isn't going to help.* "I beg your pardon, Right Reverend Cary. It's blood. Looks like more of her injuries have opened up. I've moved her too much. Sorry, love."

James reached for the fastenings of her gown but hesitated. "This is wrong."

"It's necessary, and she agrees, don't you, Katerina?"

Katerina nodded against his shoulder. Her weight was growing as her trembling legs lost strength.

"Please hurry. I'm afraid she's going to faint."

James opened the back of the gown and Christopher slid it, and her chemise, down to her waist, keeping her front pressed against his chest to preserve her modesty.

"Good Lord!" James exclaimed, and his uncle grunted in astonishment.

"There you see? Have you ever encountered injuries this bad?" Christopher demanded, his fingers sliding over one deep groove.

"Once," the bishop said grimly. "The unfortunate lady did not survive. I had to perform her funeral service. Her husband was hanged. Is that the extent of the damage?"

"No." Christopher did not elaborate. He didn't need to. "Will you issue the license now?"

"Perhaps. First I need to speak to her alone."

"James, a little help please?"

Together they worked her clothing back over her ruined flesh and fastened it. Christopher walked her back to the sofa, supporting nearly all her weight, and helped her to lie down on her only uninjured side. With gentle fingers, he smoothed a wisp of dark hair away from her ashen face.

"Don't leave, Christopher," she sobbed, finding her voice at last.

"I won't go far, love," he promised. "The bishop needs to talk to you. I'll be nearby if you need me." He stroked her cheek gently and pressed his lips to her forehead. "Be strong, Katerina. Whatever he asks you, tell him the truth."

He lingered in the doorway until James pulled him out. "She's safe with my uncle. Let's go look for a snack. I hardly got a bite of dinner and you didn't get any. Besides, you could use a drink."

Chapter 6

 Y dear," the bishop approached Katerina slowly. Tears slid down her temple into the ebony-colored upholstery, "do you swear to me it was your father, and not your young man, who hurt you so badly?"

She looked askance at him.

"Sometimes abusive men can coerce women into lying, but if you marry him, the abuse will continue."

"No." She steeled herself, using the last of her faltering strength to force the words out. "Marriage is the only way to stop it. Christopher didn't do this to me. Father did. I've only known Christopher two weeks."

"I see," the bishop replied, understanding dawning on his friendly, wrinkled face, "and those scars are much older, aren't they?"

"Some are ten years old," she elaborated, straining to move her numb lips.

"I'm sorry for all you've had to endure," he murmured, gentle and sincere.

"Thank you." Her eyelid began twitching, so she closed her eyes.

"Do you need me to summon anyone to treat your injuries?" the bishop asked, his voice not quite steady.

Katerina shook her head. "They're not as bad as they look," she replied. "I don't need anything but sleep, and to marry Christopher tomorrow."

"Very well. Rest my dear." He turned to leave the room.

Once more Katerina spoke softly, voicing the question that had been lingering in the back of her mind since Christopher proposed this mad plan. "Is it wrong of me to ask this of him?"

The bishop turned and regarded her without speaking for a long moment. Though his expression remained grim, something of hope seemed to flare in his blue eyes. "It's good of you to think of it. He's your only hope though."

Raw despair clenched her heart. "I know. I wish I had something to offer in return."

"You will someday when you're better." He patted her shoulder reassuringly.

"Will my heart ever heal?" she asked in a weak, faltering voice.

"If you want it to, if you pray and try with all your might to trust, to let go of the past, you can grieve for a season, and then begin to improve. I've seen it." He seemed to consider for a moment. "Have you ever been loved?" he asked at last.

"Before my mother's death, she loved me." For a moment, Katerina could have sworn that warm, soothing arms wrapped around her.

"Then there's hope," the bishop said with a sad smile. "Remember her love. It will show you the way."

That makes sense, but I'll have to consider it later. I'm at the end of my strength. "Yes."

"And it really wasn't Mr. Bennett who hurt you?" he asked again.

"No. It really wasn't," she choked out.

"All right. You rest then. I need to talk to him and to my nephew. I think, in the morning, you'll be free of this danger for good."

"Thank you." Glad she no longer needed to remain conscious, Katerina finally passed out.

* * *

The Right Reverend William Cary wiped a tear from the corner of his eye and left her to rest, following his nephew and Christopher to the kitchen. There, he found James slurping a bowl of soup at the rough-hewn table. Christopher leaned uncomfortably against the wall between the cookstove and doorway, staring gloomily into a glass of brandy.

Hearing the approaching footsteps, they both looked up.

"Well?"

"Calm yourself, son," he told Christopher gently. "I'll issue the license. I'll perform the wedding in the morning. Are you sure you want to do this? She'll be years recovering if she ever does."

"And if she dies because I did nothing? What then?" he asked fiercely.

"It's a terrible burden," the bishop replied, his mouth set in a grim line. "I know exactly how terrible, but we can't save everyone. Laws must be changed first."

"That will take years," Christopher reminded him. "So, in the meanwhile, I can save this woman. Will you let me?"

"Uncle," James interjected, looking up from his bowl, "listen, I know this girl. I danced with her. I had no idea… I thought she was just shy. Christopher saw right through it. I think there's something… special between them. Maybe he was always meant to be her savior."

"Perhaps," The Right Reverend Cary conceded. "He certainly wants to be."

"Is she all right?" Christopher demanded, ignoring the conversation.

"She's sleeping now. I've left her to it. I'm sure she needs the rest. I've said I'll do it and I will. Here, get something to eat." He offered a bowl.

Christopher waved it away. "I'm too upset to eat."

"Yes, I imagine," the bishop replied, ladling himself a serving. He took a seat and regarded Christopher before adding, "You're heroic to try and help."

* * *

The comment stuck Christopher as wrong, setting the pit of his stomach roiling in disgust. *Hero, ha. A real hero would have done something before this happened.* "That's not what this is about."

The Right Reverend Cary rose from the table and crossed the room to clap Christopher on the shoulder. "I know. I hope this fierce attraction and protectiveness turns into a deep and mutual love someday."

Christopher met his eyes, sure his anguish was far too visible for comfort. "I have to believe it."

The hand on his shoulder squeezed lightly. "Yes. Well if you're not going to eat, put the brandy down. It will do you no good to be hungover for your wedding. Why don't you try to rest a little? I have a guest room made up."

Christopher sighed deeply. "Very well."

He rose and headed back through the house. He had been here often enough, with Cary, and knew his way. First, he returned to the parlor, where, as the bishop had said, Katerina lay asleep on the sofa.

He knelt in front of her. "I wish I had helped you sooner," he told her as she slept, "but I swear I'll never let him hurt you again." Then he kissed her lips tenderly.

Her eyelids fluttered open. Warm brown eyes met his, and she smiled.

"Rest, love," he told her, "tomorrow is your wedding day."

Shy hope and gratitude dawned in her eyes. "Thank you, Christopher."

Since she was awake, he kissed her once more, and enjoyed her response. Then he ran his hand soothingly over her forehead until her eyelids shut again.

Chapter 7

T noon the next day, Katerina walked slowly and painfully from the hansom cab up through the wrought-iron fence surrounding the churchyard garden, which now lay dormant under the grip of a frigid London winter. Ahead of her, a small, plain building constructed of golden bricks awaited. There, she would finally shake off the burden of her father's abuse for good.

Wind ruffled her icy blue wedding dress, which she'd borrowed from the bishop's late wife's closet. It fit badly, being both too short and too generously cut for her, but there was no help for it. Her white party gown had been ruined with blood.

She leaned heavily on Christopher for support as they proceeded up the steps, through an arched wooden door in which a single rosette window of colorless glass admitted a ray of pale winter sunlight.

Her wounds, though no longer bleeding, felt stiff and fragile. She walked carefully, pain exploding with every step until they stood in front of an altar, beneath a white barrel-vaulted ceiling decorated with a wide wooden lattice.

Bishop Cary waited for them, his prayer book in his hand. He opened it, though his eyes remained fixed on Katerina, concern twisting his face as he spoke. " 'Dearly beloved, we are gathered together here in the sight of God, and in the face of this congregation...' " he glanced at the pew beyond where Katerina had noticed James sitting as they passed. He'd been biting his fingernails. Two strangers perched beside him—an older couple in rugged clothing. *Probably the groundskeeper and the cleaning woman pressed into service as witnesses,* Katerina thought idly. *No time for a congregation and I wouldn't want one if I could have it.*

Katerina felt a sudden, fierce pleasure. *Father must be awake from his drunken stupor by now. He's sick and angry and no doubt searching for me, but he'll never find me in time. Everyone who knows where I am is in this room.* The realization bolstered her confidence.

" 'Secondly, It was ordained for a remedy against sin,' " Bishop Cary continued.

Sin, ha. Some might say this very wedding is a sin, but it's not. Honoring my father is impossible. No matter how good I was, I've never been able to satisfy his demands, and now I'm was being very bad, defying him, and the rewards will be considerable.

The bishop continued. " 'I require and charge you both, as ye will answer at the dreadful day of judgment when the secrets of all hearts shall be disclosed, that if either of you know any impediment, why ye may not be lawfully joined together in Matrimony, ye do now confess it…' "

Again, the unfairness of this situation for Christopher struck her. *If there is an impediment, that would be it. I gain everything from this marriage, but what does he gain? A ruined, terrified bride.* A shudder ran up her spine, but she reminded herself that he knew what he was doing. *At least, I hope he does, and besides, I do have the option—no, the duty—to try to become a worthy wife. Someday, Lord willing, I'll succeed.*

Shaking off her wandering thoughts, Katerina focused her attention back on Bishop Cary, just as he turned to Christopher. "Wilt thou have this woman to thy wedded wife, to live together after God's ordinance in the holy estate of matrimony? Wilt thou love her, comfort her, honor, and keep her in sickness and in health; and, forsaking all other, keep thee only unto her, so long as ye both shall live?"

"I will," Christopher replied in a calm, fearless voice. He looked into Katerina's face, meeting her eyes. This time, the static shock of their undeniable connection radiated warm and deep into the recesses of her being.

It stole her breath for a moment, and it was only faintly, as though from a great distance, that she heard the bishop speaking to her. " 'Wilt thou have this man to thy wedded husband, to live together after God's ordinance in the holy estate of matrimony? Wilt thou obey him, and serve him, love, honor, and keep him in sickness and in health; and, forsaking all other, keep thee only unto him, so long as ye both shall live?' "

"I... ahem." She cleared her throat of a sudden, raspy sound. "I will."

As they had no one to give away the bride—in essence, Christopher was stealing her—Bishop Cary skipped ahead to the vows.

Again, Christopher's voice held firm and confident as he took hold hand and said, "I Christopher take thee, Katerina, to my wedded wife, to have and to hold from this day forward, for better for worse, for richer for poorer, in sickness and in health, to love and to cherish, till death us do part, according to God's holy ordinance; and thereto I plight thee my troth."

A ghost of a smile creased her lips. *He truly wants this,* she thought. *Not just to save me, though that plays a large role in the timing. No, there something about me that makes this lovely, kind man happy.* She blinked.

Behind them, the clouds parted, and a ray of sunshine fell through the colored glass of the window, sprinkling them both with joyous rainbows.

Katerina swallowed a lump in her throat. "I Katerina take thee, Christopher, to my wedded husband, to have and to hold from this day forward, for better for worse, for richer for poorer, in sickness and in health, to love, cherish, and to obey, till death us do part, according to God's holy ordinance; and thereto I give thee my troth."

He released her hand reluctantly to accept from Reverend Cary a simple gold band James had gone out earlier to purchase for them. He eased it onto Katerina's finger and repeated, "With this ring, I thee wed, with my body I thee worship and with all my worldly goods I thee endow: In the name of the Father, and of the Son, and of the Holy Ghost. Amen."

Next came a prayer, and both Christopher and the bishop had to hold onto Katerina's arms to help her into a kneeling position. Her back and buttocks burned, and her belly ached, but she persevered. *Lord, if this be your will, I will accept the pain. Only, help me be worthy of your gift—and of his sacrifice.*

After the prayer, Katerina struggled painfully to her feet.

Bishop Cary said, "Those whom God hath joined together let no man put asunder. Forasmuch as Christopher and Katerina have consented together in holy wedlock, and have witnessed the same before God and this company, and thereto have given and pledged their troth either to other, and have declared the same by giving and receiving of a ring, and by joining of hands; I pronounce that they be man and wife together, In the name of the Father, and of the Son, and of the Holy Ghost. Amen."

Christopher led his bride down the aisle, supporting her with his arm around hers.

Her feet felt numb as she stumbled and fought for her footing. *We're wed. It's done. Thank God!*

* * *

Across town, they arrived at Christopher's home; a messy and cramped bachelor's quarters never intended to be shared with a woman. The whole living space consisted of only two rooms: a parlor and a bedroom. The parlor contained sparse furnishings, as little would fit into the narrow space.

"Sorry about this, love," Christopher told her as he escorted her over the threshold into the sitting room, "I'll look into finding us a home soon." He swept a pile of jumbled papers from the sofa to the floor and urged her to sit, joining her and taking her hand in his.

"I'm just glad to be here with you," she replied, lacing their fingers together.

"Can I get you anything?" Courtesy had prompted the question, but he had little to offer in the apartment other than liquor, wine and half a loaf of bread almost certainly too stale to eat. He took most of his meals elsewhere.

"No, thank you," she replied. "Can we proceed?"

"With what?" he asked.

"I'm not really safe yet, am I, Christopher?"

He turned sharply to regard her, eyebrows drawing together, and shook his head. "You're not ready."

"It hardly matters," Katerina insisted.

"You're too badly injured," he said, not finished arguing.

"And if he finds me? Can he not take me away, have the marriage annulled?" she pointed out. "I'm young, Christopher. It would be easy for him to convince... someone that you manipulated me and remove me to his care until everything could be straightened out."

"He could," Christopher agreed reluctantly. *Does she have to be right? I don't want to hurt her more.*

"And then I would die," she stated in a hard, flat voice.

Christopher broke eye contact, tracing the pattern of vines across the upholstery of the sofa.

"Then there's nothing more to be said, is there? Let's go." She tugged on his hand.

"Kat, you don't know what you're asking," Christopher protested.

"You're right. You promised to explain it to me." She regarded him with an unruffled expression that demonstrated her powerful innocence.

"Do you have any idea what is involved in consummating a marriage?" he demanded.

"My mother died when I was nine. I have no idea."

"Oh, Lord." He sighed, steeled himself, and proceeded "Very well. This is going to be a difficult conversation. Are you ready?"

She nodded.

"All right, you know your woman's time?"

"Yes." She was already blushing.

"There's an opening there… between your legs."

"Yes." The pink in her cheeks darkened.

"I have to fill it," he said. He swallowed hard. *Making love is so much easier to do than to explain.*

She blanched and then looked at him, bewildered. "With what?"

"With my… my… let me show you." He took her hand and guided it to the front of his trousers. Her eyes widened.

"Do you feel that?" he asked.

"Yes. Of course." But her eyes still asked so many questions.

"It fits right in. And then, well, there's… a substance that comes out. I put it inside you, and, if the timing is right, and the Lord wills it, a baby is created."

"That's the consummation?" He was pleased to note she appeared curious rather than revolted.

"Yes."

"And it causes bleeding?" she asked.

Now you look worried, do you, love? Well rightly so. It's not a joke. "The first time," he replied. There's a little… blockage inside you. Your maidenhead. I break it when I enter you."

"The first time?" Her delicately arched brows drew together. "How many times do we do this?"

"Often," he replied. "It's quite… pleasurable."

She raised one eyebrow.

"You see, love?" he told her gently, "You're not ready. I married you to save you, but now you're my wife. It's for life, you know? Adultery disgusts me. Therefore, from now on, you're my only source of sexual satisfaction. I don't want you to become… unwilling because we were intimate before we gave desire time to develop."

Though confused and embarrassed, she still pressed. "There's no choice. We have to. I won't be safe until we do it."

"I know," he replied, trying to explain his vague discomfort, "but it's also our first time making love together. You're giving me your virginity. All of that matters. I want it to be good for you, so you'll like it."

She considered his words. "Even if this time is… difficult, I promise I'll let you keep doing it until we get it right. I'm a wreck right now, but I don't want to stay this way forever. I want to be a good wife."

Christopher grasped her hand and squeezed it. "Thank you, my dear. That might make the difference."

"Shall we proceed then?"

She was right, and despite his grave doubts, he knew it. "Very well."

He helped her onto her feet and led her into his bedroom. Like the rest of the apartment, it was small, barely room inside for a modest wardrobe and a bed, simple and unadorned, with good quality sheets and covers but no hangings or side curtains.

"This is normally done nude, you know," he told her.

She blushed but nodded. Turning, she let him open her borrowed dress. He dropped it to the floor, lifting her bloodied chemise over her head.

In the daylight, the wounds on her back looked even more terrible, and they extended almost to her knees. How many times had she been beaten bloody and no one tried to help? Too many.

Abandoning this line of thought, he pushed back the covers on his bed, glad to note the cleaning woman had changed the sheets.

He extended a hand and she gripped it for support, climbing onto the mattress.

"Get into a comfortable position, love," he instructed. "I'll work around what you can manage."

She lay down on her uninjured side, facing him, her arm under her head. From the front, she looked less desperately damaged, and he could focus his attention on her blushing cheeks, her pretty breasts and her soft thighs, and ignore the yellow and purple bruises on her abdomen. He undressed quickly and joined her, face to face, leaning in for a long sweet kiss.

"You like kissing, don't you, little love?" he asked, his lips inches from hers.

"Yes. Is that good?"

Her hesitant eagerness charmed him, reminding him why all this had been necessary. "It's an excellent start. You know, if you open a little, I can give you an even better kiss."

"Really?" She sounded doubtful.

She likes kissing that much, does she? Good. "Try it. Don't be startled though."

"What are you going to do?"

"You'll see."

Her lips parted. He lowered his mouth to hers again, pulling the pins from her hair to let the long dark strands fall all around her. *How beautiful she is.* Working up the desire to be intimate with her would not be difficult at all. He already desired her, but he really did want her to find joy in their marriage bed someday, and so he had to take her slowly.

Stroking the silky strands, he let his tongue touch her lips. She drew in a deep breath but didn't protest, allowing his experience to guide them. *Excellent.* He entered her mouth. She tasted of tea and woman, and he worked her mouth gently for long moments while her surprise faded. Eventually, she began to respond instinctively to his kiss, touching his tongue hesitantly with hers. He let her explore for a few moments and then drew back.

"Was that wrong?" she asked, her eyes filled with worry.

It occurred to him that in her mind, doing things wrong was not just embarrassing but dangerous. He hastened to reassure her. "No, it was perfect."

"I feel like such a bad girl, being nude in bed with you." Her eyes turned shy, though he would not say exactly ashamed.

"Ironically, the same characteristics that make a bad girl make a good wife," Christopher replied. "Now that we're married, love, you have every right and responsibility to share your lovely body and your sweet kisses with me, and I have the same towards you."

"Good. I like the way you touch me," she said as his fingers stroked through her hair.

"You haven't had enough affection in years, have you?"

She shook her head.

"I'll take care of that for you." His words made her smile, nervously, but sincerely. "Now then, are you ready for a little more?"

"Such as?"

"You have lovely little breasts. May I touch them?"

Confusion again. "Why do you want to?"

Christopher squashed his frustration. *It's not her fault she doesn't know. At least she has no preconceived notions.* "I think you might enjoy the sensation."

"Is it allowed?"

"If we had time, I would let you read Song of Solomon. If the scriptures glory in a man touching his wife's breasts, we have nothing to worry about."

Her expression turned thoughtful. "You're right. I'd forgotten that part."

"You read it?" His eyes widened.

"Yes."

He grinned. Under the crushing weight of abuse, a passionate woman waited to be released. Something told him all the time it would take for her to heal would be worthwhile in the end. And so, he ran his hand up the length of her side, skimming lightly over the bruise, and stroked up to her collarbone. He traced his fingers down to the little globe. There really wasn't an excess of flesh there, but the nipple was lovely, and he caressed it tenderly. Plucking it, making it rise under his fingers, he gripped it gently.

"Oh," she sighed, "that's very nice."

"Good."

"Christopher, may I put my arm around you?"

He beamed. "Of course. Yes."

She wriggled closer to him and laid her arm over his waist. The sensation of her warmth and softness against his body made his sex ache. *Easy, lad. You'll have your chance soon enough.*

He transferred his attention to her other breast, and she sighed again. *She likes to be touched so far, thank the Lord. I would hate it if she was protesting.* Stoking and tugging first one tender peak and then the other, he listened carefully to each soft sigh and whimper, learning how her untutored body wanted to be touched.

He claimed her lips again and she responded eagerly, opening to his questing tongue, twining hers around his, and even chasing it back into his mouth. Suddenly, her back arched, thrusting her hips forward so her pubic hair slid along his belly. The ache in his penis ratcheted up to near pain as it demanded satisfaction. Fighting down the urge to tumble her to her back and plunge in, he continued kissing her while he aroused her. *I love how her body softens and relaxes moment by moment. She's such a good girl, so willing to let me try. If only she were well, how I would delight in caressing her back, cupping her bottom, kissing her belly. Someday I'll show her all these pleasures. I'm sure now that she'll let me.*

At last, she was squirming with pleasure and it was time to move on to greater intimacy. He took her knee in one hand to lift and bend it, giving himself access to her.

"It's very important that you let me touch you here," he indicated her mound.

"Why?" This time her confusion did not surprise him.

"As I pleasure you, you will become wetter inside. Then, when I take you, it will be much easier for us both. Can you let me touch your private parts?"

She didn't speak. Her eyes closed, but her leg remained bent, permitting the access. He stroked the coarse curls for a long moment. Already there was some dampness there, on the outside of her lips. *Excellent.* He spread the folds and touched her core. *Wet. Wonderfully wet.* Finding her portal, he dipped one finger inside. *So tight, and there's her hymen, intact.* So, her father hadn't molested her. *That's one good thing out of the whole damned situation.* He probed further, and she squeaked. He sighed. *It's a thick maidenhead though, and she'll have some pain in the breaking of it.* In the meanwhile, he wanted to give her more pleasure. His fingers slid through her folds, upward, until he found what he had been seeking, a little erect nub of exquisite sensitivity. She gasped, and he could tell she had not realized the spot existed before this moment.

"Are you sure this is right for us to do?" she asked again in a breathy, uncertain voice.

"Yes," he replied.

"How do you know?"

How to respond? The inspiration came like an answer to prayer. "My dear, if the Lord didn't intend women to experience sexual pleasure, would he really have equipped them with an organ that has no other purpose?"

"I suppose not," she replied, struggling through a visible blend of embarrassment and arousal to try for a neutral answer. She did not succeed in any way.

Christopher grinned. *I'm doing something right.* "Please let me touch it," he urged. "The more I caress you, the better our joining will be."

And then he kissed her while his fingers worked gently between her thighs. *Again,* she submitted without question, and just as he had predicted, moisture surged. Her breathing grew unsteady and ragged.

"If you feel something building, don't be alarmed," he advised her. "It's a normal, desirable part of the process. Let it happen."

Her thighs tensed as the pleasure he was stoking built and built… and then burst.

She squealed in startled delight as her belly contracted and her intimate flesh throbbed. He worked her through the peak tenderly; thankful he had been able to get her to orgasm under such desperate circumstances. "Very good, love. You're doing wonderfully. What an excellent wife you are already."

"Oh, that was lovely," she sighed, her body relaxing.

"Now do you understand why people want to do this?"

"Yes." Her cheeks glowed, but with satisfaction rather than embarrassment this time.

He let her lean against him for a long moment, basking in the glow. He rested his arm on her hip and toyed with the ends of her hair. *I'm so glad you let yourself enjoy this, love. I hope the rest won't be too upsetting.*

At last, she sighed. When she met his eyes, he could see reality had returned. "That wasn't really it, was it? You didn't do… what you told me about."

"You're right," he agreed. "But now you're more ready. All right. Now, how do we do the rest? Normally I would have you on your back, but that won't work. On the side is too difficult, and I don't want you standing. Hmmm. How shall I take you?"

Suddenly inspired, Christopher piled up a mound of pillows.

"Here, roll over and lean on this."

She obeyed.

"That should take some pressure off your back. All right, I'm coming behind you."

Damned strange way to take a virgin, he thought, surveying her whole damaged back, bottom and thighs while he positioned himself. *Poor darling*. The terrible sight dampened his desire considerably, but it also reminded him why this was necessary.

At least he was able also to look at her intimate folds. *What a pretty flower she has, innocent and untried, but drenched from her first orgasm.* He spread the lips again, this time finding her virgin portal and aligning his sex with it. He pressed the tip into her, and she gasped.

"Katerina, I know you have some experience tending injuries," he said, or rather moaned as her luscious tight heat engulfed the tip of his sex.

"Yes, why?" Her voice turned thin with nerves.

He reached her maidenhead and nudged against it. It held fast. "When a bandage is stuck to a wound, is it better to rip it off, or peel it slowly?"

She hissed and then replied in a wavering voice, "Well, if it's a bad injury, you have to soak it, or you open the wound again and have to start over."

Damn it, come on. "What about if it's small?"

"Rip it. Get the pain over with quickly."

"All right then."

He braced one hand on her uninjured hip and penetrated her with a hard thrust, tearing her hymen apart and filling her to the limit.

She squeaked in protest.

"I know that hurt, love. I'm sorry." He stroked her hip. "That was the blockage I told you about."

"Are we consummated now?" she asked breathlessly.

"Yes."

"Good."

And she's probably ready to be finished. I should withdraw, let her recover, he thought as her sex clenched and fluttered in protest of his girth. He groaned. *Forgive me, love. I need you.* "Are you able to take a few more moments?"

"Of what?" she asked, and then sucked in a breath as he slowly withdrew.

"Remember how good it felt when your pleasure peaked?" he asked, easing back in. His breath hissed between his teeth as her clinging passage caressed his erection inch by glorious, tortuous inch.

"Yes."

"I want one too." He eased back.

"What do I do?" she asked. Then she whimpered as he pushed in again.

"Just stay still. I'll take care of it."

She stayed still. He pulled back and thrust into her again. *No wonder some men pursue virgins.* Her tightness tantalized him. She caressed his erection with wanton sweetness as he carefully increased the speed and force of his thrusts. Each inward drive coaxed a whimper from her and an answering squeeze of her sex. Christopher clutched his wife's hip, shuddering and gasping in the hardest, longest, most earth-shaking climax he'd ever experienced. He groaned as his seed spilled, filling her belly.

And then he gently withdrew from her clenching sex, lifting her from the pillows and arranging her on her bottom on the bed. She winced as her bruised buttocks landed on the sheets.

"What are you doing?" she asked.

"Making a bloodstain. Stay there." To keep her still, he kissed her mouth. "Well, little wife, what did you think of that?"

"Interesting," she said, and then giggled a bit hysterically.

"Did you hate it?" he asked, now feeling uncertain. *Was it bad of me to ask for my own satisfaction? Was that selfish?*

"Of course not," she replied. She stroked his cheek. Then another thought chased across her face. "Um, it won't always hurt like that, will it?"

"No," he promised. "I'll give you some time for the soreness to subside before I take you again. After you recover inside, the penetration will feel good for both of us."

She considered, worrying her lower lip with her teeth. "Have you done this often before?"

"Fairly often, yes," he admitted.

"Ah."

"But we're married, Katerina. From now on my only partner is you." *Believe me, sweet girl. I mean it.*

"I doubt I can live up to what you've had."

Not doubting my fidelity, but her own worth. She's so uncertain of her value, poor darling, but she can't be more wrong. Her innocent willingness had been quite pleasing, rather more than the jaded experience displayed by his previous lovers. Giving her a tender smile, he said, "Actually, dear, it was perfectly lovely. Equal to anything I've done before. Remember, you're mine, my wife. That's very special." It *had* been special, and much more powerful than he had realized it would be.

She smiled. Then she yawned hugely. "Sorry."

No surprise. She's had a hard time of it. "Think nothing of it. Would you like to sleep for a while?"

"Yes please."

She stretched out on the bed and Christopher covered her with the blankets, noting in passing that they had succeeded in making an obvious mark—her virgin blood mixed with his semen—on the sheet. *Proof. Excellent.* He kissed her cheek, then realized there was something important he had to do. Quickly washing himself, he pulled on clean garments, headed out into the hallway, and summoned the hotel's housekeeper, Mrs. Bristol and his valet, Mackenzie.

Within moments of him ringing the bell, a quiet scratch on the door revealed a plump, smiling woman in a gray dress, silver side curls bouncing around her face from under a white mob cap. Close on her heels, Mackenzie entered the sitting room, his uniform and hair rumpled, yawning hugely.

"Sorry, boss," the man said, the sounds of Yorkshire laying so heavily on his voice, Christopher almost couldn't understand him. *It's always worse when he's tired.*

"Not to worry," Christopher replied. "When did you get back?"

"Around two in the morning," Mackenzie said, rubbing his eyes. Their redness made the cornflower irises look even brighter. The young man tugged at his uniform.

"Is your mother better?" Christopher asked.

"Aye," he replied, rumpling his already-messy reddish hair so it stood up like the flame of a candle.

Christopher nodded in acknowledgment and got straight to the point. "I have a difficult request to ask of you both. I have married a lovely young woman who has suffered more than anyone should ever have to suffer. The abuse she has endured is beyond imagination. But she's mine now, and I will not allow her to be harmed again. As of a few minutes ago, we were married beyond all redemption. Do you understand?"

They nodded, faces wreathed in questions.

He continued. "First of all, no one is to know of the abuse. I don't want her embarrassed. If anyone asks, please say we were struck with a mad passion for each other and could do nothing other than marry as quickly as possible. It's not a lie, you understand?"

"Yes sir," Mackenzie agreed. Mrs. Bristol nodded again.

"And then, I want you both to gossip like never before. Tell everyone who will listen how very… passionate our marriage is. Soon, I will take her out for a while. Mrs. Bristol, there is a bloodstain on the bed. You understand what this means."

"I do," the woman replied, her plump cheeks turning pink even as her lips curved into a smile. The skin around her blue eyes crinkled.

"It is vitally important that everyone know it was there. In fact, if you would be so kind as to save the sheet without cleaning it, it might be beneficial. But you must tell everyone how very… physical my wife and I are together. There can be no doubt, in the interests of her safety, that our marriage is completely legal. Can I count on you both?"

"Oh yes," Mrs. Bristol said, and Mackenzie agreed easily.

The uncomfortable conversation finished, Christopher dismissed the two and flopped gracelessly on the sofa. At last, he'd accomplished his goal of ensuring Katerina's safety, and now, he suddenly felt overwhelmed by the events of the last twenty-four hours. As the adrenaline faded, his mind cleared. A square of paper caught his eye. He lifted it; the marriage license.

Dear Lord, I really married Katerina. What was I thinking? For the last eighteen hours he had been caught up in a frenzy of protectiveness towards this young woman, but to what personal cost? He desired her, but he barely knew her. *And now she's my wife, my utterly irrevocable wife.* Perhaps this impulsive act was not the only way to save her, but try though he might, he could think of no other. In order to preserve her, he had sacrificed himself; his future, his ability to choose a wife later, when he was ready. If she never healed, if she remained wary and damaged, or worse, went mad, there would be no recourse.

But then he remembered all their brief encounters. *How sweet she is, how eager to be loved, to be touched. She even enjoyed being bedded.* There was every chance that, in time, her natural passionate nature would emerge, and she would be a perfectly adequate wife. He imagined making love to her in the future when her back was better, her bruises faded and when she was no longer sore. She'd done well all things considered, and it would be better the next time. A slow smile spread across his face. *Passionate lovemaking is not the worst way to start a marriage.*

A knock sounded at the door, actually, a loud hammering. *Someone's beating with a fist.* He hurried over, not wanting Katerina's rest to be disturbed. Easing the door open a crack, he found himself face to face with a thickset, dark-skinned man whose silver-streaked black hair had been slicked into submission with copious pomade.

"Can I help you, sir?" Christopher asked coldly.

"Where is she?" The breath issuing from the interloper smelled strongly of liquor.

Christopher made a face at the unpleasant aroma and drawled rudely, "Whom do you seek."

"Don't pretend you don't know," the stranger snarled, the sounds of Italy heavy in his voice. "You have my daughter. I want her back."

Christopher's jaw clenched with icy rage. He leaned insouciantly against the door frame and challenged the other man with a sneer. "No."

Signore Valentino's face turned red. "I'll have the law on you."

"Go ahead," Christopher offered, examining his fingernails. "You no longer have any legal right to her."

"What?" The dark face contorted in rage.

"We're married, Katerina and I. She's safe from you." Christopher met the dark angry eyes with a bit of his own ill will.

The other man's eyes shifted nervously. "Safe? What do you mean?"

"I saw what you did to her," Christopher said, letting more of his anger show, "but you'll never hurt her again."

A vein in Valentino's temple began to throb. "Did that lying little whore say I did something to her?"

Christopher wanted to hit him. His fingers actually itched with the urge, but he forced himself to hold back. "To the best of my knowledge she's never lied; *someone* did something terrible to her. And as for her being a whore, not likely. She gave me her first kiss. Her virgin blood is staining my sheets as we speak. So, you see, Signore, Katerina Valentino no longer exists, only a very satisfied Mrs. Bennett. Good day to you."

This provoked an extended round of Italian curses, which Christopher found utterly unimpressive. He began to close the door. A heavy fist clamped onto the wood.

"You'll never be free of me, Bennett. I keep what's mine."

"Then you should have treated her better. She's not yours anymore. Now release the damned door or I'll close it on your hand."

The hand disappeared, and Christopher slammed the door shut and locked it.

A soft sound emerged from the bedroom, and he followed it. Katerina sat up in the bed, tears streaming down her lovely face, her shoulders shaking. He slid into the bed beside her, taking her in his arms. She shook in like a leaf in a thunderstorm.

"Did you hear that, love?" he asked tenderly.

"Ye...yes," she managed to choke out.

"He's gone. You're safe." He stroked the scars below her shoulder blades.

"No one has ever protected me," she sobbed, struggling to hold back a flood of grief. "Not since my mother died."

"Everything is different now," he reminded her. "You're my wife. Your safety is my responsibility." *I don't regret that,* he realized. *I'm happy to have made this decision.*

That she reached out to him for comfort caused warmth to spread out from the vicinity of his chest, until it warmed every finger and toe. But despite the power of the moment, she still had much ground to cover. "You've been through hell, haven't you?"

"Yes," she admitted choking on the word.

"Then let it out. Don't hold back. You're allowed to grieve. Your childhood was a nightmare. Your future is much brighter, but you have to grieve your past so you can build a better future. Let go, darling."

He stroked her hair, and the tender touch lanced deep into her soul's festering wounds. A lifetime of misery came tumbling out of her in hysterical, wracking sobs. She cried and cried until at last, she cried herself to sleep in the safety of her husband's arms. He lowered her to the bed, positioning her gently on her side. *That wasn't the end of it,* he realized. *Not even close. There's no way to cure a decade of abuse in a single good cry, but it's a start. She feels safe enough with me to share the vulnerability of her tears.* Suddenly exhausted, Christopher lay down beside his wife and succumbed to slumber himself.

* * *

Giovanni cursed to himself as he stormed out of the hotel. "*Damned interfering son of a bitch," he muttered in Italian, ignoring the stares of passersby. "How dare he meddle with my property? Does the gall of these self-important peasants know no bounds?*"

He shook his head vigorously as he stomped down the street, boots crushing every leaf and twig and crunching in the gravel. "We are royalty, descended on my mother's side from a long line of the highest rank in Florence, all the way back to the Medicis. Granted, it's not exactly a legitimate line, but real and traceable, nonetheless."

Reaching an intersection, he turned at random, still pontificating under his breath to an audience of one. "Despite this, and despite the sizeable income generated by my father's shipping line, which runs itself beautifully, providing my income while requiring little interference, the foolish peasants in Italy didn't understand how fortunate they were to have us."

He growled, examining the street signs without reading them before making another random turn. "No longer welcome in Florence, we relocated here, hoping England, with its powerful queen, would be more respectful of my elevated rank. But here, like in Italy, jumped-up farmers and working-class rabble have risen above their station and are challenging the right of those ordained by heaven to rule. Now, one of them has even had the gall to lay hands on my daughter! That whore will pay in pain and blood."

Deep in his ruminations, he failed to notice a young clerk hurrying in the other direction with a sheaf of papers clutched in his arms. The two men collided, sending the sheets fluttering in all directions. Giovanni growled in annoyance at the youth's clumsiness, and hurried on, deliberately planting his wet and muddy boot on one of the meticulously prepared documents, reducing it to trash.

"What is wrong with people? Even my own wife struggled for years against my God-given authority. *Silly cow. She never understood what a favor I'd done her, lifting her from the dirt of her father's olive farm and allowing her the privilege of carrying my child. If only she'd given herself over to my authority, as she should, she might not have died of infection, from the wounds she brought on herself. Katerina has always been better, more submissive.*"

Giovanni shook his head. Ugly rage roiled in his head until the world seemed bathed in a dark and ominous haze. "*I need another drink, and I need to hit something, get rid of this anger so I can think straight. But what to do? Ah yes, my favorite brothel. They will have a whip and a girl.*" *That will definitely help.*" As he walked along towards the discreet townhouse, he considered what must be done. "*This insult cannot go unpunished.* My whore of a daughter and her disrespectful cotton weaver will pay for this insult."

Chapter 8

ATERINA woke suddenly as the late afternoon sun began slanting through the window across her face. She felt warm and comfortable... and nude; completely naked in bed with her astonishing husband. She took a moment to admire his handsomeness: his dark brown hair, nearly as dark as hers, his finely chiseled face, almost angelic in its symmetrical proportions, his flexible lips, which felt so wonderful pressed against hers, his beautiful silver eyes, now closed in slumber, long lashes resting on his cheeks. *He's glorious, and he's mine; my savior, my lover, my husband. He sacrificed himself for me.*

His eyes opened, showing their lovely, misty color, and the corners crinkled as he smiled at her.

She smiled back shyly.

"Did you rest well, sweet girl?" he asked.

She smiled a bit wider. "Yes. I feel very good. You?"

The corner of his mouth turned up. "Excellent. Are you sore?"

"Where?" she asked, her cheeks heating as various interpretations flitted through her mind.

"Everywhere."

Katerina took stock of herself. "I think my back is a little better."

He gave a brief nod. "Good. Your belly?"

She pressed against the bruises. "It hurts, but not as much as yesterday."

"And here?" His fingers trailed through the hair at the apex of her thighs.

Her face heated. "Sore. Quite sore."

His boyish half-grin turned regretful. "Not surprising. You were rather hard to deflower."

Katerina studied the eyelet pattern of the bedspread. "Sorry."

He lifted her face with one finger under her chin. "It's the way you were made, love. I just hated hurting you."

Every time he opens his mouth, he says something even sweeter. "I didn't mind, honestly. I have a pretty high tolerance. It wasn't the worst thing I've felt."

"I can imagine," he replied grimly. "And now, are you hungry?"

At the mention of food, her stomach gurgled loudly. "Yes, I am. Famished actually."

"Me too. I have an idea. Shall we see if my parents would be interested in having us for dinner?"

Parents? Oh dear. What will Julia think about all this? "Will they be upset?"

"About what?"

"That we married without telling them," Katerina explained.

Christopher shook his head. "I doubt it. Mother wanted us together. She understood the urgency. She'll explain it to father. All will be well, love. You're a Bennett now."

Katerina smiled. "That sounds perfect."

"Then get dressed. You look lovely, but it's rather much for going visiting."

She laughed, startled to notice it felt a bit rusty. It had been so long since she'd been comfortable enough to laugh. Scrambling stiffly from the bed, she lifted her chemise and examined the stained fabric with a frown. "This is disgusting."

"Yes," he agreed, grimacing at the sight of it.

What to do? "I'm sadly lacking in undergarments. In everything really."

"What about at... your father's house?" Christopher asked.

"My entire wardrobe is there, but I don't fancy going after it. Besides, after you dismissed him, he probably did something rash, like burn them." *I'll go naked before I set foot in that hell hole again.*

Christopher rolled his eyes heavenward. "No doubt. Just a moment, let me see if the housekeeper can find you something to borrow. Here." He retrieved a shirt from the wardrobe and tossed it to her. "Cover yourself so you can meet her."

She slid the shirt around her slender body. As she was tall for a woman, it fluttered around the middle of her thighs, but it was enough, barely, for decency. Christopher took her hand and led her out of the bedchamber and into the front room, where he summoned his housekeeper.

Mrs. Bristol flitted around the room, scowling at the slovenly mess Christopher had made on and around the coffee table. "Your man should be fired."

"He's been on holiday," Christopher explained. "I believe he got back last night. This is all my doing."

She glared at him and he held up his hands in mute apology. The pseudo-serious pantomime shattered when both of them broke into laughter. Mrs. Bristol, in particular, laughed so hard her whole body shook, sending her white side-curls dancing. The plump, smiling woman put Katerina instantly at ease, despite the fact that she was standing in front of a total stranger wearing her husband's shirt, which covered her only to mid-thigh, and nothing underneath.

Christopher settled down to business. "Mrs. Bristol, this is my wife. In the process of removing her from a... terrible situation, all her clothing was lost. I will take her shopping tomorrow, but in the meanwhile, do you know of anything she can borrow?"

"Yes," the woman replied as she clasped Katerina's hand. "My daughter was built a little like you. She left some old clothes with me. I keep them downstairs. Does that interest you?"

"I can't be choosy," Katerina explained. "I'll be thankful for whatever I can get."

"Just a moment. I'll be right back."

A short time later she fluttered into the room with a pile of garments: a white nightgown, a clean linen chemise, threadbare but serviceable pantalets and two dresses. Katerina nodded in gratitude. "Thank you so much."

"You don't need a corset, you're so slender," the woman said.

Katerina smiled. "I wouldn't be able to fasten it anyway. Just a moment." She hurried into the bedroom and emerged a short time later, comfortably clad in the undergarments and one of the dresses, all unfastened down the back. Mrs. Bristol circled her to help.

"Dear Lord, child, what happened to you?"

Drat, Katerina cursed in her mind, realizing the oversized chemise had dipped too low, revealing scars. She closed her eyes in shame.

Christopher gave the housekeeper a hard look. "I already told you."

"You're a very good man, Mr. Bennett," Mrs. Bristol said fervently.

"He certainly is," Katerina agreed.

"Won't it hurt you if I fasten this?" Mrs. Bristol asked, and her kindness brought tears to Katerina's eyes.

"Maybe, but it needs to be done." She controlled her desire to wince as Mrs. Bristol bustled around tightening the tapes until the garment lay in position on her slender body. *It does no good to make others suffer with me,* she reminded herself each time a bruise or cut began to throb.

At last, Katerina's clothes had settled around her body, covering the scars and lending her a semblance of normalcy. The housekeeper smiled sadly at her and left the room, scrubbing her cheeks and muttering under her breath.

Kind woman. I pray she receives a blessing.

Then Katerina continued her preparations on her own. There didn't seem to be a hairbrush anywhere in the apartment, so she borrowed her husband's comb and smoothed out the tangles. She gathered up as many of the scattered hairpins as she could find and simply pulled her hair back away from her face, twisting it into a bun.

She struggled into her boots, groaning as she bent forward, and the scabs stretched.

"Do you need any help, love?" Christopher asked, hurrying towards her.

She waved him away. "The scabs feel solid today, and I didn't want to risk the new scars on my back becoming too rigid as they form," she informed him. This discomfort is necessary, I'm afraid."

A strange blend of understanding and anger crossed Christopher's face. "I see," he said.

She sent him a rueful smile and returned to tugging her boot laces. Then she tried to rise, but a jolt of pain locked her into a bent-over position, like a crone.

This time she did reach out to her husband, and he helped her to rise without complaint, taking advantage of her proximity to lay his hands gently on her hips and kiss her forehead. Katerina regarded his face for a long moment.

Christopher shook his head. "I can't resist you, love." His lips claimed hers. Pleasurable heat flared in Katerina's core, radiating outward to her extremities. If their stomachs hadn't growled in tandem, who knew what kind of shenanigans they might have committed.

Christopher smiled ruefully with one side of his mouth, and Katerina compressed her lips in a similar expression. Then he took her arm and led her from the room. They stepped into the growing darkness as a brilliant orange sunset broke over London.

A hansom waited in the street, and Christopher escorted her to it, handing her up into the seat. She groaned and bit her lip at the uncomfortable movement but reminded herself of the importance of remaining flexible. When her husband joined her, she slipped her hand into his. The driver snapped the reins over the back of his bay gelding, and they began their journey across town.

Less than twenty-four hours ago I defied my father to attend a poetry party with my secret suitor of only a couple of weeks. Now we're married. My whole life has changed in the blink of an eye, so fast I still feel dizzy with it. Thankfully it was dizziness of the mind, not the body. Without a corset cutting off her breath, no longer bleeding, and knowing, objectively at least, that she was safe, her hands and feet had never felt so steady.

On the other hand, the temperature had dropped with the approaching night. Her shawl had been forgotten in the parlor of the Wilders' home and her warm winter coat remained in the Valentino house, abandoned for good. She shivered.

While they traveled, Christopher engaged her in conversation, asking, "Now then, love, clearly we can't stay in my cramped lodgings for long. How would you like to live? Do you prefer rooms in a hotel or a house?"

Katerina blinked at yet another new and unfamiliar thought. "I scarcely know. I've never lived in 'rooms.' My father rented a house when he and Mother came to England, and we've lived in that very house ever since. It's the only living quarters I know."

"Is it very large?" he asked.

"Yes." She swallowed at the memory of the cavernous space. Sounds echoed there, making it nearly impossible for her to keep her location secret. *I didn't like that.* Carefully choosing her words, she said, "I think I would like a house. Perhaps a row house?" she paused while thoughts bounced around her head and finally settled into a coherent idea. "Not too large, please."

"Why not?" he asked, puzzled.

She struggled to put her fear into words an utterly confident, unabused man could understand. "It's helpful for me to know where everyone is. The more space we have, the harder it will be to keep track of all the rooms."

"Is it so you know where *not* to be?" he guessed.

"Precisely," she replied.

"You don't need that anymore, you know," Christopher pointed out.

She nodded. *He's right.* And yet the fear refused to leave her.

She could feel his gaze on her profile. "All right, Katerina. Tell me what you're thinking."

I suppose I didn't suppress my feelings well enough. She regarded the buildings in silence while she pondered her words.

He ran his fingers down her cheek, capturing her attention again. "Tell me, love. I can see you disagree. You do need that kind of control, don't you?"

His gentle touch and soft voice disarmed her. She closed her eyes and told him the truth. "Yes, I do. For now, I do. I wish I could simply turn a gear and just like that, everything changes, but I can't."

He treated her to a rueful smile. "You're right. I'm sorry I second-guessed you. I think a modest row house would be very nice. Perhaps with a little garden; a green space is a blessing in the city. Tomorrow, I think, we can go and look for a suitable place to rent."

"We?" Her eyes widened in surprise. *Does he actually mean to consult me about the choice?*

"Naturally. I'll be at work at the factory many days a week. You need to be comfortable in our home. Of course, I want your opinion." He spoke as though the answer were obvious as he slid his fingers into her hand and squeezed gently.

"Are you real, Christopher?" she asked, turning to examine his face.

He screwed his lips to the side and furrowed his brow. "What on earth do you mean?"

"You seem too good to be true," she said simply, closing her fingers tighter around his as though fearing he would disappear if she let him go.

Even in the shadowy interior of the cab, she could see his cheeks darken. "I'm not. I'm just an ordinary man. Nothing at all out of the common way." He met her eyes. "I'm sorry to tell you this, love, but the way you grew up was nothing like normal. Your father is… evil."

"Yes." *Knowing that and believing it are two different things, but I do know it.*

"I'm not too good to be true. I have a number of bad habits," he admitted.

"What are they?" She looked into his eyes, curious to know what he saw as flaws.

"I'm always late, for one thing. I'm famous for it. I also have a temper."

A frisson of fear clenched her belly at the admission.

"Don't look at me like that; I would *never* hit a woman. It's a cowardly thing to do. I'm not a bully. Now, if a *man* makes me angry, I've settled it with my fists from time to time. Less now that I'm an adult, but in school, I got into quite a few scuffles. I've even studied pugilism since you never know when a threat might arise." He paused, waiting for her to relax before he continued. "I curse. And I despise tobacco. I find it so disgusting I can hardly help but object to people smoking in the same room as me, and snuff is worse."

Katerina grinned. "What a terrible monster you are." She leaned over and kissed Christopher on the cheek.

The look he turned on her simmered with possessive heat. *You're mine,* it seemed to say, *and I intend to claim you over and over until all other claims fall away.*

She shivered, but not with fear.

"I also have a strong appetite for lovemaking. I hope you're prepared for it." His lighthearted tone gave way to an intensity that matched his expression.

She had noticed, but honestly, the process hadn't been disgusting or unduly frightening. Just new and a little... surprising. Now that she knew what to expect, she felt perfectly willing, though the thought did make her cheeks color a bit.

"Yes, I think I could try it again," Katerina said, biting her lower lip, "though perhaps tomorrow night. The ache is still quite strong."

He patted her hand. "No doubt. Tomorrow will be fine. I can wait that long."

They pulled up in front of the Bennett family home, and Christopher helped his bride descend from the cab. Then he walked her up to the door, his arm wrapped gently around her waist to shield her from the cold.

An elderly gentleman answered his knock.

"Good evening, Tibbins," Christopher said, treating the servant with a courtesy normally due to a social equal. "Are my parents in?"

"Yes, sir," the man replied. "They're in the music room this evening."

"Very good. And how are your knees?"

His concern further astonished his bride. *If this is how he treats servants, maybe I really am safe.*

"Fine. Better actually thank you. Tonight, it's my arm that hurts." He clutched his withered bicep in one trembling hand and dug in the fingers.

"Heavens, we can't have that. Take care of yourself," Christopher insisted.

"I'll do that, sir, and thank you."

Now that they had found shelter from the biting wind, Christopher took Katerina's arm properly. Though she knew the layout well enough, having visited the sizeable house on more than one occasion, she allowed her husband to steer her. Her mind focused on the meeting, on worrying over the reaction of her dear friend to the rash and impulsive decision she'd just made.

Christopher led her to a familiar room and opened the door. Only three weeks ago she had visited for tea and played the lovely carved and painted harpsichord for Mrs. Bennett and Mrs. Turner.

"Good evening, Mother, Father," Christopher addressed his parents. "Is there any chance of a couple of weary souls finding food on such an icy night?"

"Of course, son," Julia replied, jumping from her seat and hurrying forward to greet the new arrivals. "But... Katerina, what on earth are you doing here? This is really too great a risk, my dear."

"It's fine, Mother," Christopher answered. "I remember you told me how great the danger was where Katerina was concerned, and I have applied myself to getting to know her as quickly as possible. We need to talk to you both to be sure we are all in agreement about how to proceed." He squeezed Katerina's fingers gently, as though sending a silent message.

"What do you mean, son?" Adrian asked, eyebrows like storm clouds.

"Well, should there be a sudden crisis, and I needed to take her out of the situation on a whim, with no time spent in preparation, just whirl her off to the bishop and marry her, would anyone object?"

What on earth is he doing? Katerina wondered.

"Hardly. And such a crisis is a real risk." Julia agreed grimly.

"I know," Christopher said grimly. "Father, you understand what we're talking about, do you not?"

Adrian nodded, his expression serious.

Katerina's cheeks colored. *So, everyone knows? I don't like that. And this conversation is ridiculous.* "Christopher, stop teasing your parents. Mr. Bennett, Mrs. Bennett, Christopher and I got married this morning."

Both of the elder Bennetts blinked in surprise. Julia recovered first. She jumped to her feet, chattering as she approached. "You did? Oh, very good. It takes a huge weight off my mind. I was so terribly afraid for you my dear."

Though her friend's kindness made Katerina want to weep, she swallowed the urge and replied in a calm voice, "You had cause. Thank you for sending him in my direction." She smiled, shyly because Mr. Bennett was there, and his intense and faintly disapproving expression made her uncomfortable.

Julia, exuberant as usual, scooped her new daughter-in-law into her arms and hugged her. Katerina returned the embrace and again tears threatened. Julia smelled and felt like a mother—like the mother Katerina had lost a decade before.

Then the embracing arms compressed a sensitive spot and an agonized squeak crept past Katerina's defenses. As she breathed deeply trying to dispel the pain, she could feel Adrian's curious stare from across the room.

"What's wrong?" Julia asked, studying Katerina's face with concern.

Katerina exhaled. "Well, there was a crisis, just as Christopher said. That was why we needed to act so quickly."

Warm dark eyes searched hers. "Are you injured?"

"Yes, but I'm healing," Katerina replied, trying to ignore the throbbing in her back.

Julia noted the bruise on Katerina's cheek but said nothing more on the subject. Instead, she kissed her on the other side. "Welcome to the family, love. We're so very glad you're here."

It was more than Katerina had expected. Her throat burned, but she suppressed it. She would have need of more tears, but hopefully, most of them could be shed in private. Too many people knew her sorrow already.

* * *

"Married, eh?" Adrian looked at his son's wary and damaged bride. He had not been entirely in agreement with his wife's plan to match those two together, but the obvious, dark bruise on her cheek made him powerfully angry. Her stiff uncomfortable movements spoke of other, more painful injuries. He turned to regard his son.

Christopher was watching his wife closely, and as soon as Julia stepped away, he swooped in, gathering up Katerina's hand in his and lacing their fingers together.

He's possessive of her in a way that speaks of intimacy. Looks as though the deed is done, so there will be no chance of an annulment. He hoped Christopher was prepared for the problems sure to come from marrying such a woman.

* * *

A serving woman ducked into the parlor. "Dinner is ready, sir, ma'am."

"Thank you, Marsden," Adrian replied. "Please set two extra plates."

She nodded and scurried away.

Meanwhile, the couples made their way to the dining room; darkly papered and with a heavy, brooding fireplace, but lightened by a cheerfully glowing chandelier and a table set in a crisp white cloth. Miss Marsden had arrived ahead of them and was setting two more blue and white plates along one side of the table as each husband escorted his wife to a simple, wooden chair.

A lovely smelling tureen filled with soup perfectly started the meal. Katerina was so hungry she ate surprisingly well, and as she did, it struck her how unusual it was for her to have such an appetite. Normally, she picked at her food, since dining with her father inevitably proved to be a stressful experience. As the wine flowed freely, weakening his already precarious control, the danger increased. Taking the time to savor a meal had always been unthinkable. She could not remember a time when she had; instead, she tended to gobble just enough to stave off starvation and then bolt for the marginal safety of her bedroom. But though the Bennetts' dinner table felt almost as nerve-wracking, trying to heal from her wounds, along with the turmoil of the hurried wedding and physical exertion of her first sexual experience, she could not deny her appetite.

As she sat at the table, trying to make herself chew slowly and not bolt her dinner, she realized the pain in her backside had significantly decreased. *Thank heaven. Bruises heal faster than cuts but sitting on them is deeply unpleasant.* Her internal soreness was fading as well and was quickly being replaced by a hint of curiosity. *We'll be trying 'it' again soon, I'm sure.*

Christopher had made it clear that he wanted her to be willing, which would be no hardship. *Those were the most interesting touches I've ever experienced. Pleasant, even, most of them. I'd like to know more.* He had mentioned having her on her back, and she imagined what it would be like, lying open under her husband's body as he thrust inside her. The thought made her cheeks warm with a combination of embarrassment and arousal. To cover it, she took a sip of wine.

She didn't say a word during the soup, nor the succulent beef roast that followed, but afterwards, Julia bounced from her seat, took Katerina's arm and hurried her into the parlor for a cup of tea and some serious conversation.

* * *

Christopher and his father remained at the table for glasses of port.

"What have you done, son?" Adrian asked without preamble, his voice grim with concern.

"What I had to do," Christopher replied.

"Why did you have to?" Adrian pressed.

Christopher shook his head. "There was no choice. She might not have survived another beating. The one she endured was bad enough, and it wasn't the first by any means."

"I know. Do you really think such a terribly abused woman is going to be a satisfying wife?"

Father knows how to ask the difficult questions. He responded with one of his own. "Do *you* really think I would be able to live with myself if she were murdered because I didn't act when I had the chance? Listen, Father, I know what you mean, but she wants to heal. She has promised to try. Do you think there is no hope?"

Adrian shook his head. "Hard to say. She's young. Hopefully, her fearfulness is not set into her for life. Perhaps she can overcome it in time, with your help."

Christopher nodded once. "That's my wish. I'm willing to work through this with her."

Adrian closed his eyes and pinched the bridge of his nose between two fingers. "How on earth did you get to such a place? You barely know this girl."

"I realize that. I didn't want to do it this way. The initial attraction was... promising. I wanted to get to know her slowly, court her, marry her when the time was right, maybe in a year or so," Christopher explained.

"That would have been the better way," his father said dryly, one eyebrow winging toward his hairline.

"It couldn't be," Christopher insisted. "I know she looks all right now, but you should have seen her yesterday. You should see what's under her dress. He damn near killed her, Father. I'm not exaggerating that it was a matter of life and death. The beating she took to the belly alone could have been fatal, not to mention if one of the wounds on her back festered..." Christopher shuddered.

"She does *not* look all right now," Adrian retorted. "She looks injured."

"She is," Christopher agreed, "but she's better than yesterday."

Adrian frowned.

You can't hide it, you tender-hearted old man. It bothers you too. Where do you think I learned my virtues from?

Then, with a sigh, Adrian shook off his dark contemplation. "Well, I can see there's no undoing it. You're married. And, from the way you look at her, I would guess, fully consummated as well."

Christopher met his father's eyes with a challenging stare. "Yes."

"So, there's nothing to do but move forward. How do you plan to turn a rescue into a marriage?" his father asked him, unfazed by his son's aggression.

With a sigh, Christopher flopped back against the chair. His port sloshed in the glass. "I'm not really sure." The sense of bewilderment he'd experienced earlier washed back over him. He took a sip of his drink and added, "I would appreciate some advice."

Adrian thought for a moment and then compressed his lips. "I don't know if I have any to give. It seems to me that gratitude is not enough of a basis for a vital relationship."

"No. I don't want us to remain mired in this sorrow forever."

"Naturally." Adrian pondered some more. "This thought occurred to me. She's certainly not used to expressing her feelings or asking for what she wants, so you run the risk of developing congenial parallel lives that really don't touch each other."

"How dreadful. I don't want *that*. How do I become… real to her?" He had been toying moodily with his glass, but now he met his father's eyes.

"I don't know," his father replied, blunt as always. "I suppose you're going to have to observe her closely. She won't ask for anything, so you have to figure out what she needs. It will be difficult, but if you don't do it, I'm rather sure she will withdraw from you and just live inside herself for the rest of her life. You'll need to draw her out gently and slowly, so she doesn't panic. In short, son, you've undertaken a monumental task. I hope you're up to the challenge."

Christopher rolled his eyes toward heaven. "So do I, Father."

Chapter 9

"OU'RE not upset, are you, Mrs. Bennett?" Katerina asked as she settled onto the bench of the harpsichord in the Bennetts' music room. *This room is my favorite in the house, the one where I feel most comfortable.*

"Upset, Katerina?" her mother-in-law replied, sinking onto the settee. "About what? And please do not call me Mrs. Bennett. It's your name too now, my dear. I'm either Julia or Mother to you."

"Mother, then," she said, pleased by the smile her words elicited. "About Christopher and me getting married without consulting you."

"Oh, no!" Julia cried, gesturing with her teacup and sloshing a little tea onto her dress. "I'm upset you had a... crisis. I was afraid something like this might happen. I hate how badly you've been hurt, but I'm delighted you're finally safe, my dear. I wanted this for you, for both of you. I think, once you've recovered from your ordeal a bit, you and Christopher will be excellent together. I do wish there had been time for us to talk a little, before the actual... marriage took place. I assume you're... fully married at this point?"

Katerina colored. "Yes."

Julia nodded. "Good. Did you know what to expect?"

The burn in her cheeks intensified. "Not at all, but Christopher got me through the process well enough."

"Oh dear. I imagine that was awkward." Mrs. Bennett's lips twisted at the thought.

"Yes." *And so is this line of questioning. Please, don't carry on.*

Julia, it seemed, was not finished, though she hesitated before asking, "Was it... all right?"

Katerina nodded, her hands pressed to her cheeks. "I didn't hate it."

"Good. That's a good start. Husbands like their intimacies very much. It's good if their wives do too."

"This is a very uncomfortable conversation."

"You're right," Mrs. Bennett agreed, though her own porcelain cheeks remained uncolored by any discomfort she might have felt, "but you don't have a mother. I want to be sure, since you're embarking on married life, that you understand what is needed. Do you have any questions?"

Katerina thought for a moment. "How do I fall in love with my husband?"

Julia blinked in surprise, and then a wide grin split her face. "What an excellent question, love. Here's what you do. First, don't rush yourself. You have a lot to get past before you can be open with anyone. But while you're healing, look at your husband. Every person has good and bad qualities. You need to understand the bad ones, how you feel about them, so you won't be surprised by them. And then you need to see what is good about Christopher, glory in it. Roll his goodness around yourself like a blanket until you feel warm and safe and happy with him."

"I already do," she replied. *And with every act of kindness he performs, almost without thought, I feel it more.*

"Do you?" Mrs. Bennett beamed. "Excellent. Keep doing it. And if you sometimes have to retreat, to pull back, don't fret. You can always return. A setback is not a defeat, and even the healthiest couples have them. Learning to make one out of two is difficult, but if you make yourself open to it, if you learn to trust, eventually you will succeed."

"I feel like I'm taking terrible advantage of him," Katerina admitted.

Mrs. Bennett dismissed the question with another wave of the teacup. This time the liquid remained inside. "You're not. Every man wants to be his lady's hero. He's fortunate; he's already yours. Isn't he, Katerina?"

"Oh yes. He saved my life," she replied fervently.

Her mother-in-law set the cup in a saucer, so she could continue gesturing safely. "He did. Now you dedicate your life to pleasing him, and I'll encourage him to do the same for you."

"Oh, he can't do any more for me," Katerina protested, pressing her hands to her cheeks. "It's too much already."

"Do you really think this one act is enough to sustain you for a lifetime?"

She nodded.

Mrs. Bennett gave her a sad, kind look. "It isn't. He wants to give you more. Let him. Let him fall in love with you too. You really are worthy of it, you know."

The conversation ended there because the men meandered through the door. Christopher took Katerina's arm and eased her from the harpsichord bench, leading her to the settee where he urged her to sit, joining their hands in his lap while Adrian perched beside his wife.

"Well, dear ones, I think we should host a reception in honor of this marriage," Julia said. "I understand why such a small wedding was necessary, but there should still be a celebration."

Katerina swallowed hard. A party in her honor sounded like... a nightmare. She hated people staring at her. She looked at her mother-in-law with panicky eyes.

Mrs. Bennett read the expression easily. "What, dear, don't you want a party?"

"No thank you," Katerina replied, desperately trying to sound calm. "You needn't go to all the trouble."

"It would be no trouble," her mother-in-law assured her. "I enjoy planning parties."

She's not understanding. "Please. You don't need to do that."

"Mother, listen. She's telling you no." Christopher said. "Kat, you can say no to my mother. No one will be upset. Tell her what you want."

Katerina shook her head. *This is already too much attention.* She closed her eyes for a moment, blocking everyone out.

Christopher noticed her increasing discomfort, and pulled her into his embrace, letting her hide her face on his shoulder.

"Looks like we've had enough togetherness for one day. We'll be back soon, I promise. Come on, love, it's time to go."

She nodded against his shirt, not wanting to meet anyone's eyes.

He helped her to her feet, and she suppressed a groan as her muscles and skin stretched. *I sat too long.* Opening her eyes as they began moving toward the door, she saw Julia regarding her with a worried expression, Adrian with an unreadable one. Focused on her own discomfort, she didn't spare much thought for either one.

Christopher escorted his bride outside. Katerina inhaled deep breaths of icy air as the breeze teased her borrowed clothing and cooled her overheated cheeks. She shivered. Christopher tightened his arms around her. She drew herself inward, blocking out sight but listening to the soft murmur of wind through fabric, the groaning of naked branches. The symphony of nature sufficed to soothe her better than any spoken reassurance. *Especially if it involves Christopher's arms around me.*

A distant clatter of hooves and jingle of reins cut into the quiet as a hansom approached. With a crunch of wheels, the conveyance stopped along the curb.

"Come on, love," Christopher urged, moving her toward the hansom and helping her into the seat. As they progressed back towards Christopher's lodgings, a burning shame fell on Katerina.

"I'm sorry," she said softly.

"For what?" he asked, puzzled.

"I ruined your evening." She swallowed hard at the admission.

"How?" he replied, clearly not understanding her.

Maybe, since he doesn't follow, it really wasn't a problem? But she explained anyway "I'm such a rabbit. I have no courage. I can't even hold a normal conversation."

"I understood," his arm snaked behind her back, "and I'm not upset. Mother should have known better. You hate to be the center of attention, don't you?"

"Yes."

Christopher contemplated. "Is attention a threat? If someone notices you, they might realize you've made some kind of mistake and tell your father?"

Is that why I don't like crowds? Because I don't know what they're going to do? "You may be right. I've never thought about it."

He pulled her closer. She rested her head on his shoulder. "But everyone was looking when you played. Why was that different?"

More questions. He wants very badly to understand. It's a pity I don't know the answers well myself. She considered. "I've been playing for Father's friends forever. I'm used to it."

"I see. Well," he continued, returning to the point, "we don't have to have a party. There's no great reason for it if you don't want one. But it's going to be important for you to work on telling people what you want. Don't hint quite so subtly my dear. It's hard to understand."

"Sorry." Her shame increased.

"No, don't be sorry." He caressed her cheek, wanting to soothe her. "It's not a judgment, just a suggestion. One step towards your new life as the happy and confident Mrs. Christopher Bennett."

She smiled ruefully. "That sounds good. Um, Christopher, do you think it's too late for me to have a bath when we get back?"

"No, it's not late really. Why?" he asked.

Ah good, an easy question. "I'm stiffening. A hot bath really helps."

His arm around her tensed. "Certainly, you may."

"Thank you."

"In the meanwhile, love, are you cold? Be honest."

"Yes." As though her teeth weren't chattering audibly in the frigid interior of the cab.

"Then come over here and let me warm you."

She scooted against his side and he embraced her, his arms resting lightly on her back. "Does this hurt?"

She considered the sensation of pressure against bruises and scars. "No."

"Truly?" He looked deep into her face as though testing her honesty. "Truly. It's fine."

"Good." His gaze fell to her lips. "Would you like a kiss?"

"Yes, please," she agreed eagerly.

He lowered his mouth to hers, touching her lips with the tip of his tongue and asking her to open. She did, and he treated her to a long round of passionate loving inside her mouth.

The cab pulled to a stop outside the hotel and Christopher reluctantly released his wife's lips, paid the fare, and escorted her back to his rooms, ringing for a bath.

Soon a portable tub filled with steaming water and Epsom salt filled up nearly all the available space in the sitting room, awaiting Katerina's sore body. All the furniture had been shoved into the corners to make room for the supposedly portable slipper bath, and the curl of lilac-scented steam coiled itself around her, making her shiver. She could hardly wait, but her borrowed dress had complicated fastenings, and she needed another set of hands to open them. Christopher, naturally, looked delighted at the thought of undressing her again.

"You know," he told her, looking at the tub, "I would love to share a bath with you."

She considered the possibilities and her cheeks began to burn. "Is that done?"

"Certainly, if you want," he replied, unflustered by the intimate thing he was requesting.

"I don't know." Her dithering was wasting the heat, but what could she say?

He seemed to sense her discomfort. "Tell the truth. Do you want me to be here, or do you want some privacy?"

She closed her eyes. "Privacy," she more mouthed than said.

He nodded, a little crestfallen but neither angry nor surprised. "That's fine, I'll wait in the bedroom. You enjoy your bath. I'm so proud of you for saying what you want." He kissed her gently and left her in peace.

Thank the Lord he's gone. At last, she could do what she needed. Stripping off her borrowed chemise, she sank into the water. Heaven. The salt stung on her cuts, but it also soothed her bruises and knots and the dainty injury her husband had inflicted between her legs.

As the pain and tension faded, her body relaxed, and it was a powerful relaxation the likes of which she could scarcely remember ever feeling before. She began, in some small part of herself, to understand what safe meant. Safe. Without warning the cry that had been threatening for the last several hours breached her defenses and she sobbed. It felt marvelous to release it.

"Kat?" Christopher knocked on the door, "are you all right? Do you need anything?"

Do I want his soothing? No. I want to work through this alone. "No, thank you," she called back in a wavery voice. "Nothing."

"Let me know if you change your mind, you promise?"

"Yes."

He left her alone. *Finally. I don't know how much longer I could have held on.* With a relieved groan, she sank into the water until only her face remained above the surface and let herself cry. Giving herself over to the power of her raw emotions, she allowed the overwhelming whirlwind of grief, fear, sorrow and confusion wash over her. As she wept, she realized it wasn't enough to fix her for good, but it was enough for today. Long minutes she gave to the catharsis until she felt... washed clean. *I'm embarking on a new life, with new opportunities. I can make myself into whatever I want to be, learn new reactions and new habits.*

The startling revelation brought a watery smile to her lips. For a decade she had lived like an animal, reacting, hiding, trying to avoid being noticed. She had not lived, merely survived as best she could, but that was no longer necessary.

I am not a mouse or a rabbit, I am a woman, and I have the potential to think, to observe, and to choose my actions, and behaviors. Self-awareness dawned like sunrise, bringing hope, a hope she had never expected. She could be more than a frightened animal. *I can be Katerina, whoever that is, Mrs. Christopher Bennett... a whole new identity.* She could tell her mother-in-law she didn't want a party, she could request something that suited her, or she could compromise. She could choose something uncomfortable to please others, but she didn't have to in order to avoid danger.

Her meandering thoughts turned to the source of her newfound freedom; Christopher. He had asked a little while ago for the intimacy of sharing a bath. In order to avoid conflict, she had been inclined just to let him make the decision, but he had begged her to be honest, and honestly, she had wanted to be alone. *He wasn't angry. He was disappointed but acquiesced to my wishes. He listened to me!* He had listened in bed too, she remembered, taking her quickly to minimize the pain, just as she had asked.

Affection towards her husband stirred within her. She had been attracted to him because he was handsome and soothing and represented safety. But suddenly she liked him. *I want his company because he's Christopher. He's safe and kind and he draws me in ways I don't fully understand. These are good thoughts, and I like them. I feel content.* Perhaps someday she would understand happy. For today contentment measured among the most pleasant things she had ever felt, like this soothing salted bath, like crying when she needed to, like the lovely pleasure she had felt earlier today when she let Christopher touch her.

I should let him touch me again, she decided. *He wants to, I'm sure of it.* She also felt again the shy curiosity about the act. He said that once her soreness faded, she would enjoy him putting... that inside her. *It's hard to imagine,* she thought, *it stung and burned so badly the first time.* Perhaps now, since she was open, the discomfort would not recur.

She had been sore all evening, a lingering embarrassing reminder that she had taken all her clothes off and been naked with a man who had touched her intimate parts and then thrust himself inside her. But the ache was fading in the warm water, and the man was her husband.

We pledged our bodies to each other, forsaking all others. That means I owe him access to mine. The realization that he also owed her access to his made her smile as a confusion of images and sensations filled her mind; of eyes filled with flattering desire, lips kissing her, arms embracing and supporting, fingers eliciting naughty pleasure from her unmentionable places. Heat coiled in her belly.

She sat up taller, her breasts breaking the surface of the water, the nipples hardening in the cool air. *I liked it when he touched me there, and he liked to do it.* She hesitantly stroked one bud. *Nice, but not really the same.* And lower, *am I ready to be touched there again?* Her hand slid under the water, down her belly. The bruises hardly hurt anymore, but touching herself proved too daunting, and she stopped. *I'll leave the intimate caressing to my husband. I suggested waiting until tomorrow, but right now I want to be touched. Am I brave enough to ask him?* she wondered. Then she shook her head. *Not really.* However, her nightgown remained in the bedroom. *I can emerge nude.* That might be clue enough.

Finished bathing, she stood and picked up a towel, pleased to be able to bend over. Then she dried herself quickly. The chill in the room from the drafts of wintery air filtering around the windows stung her, and her nipples hardened further. *Good.* Before her nerves could stop her, she walked quickly through the front room to the bedroom. Christopher reclined on the bed, reading a novel. He glanced up, and she grinned to see his eyes widen and his jaw drop.

"Did you have a good bath, love?" His calm voice seemed at odds with his stunned expression. Clearly, he had not expected a move this bold.

She smiled sweetly at him. "Yes. I really needed that. Perhaps, sometime, we can do… what you suggested."

"Let me know when you're ready," he told her eagerly.

"Is it normal for a husband to give his wife so much power over the choices?" she asked, surprised again by his generosity and consideration.

"How do I know?" He shrugged, his lips curling into a white-toothed grin. "I've never been married before. But I doubt it matters. Others have their marriages, but this is ours. I know what I want it to become, and I won't get there by being controlling."

She climbed onto the bed beside him. "The sheets have been changed."

"They have," he agreed.

Katerina blushed. "Well, it did have a significant mark," she said.

"Indeed," he winked, "and no wonder. Someone was deflowered here."

She put on a shy, innocent expression that was only half feigned. "I think it was me."

"You think? Aren't you sure?" He raised one eyebrow, and something about the position of his lips suggested he was concealing a smile.

"You know, I'm not," she teased.

Christopher grinned before adopting a playfully wounded air. "If you've forgotten, perhaps I should remind you."

"Perhaps you should." *Did I really just say that? What a hussy I've turned out to be.* But she couldn't help beaming. An unknown sensation rose up in her—an unexpectedly pleasant one.

His wolfish expression turned concerned. "How's your back?" he asked.

She rolled her shoulders. "Better."

"Let me see."

Blushing, she turned reluctantly. *I wish my scars would just go away. I'm no beauty, but at least, from the front, I look... normal. From the back... words cannot describe.*

"It does look better, I think," he commented, trailing one finger along her skin. The deadened sensation told her he was touching scar tissue. "The bruises are all yellow. Nothing's purple anymore, and all the scabs are solid. Can you lie on it comfortably?"

She lowered herself to the cool sheets and positioned herself. "Not too bad." *And completely hidden. That's even better.*

"Good. Your belly?" He trailed his fingers across the skin.

She squirmed at the tickling touch. "Much better. Really, that part wasn't as bad as it looked. His strength was about gone at that point, so those bruises were colorful but not very deep."

His palm came to rest on her skin. "I'm glad to hear it. I was worried about you."

"I was worried about me too," she admitted. "I think the corset didn't help."

"Likely not. No more of that. You're slender enough without it." He leaned over her, lowering his mouth to hers and kissing her again.

She slid her arms around his neck and pulled him closer.

"Kat, are you feeling better here?" He slid his hand down to her mound.

"Yes," she admitted through her blush. "It stopped aching in the bath."

Uncertainty chased across his features. "Would you like to be close again?"

Steeling herself against her own discomfort, she hastened to reassure her husband. "I think... yes." She colored prettily. It felt wanton to be asking for his intimate caresses, but she couldn't help herself. So many slaps and punches, so few hugs had left her deprived, and she was hungry to be touched.

He sat back, stripping off his clothing and shedding it wildly all over the floor. Then he joined her again, stretching out beside her. He cupped the delicate arch of her neck in one hand, turning her towards him for long arousing kisses.

"Are you feeling brave, love?" he asked at length.

"What did you have in mind?"

"I want your tongue in my mouth again. Can you do that?"

"Oh." Recalling the deep kisses that had so wonderfully enhanced their last lovemaking, she smiled. *Yes. I can do that.* She leaned toward him for the kiss and did as he had requested, tasted him timidly. Like the shy girl she was, she showed him she wasn't sure how to cope with her own desire but felt it, nonetheless.

He let her explore the growing sense of her own boldness, and then finally pulled away. "Well done, love. You're learning so fast. And now, let me turn my attention to these pretty little breasts of yours. They look... lonely. See how they reach for me? Do they want to be touched, Kat?"

"Please." Her back arched in eager anticipation.

He cupped one in each hand and lowered his face, pressing his lips to the silky skin between. Her breath caught as he slid his mouth over the dainty globe, wetting it in a burning line. He snaked out his tongue and teased the nipple.

"Oooh," she breathed, "how nice."

"And this?" He sucked the sensitive peak into his mouth.

She had no words, but really, she didn't need them. Her soft sigh told him what he needed to know. He tugged and licked and teased her, and she responded eagerly, clutching the back of his head and pressing him closer. This touch had the intensity she had missed in the bath. A partner made all the difference. *Christopher makes it different.* She was not alone anymore. She was part of a family, a real family.

"That feels nice," she murmured.

"Good." His voice rumbled against her breast, "I want you to feel wonderful."

His hand shaped and gently squeezed the other side. Finally, he released the wet, straining nub and turned to the other.

She sighed again as he pleasured her. Each tug on her breast created an answering sizzle low in her belly. Arousal grew, bringing wetness that signaled her readiness for her husband.

Her hands left his hair and stroked down his back, feeling the bunched muscles under the smooth skin. *He's a beautiful man, and astonishingly, he's mine.* This tender lovemaking would be available for her to enjoy for the rest of her life. *Perfect.*

Suddenly he shifted. Leaving her nipples bereft he trailed his lips over her belly, kissing the partially healed bruises and teasing her navel before moving lower still, his hands parting her thighs.

What mischief is he up to now? "Christopher?"

"Trust me, love," he replied. "I want to make you feel good."

He can't be serious. "Like this?"

Their eyes met across the plain of her belly, and she noticed the hungry gleam in his silver gaze. "Yes. I can't wait to taste you. Open."

She tensed, then made herself relax. *His touches so far have been good. He wouldn't ask me to do anything that was wrong or bad. Trust is a choice, isn't it?* She closed her eyes as his fingers opened her, baring her intimate parts to his gaze.

"You're very wet, little love," he told her gravely.

Oh no! What have I done now? "You said that was good," she reminded him, fighting down panic.

Christopher dropped his teasing air. "It is," he reassured her. "Kat, do you... like... to be made love to?"

"I do. Am I a bad girl?" she asked, her voice hesitant as fear threatened to overwhelm her. She suddenly wanted not to be lying naked and vulnerable before this man, but to hide in the wardrobe.

"No. You're a good wife," he replied firmly.

And then he lowered his lips, stopping her voice. He made love to her with his mouth, kissing and licking her in that tender spot he had caressed earlier, and it felt even sweeter than she remembered. Gradually, fear gave way to pleasure, to trust. She recalled, at last, why she'd put faith in him to begin with. *It wasn't desperation, it was instinct deeper than fear. Christopher will never harm me.* Knowing again that she was safe, Katerina forced herself to relax and let him play.

* * *

"And now, let's see if you're really better." Christopher slid a finger deep into his wife's body. Her back arched as he penetrated her. *Very nice. She likes that, but can she handle a little stretching?* He pulled out and returned, with two fingers this time, and he could see from the faint clenching of her teeth that it did sting a bit; after all, he'd removed her maidenhead earlier that day. But then she relaxed, arching into it, liking the pleasure more than she feared the discomfort. Satisfied she would be able to take him in when the time came, he returned his attention to loving her, working his fingers in and out to prepare her while he licked and suckled.

"Christopher?" she called out in a voice that had a hint of a wail to it. "Love?"

"It's happening again." She squirmed, shifting her hips, and he understood what she meant.

"It will be good again. Let it happen," he urged, glad her moment of panic had passed.

Katerina tossed her head on the pillow, seemingly aching for release, and he worked diligently to get her there. She hovered on the edge, so he spread his fingers and sucked hard, and she orgasmed with a sweet cry. She arched her back, completely undone and unashamed at her response. And then he slid his fingers out.

She lay panting as he bent her knees, positioning them widely apart. He aligned himself, feeding the tip inside her again. He didn't want to risk reopening the wounds on her back by rubbing her body on the sheets, so he slid one arm under her shoulder blade to keep her stationary as he pressed slowly into her. *If I do this correctly, there should be no pain.*

Katerina closed her eyes and took a deep breath. She still felt very tight, and his entry must have stung a bit, but she accepted it. He paused for a moment to let her catch her breath and then slid to the hilt inside her. She made a soft sound.

"Is that all right, love?" he asked, stilling his motion again.

"Yes. What an odd sensation." Katerina rocked her hips to one side and then the other.

"You'll adjust." He worked his other arm under her, pinning her completely so she lay captive to his passion. She shifted, instinctively wrapping her legs around his thighs.

He met her eyes, startled. Then he lowered his mouth to hers for a long kiss while he began to thrust inside her. The friction of his movement seemed to please her. She whimpered and sighed each time he surged deep. She met each inward glide with a sideways shiver. The movements added spice to her enticing heat and wetness. Her flesh fluttered around him, ratcheting his own pleasure to greater heights until at last he moaned and emptied himself inside her.

"Was that good?" she asked him as his climax faded.

He had to take a moment to catch his breath. "I think… I'm going to like being married. What about you?"

"I'm starting to think there might be reason to hope."

"Good. I'm so very glad you like to be touched." He slid out of her, rolling to his side and pulling her into his arms. "Let's sleep, love. It's been a long day, and we have much to do tomorrow too."

"Yes," she agreed, snuggling into his embrace. "Our wedding day is over. Our marriage is beginning."

"It is." He kissed her lips.

* * *

A few blocks away, Adrian Bennett stretched out in bed beside his wife and took her in his arms, stroking the fiery silk of her hair. "Julia?"

"Yes, my darling?"

"Why did you do this?" he asked, his face wreathed with concern.

"Do what?" she replied, feigning innocence.

Her attempt did not fool her husband. "You know what. You orchestrated the whole thing. Why was Christopher supposed to marry that woman?"

"She needed it," Julia replied simply.

He raised one eyebrow. "And what about him? She's a ruin. How is this going to be good for him?"

Julia thought about her words carefully. "She's not a ruin, at least I don't think so. She's hurt, to be sure, but I think there's hope. I mean, I've been her friend for the last year. I know she was very shy tonight, but it was probably because you were there. When she's comfortable, she's quite charming and sweet. There's a real woman there, under the pain. Once she heals a bit, they'll be quite good together. If I didn't think so, I wouldn't have done this. Besides, Christopher has always been a little... self-centered. He knows how handsome he is, how easily women fall into his arms. It will be good for him to focus on someone else's needs."

"What?" he asked, concern hardening to a pointed, narrow-eyed stare.

Oh dear, I didn't suppress that feeling deeply enough. "It's nothing."

"Tell me, Julia."

She attempted again to prevaricate, feeding out a partial truth. "Well, he's always been a bit of a rake, you know? The gossips say he had an... indiscretion with an opera singer a few months ago."

Adrian shrugged. "And? He's young. These things happen."

Julia compressed her lips and gave her husband a speaking look. "I don't like that they do. He doesn't need to cheapen what is best between a man and woman. It's time for him to grow up and understand how much better love can be. Katerina has many fine qualities. She'll be as good for him as he is for her."

Adrian smiled.

She knew that, like his son, he'd sown quite a few wild oats when he was young, but Julia wasn't backing down. The passion between a husband and wife was so much better than flings with loose women. He'd admitted as much more than once.

"Come now, love," Adrian urged, "I won't believe you did this because of a months-old affair. Tell the truth, Julia."

"Fine." Her voice was suddenly fierce. "I want her for myself. I want to be her mother. I love her like a daughter and..."

"And you've missed having one all these years?" Finally, Adrian understood, if the look on his face was any indication.

"Yes," Julia admitted, bitter grief twisting her lips and stinging her eyes. "She would have turned nineteen in March. It's only a few months difference."

He gave a single, slow nod. "Julia, Katerina can't replace Andrea."

Her voice wavered as she answered. "I know, but she's special too."

"And now she can be yours?" he guessed.

"Yes."

"Are you certain she's capable of becoming the kind of wife he needs?" he pressed, aiming straight at the heart of the matter.

"She already is," Julia insisted, "and I'm sure she will get better as time goes on."

"I hope you're right," Adrian said in a voice that spoke clearly of his doubt.

A hint of worry flared. "So do I, darling. So do I."

Chapter 10

ATERINA was enjoying a simple but tasty breakfast of hot buttered toast and tea, accompanied by the unrivaled pleasure of looking at her husband across the little table. Dark stubble spread across his cheeks, making him look rakish. Bed-messy hair added to the illusion. He pored over a newspaper in search of rental advertisements. They'd had a breakfast tray sent, wanting to linger a while in the apartment and savor their closeness rather than joining the throng in the dining room.

She took a sip of the dark unsweetened brew and sighed.

The sound brought his head up. "Are you well, love?"

She gifted him with a shy smile. "Yes. I feel wonderful. I don't know that I've ever slept so peacefully."

He grinned, and there a hint of masculine possessiveness slipped into it, though his words, when he spoke, sounded ordinary. "That's good to hear. So, are you up for seeing a few properties today? This setup was cramped when it was just me."

Katerina rolled her shoulders experimentally. "I think so."

"You seem to be moving more freely today," he commented.

"Yes. The bath helped immeasurably, and you also... relaxed me." Her cheeks burned, but not as much as she had expected. *Hussy,* she chided herself, but even in her own mind, it was a jest. She felt amazing.

He smirked and winked at her. "Any time, love."

She colored prettily.

And then, breakfast finished, she dressed while he shaved. Soon the newlyweds were ready to search out a place to make their home together.

* * *

"Well, love, what do you think so far?" Christopher asked from his seat beside Katerina in the hansom.

She shrugged. "Um, I suppose the small one was best so far, though I don't fancy the thought of all those stairs. Walking directly into the kitchen isn't my favorite either. It isn't good for entertaining. I wonder who designed such a structure."

"I agree. It wouldn't be much of an improvement over my rooms. Each floor is about the same size, only there are more of them, but at least it's furnished. What about the larger place?"

"It needs too much work," she pointed out. "Those holes in the walls and floors will leave us either marooned in the hotel for weeks or living in the middle of the renovation. And *then* we'd still have to furnish the whole thing, and it's *huge*."

"Astute observations, love."

"And the rooms in the other hotel?" she suggested. "The size is right, and it's quite luxurious."

"Too expensive," he replied. "I don't want to spend so much of our monthly income on housing alone, even if it is furnished. I hope this last place is better."

"Well, the location is convenient," Katerina commented. "In the last minute, we've passed a greengrocer, a butcher and a bakery."

The hansom rolled to a stop with a jingle and clatter, and the couple stepped down.

"Wait again, sir?" the driver asked, grinning at what a profitable morning he had spent with the Bennetts.

"Please," Christopher agreed.

The man tipped his hat.

The cold wind had died down to a shivery breeze and a pale sun seemed to be trying to warm her, though it would be several months before any discernable heat would appear. Christopher withdrew the key he'd received from the agent.

Katerina crossed her fingers as she took in their last option. The neighborhood consisted of a single continuous string of identical two-story structures, all red brick with white plaster columns supporting white balconies. The windows had been shaped into triangular peaks for added interest.

"This place is charming!" Katerina exclaimed, resting her hand on the iron pole of a gas streetlamp.

"It is," Christopher agreed, "and the location is quite good. Close to my parents, far from the Thames and the factory."

"Doesn't that mean you'll be longer getting to work?" Katerina wondered. "The weather is still quite cold."

He shrugged. "Once I find my gloves, I'll be fine. Living far from the factory is a blessing unless you fancy darkening your hair in a shower of ash."

"Your gloves are under the bed," Katerina replied, smirking at his sudden, thunderstruck stare. "I noticed them this morning when I was trying to find my other boot, and I see what you mean about the ash. Very well. Shall we go in?"

Inside, the lower level consisted of a series of rooms arranged along a central hallway with creamy plaster on the walls and polished wood on the floors. First, a small parlor waited to greet guests. Katerina could imagine a comfortable, stylish sofa, a few armchairs and a little table with a vase for flowers. The size precluded fitting in any musical instruments. Even a diminutive harpsichord would have no place once the furniture arrived. Across from the parlor, a room with built-in shelves seemed to be a study. She smiled to imagine Christopher sitting behind a heavy, masculine desk, a glass of sherry nearby, bent over a pile of correspondence. Behind the parlor, a long dining room dominated the rest of the house, large enough to invite the entire poetry group to dinner, should an alternate location become required.

At the back, opening to the outdoors, the kitchen retained a pleasing aroma of previous meals, like a ghostly yet friendly hug.

"Do you cook much?" Christopher asked.

Katerina shook her head. "A few things, but not many. Father has a great deal of money. You see, *his* father had a shipping business, which he inherited. Since it runs itself best without his interference, he simply collects the money and does whatever he wants. Father does have trouble keeping servants because of his temperament, but he always manages to replace them. My duties in the household were… limited."

Christopher's gaze turned inward as he leaned against a cold and dormant cast-iron stove and Katerina could almost see the gears turning in his head. *Probably refiguring the budget.* "I think we can afford a cook-maid," he said at last, confirming her surmises, "and of course, my man. Can you get by with that?"

She nodded. "Certainly. Especially if I have mostly clothing that does not require help to put on."

"Which I'm sure you would prefer," Christopher commented.

He's right, she realized. *I always hated my maid Marietta seeing my back and making judgmental comments. Even if I found a maid who kept her own counsel, I would still wonder what she was thinking.* "Would it bother you to have me dressing like a governess?" Katerina asked.

Christopher turned, his eyes intense as he looked her up and down. At last, he shook his head. "Of course not. I know you won't be happy if you're uncomfortable, and in my circles, there are plenty of women who prefer simple, modest clothing. You wouldn't be alone in that."

Katerina smiled, but inside her sense of disbelief grew. *This is too good to be true. How can I trust it?* Shoving the nervous voice away, she considered the kitchen. "So far this place seems quite good," she said, changing the subject.

Christopher accepted her dodge with a wry twisting of lips and escorted her from the room. Across the hall from the kitchen, tucked behind the dining room, a small box of a room seemed to serve no purpose. Shrugging, Christopher led her to the staircase at the very back of the building and up steep stairs with a pretty, if slightly threadbare black and red rose runner.

Upstairs were two small bedrooms and one large one. In the attic, two even smaller bedrooms would suit the yet-to-be hired cook-maid and Christopher's man of all work. They returned downstairs to the main floor and stood in the hallway. Christopher turned a slow circle. "I think this one will do," he told her.

"I agree," she replied, enjoying the coziness of the house. Very little draft seeped in, and even without a fire, the inside felt warm.

"Unfortunately, it's not furnished," her husband continued.

"We'll work on that," she replied. "What comes with you from your rooms?"

"Everything, but one can hardly furnish a home with a sofa, two chairs, a table and a bed," he said.

Katerina heard something of a whine in his voice. *Seems my husband does not enjoy shopping. Perhaps I should take the burden from him. How exciting to pick out furniture for my own home.* "True, but it's enough to get started, and we can work on the rest later." She trailed her fingertips down his arm and grasped his hand.

"There's only one thing I don't like about this house," he added.

"What's that?"

"Come on." He led her to the little room near the kitchen. "What a waste," he said, waving at the plain plaster walls.

"Oh, but it's perfect!" she exclaimed.

He gave her a confused look. "It is? What is this room to you, love?"

"It's a music room! What a pity you don't have a pianoforte." *It would sit right there, between the two windows, with red velvet draperies and a painting above.* She whirled around imagining the rest of the space. *Two armchairs to match the draperies, some small tables, and a bookshelf filled with songbooks and sheet music floor to ceiling.*

"A music room?" Understanding dawned on Christopher's face. "Of course. You do need one, don't you? Don't fret for a moment, love. I know just how to acquire a pianoforte for you. I won't let your music get away from you. But first, let's secure this place before someone snaps it up."

"Yes, let's." Katerina bubbled with excitement over her new home. *My home. Mine and Christopher's.* In this house, they would begin forging their marriage, and hopefully, the shadows of her childhood would begin to fall away. It was such a lovely house, and she adored it.

The signing of papers and paying of deposits only took a short time. Soon, Christopher escorted his wife down Bond Street, where the shops crowded closely one upon the other. At their first stop, he bought her a warm winter wrap. Snuggling gratefully inside the folds of amethyst fabric, she took her husband's arm and he led her to an auspicious-looking shop called Channing & Company. Of course, Katerina had heard of them. Not only did they make well-known instruments, but they also published sheet music. All serious musicians knew the Channing name.

Inside, the room smelled of wood and wax; the comforting aroma of pianos. A salesman who appeared to be about forty, with dignified silver wings in his dark hair approached the couple. "Hello, sir, madam. How can I help you?"

Katerina looked at the serious man and began to feel anxious. *What do I know about buying a piano? Nothing.* Anxiety twisted her insides.

Christopher stroked her hand gently and then he addressed the salesman. "I've just married a very accomplished pianist, and I thought there could be no better wedding gift than a pianoforte of her own."

"Ah, well we have some lovely models over here," the man replied, slipping seamlessly into his pitch. He led them to a corner of the showroom where ornate instruments stood gaudily about, drawing the eye. Katerina walked slowly towards one. Its curved legs struck her as quite pretty, and its open lid invited passers-by to examine its intricate strings.

"May I?" She indicated the bench.

The salesman looked askance. "What do you mean, my dear?"

"I want to play this piano and see how it sounds." *Does he really expect me to buy it without playing it, based on its looks alone? How odd.* Again, anxiety made her belly swoop. *Perhaps I'm not supposed to play it? Is it wrong to ask? Why don't I know these things?*

"Very well." He pulled out the bench, cutting off her nervous internal monologue, and she sat. *Well if it was wrong to ask, it's too late to worry about it now.* Katerina warmed up her fingers by playing a few rapid scales and then she shook her head.

"What's wrong with it, love?" Christopher asked her.

"It's out of tune," she said softly, "and the tone isn't very good."

The salesman gawked at her but touching the white ivory keys had shattered her nervousness and made it possible for her to take command of herself. She rose and moved to another instrument. This one was ridiculously ornate but had such a poor tone even Christopher winced to hear it. She tried another and another to no avail.

"I'm sorry, sir," she told the employee. "These pianos just don't sound very good. Do you have anything less... fancy, but more playable?"

He shook himself, blinking his staring eyes and closing his gaping mouth with a snap. "Yes, of course. I apologize. Usually, when young ladies come in here, they are more interested in the looks of the thing."

"I am not most young ladies then," she said dryly, offended by the sound of the poorly made pianos.

"I suppose not. Here, come with me. I'll show you our professional model instruments, ones used by orchestras and theaters. They aren't showy, but the sound should suit you much better."

He led them to a different part of the building, where plain, unadorned black instruments gleamed in the faint January sunshine. Katerina walked among them, running her fingers over the polished surfaces. She eventually stopped at one, seemingly at random, and seating herself dreamily on the bench. Fingers tingling, she touched the ivory keys. And then, without warning, the crashing opening chords of the Sonata Pathetique rattled the windowpanes. The last time she had played this piece, wounded and half-fainting, she had demonstrated exceptional power and skill. Today the music in her soul poured out through the keys. Submerged in a symbiotic connection with the flawless instrument, she lost herself completely and became living music.

When the piece ended, she felt like weeping. She took several slow deep breaths. *Get ahold of yourself, girl,* she told herself fiercely. *It's only a piano. Crying over it is too much.*

"This is the one, isn't it, love?" Christopher asked, laying a hand on her shoulder.

"Yes," she replied, the word catching in her throat.

"All right. It will be at our house by tomorrow."

She nodded. "Thank you, darling."

He gifted her with a tender smile. "You are very welcome."

"And you, sir," she told the salesman earnestly.

"No, my dear, thank you," he replied. "I never grow tired of hearing a pianoforte played well."

She smiled and let her husband lead her from the showroom, back down the street under vast rows of multicolored awnings. They walked past the display windows of a toy shop, from which dolls and teddy bears regarded the street with black button eyes. A greengrocer teased the frozen inhabitants with a pyramid of oranges imported from Spain. A bookseller displayed the latest collection of poetry against a backdrop of rather dusty black velvet. At last, they arrived at a garment shop.

"Now then, my dear, I believe you said you were lacking in clothing?" Christopher said, indicating the display window with a wave of his hand.

"Yes, terribly, but we've spent enough."

He smiled indulgently. "Love, my father *owns* a cotton mill," he reminded her. "I'm his second in command. We're hardly lacking in funds. I've been saving for years."

"Why?" she asked. *Saving money? What a novel concept.*

"Common trait of the middle class," he replied. "I don't believe in wasting all my money on dissipated living. I knew I would want a wife someday, and a family, so I set money aside each year in preparation, which means that now I can afford a few new things for you. Besides, our company supplies this woman with fabric, and in exchange, she gives us a discount. Good thing, since you need all new undergarments as well as dresses for various occasions. Do you ride?"

She shook her head. "No." The thought of the large animals made her shudder. *I prefer my own two feet.*

He seemed not to notice. "All right. You won't need a riding habit then. Ah, here's the modiste." He turned towards a dark-haired woman with a sharp nose. "Madame Olivier, my wife is in need of a complete wardrobe. Please outfit her with everything. Love, do you mind if I step out? Women's clothing shops suffocate me. I'll be back to collect you soon."

Katerina swallowed hard, her face growing hot, but she bravely consented. "Very well, Christopher."

He turned to leave, but said over his shoulder, "Remember, no corsets. You don't need them, and I like you to be able to breathe." He swept out, leaving his bride blushing in the stuffily close environment of the shop, in the care of a stranger who quickly had her stripped down to her borrowed undergarments, tutting over her lack of womanly endowments. Katerina kept silent but dared to admit to herself that her husband had found no cause to complain.

"Oh, mon Dieu!" the woman exclaimed from behind her.

Katerina sighed. "Je sais, madame. Ils sont horribles, n'est-ce pas? S'il vous plaît, madame, aidez-moi avec des vêtements qui peuvent les...cacher."[1]

"Yes, you're right." Mme Olivier switched to English. "I apologize. I was... startled. Of course, we can. It's fortunate that... they don't come up any higher, or it would be hard to find you anything fashionable to wear. Also fortunate that the style these days is only a little open in the back. But was your husband serious? No corset?"

"Yes," Katerina replied, shuddering at the memory of painful injuries compressed by whalebone. "I have no need to be too fashionable. I

---

1. They are horrible, aren't they? Please, ma'am, help me with some clothing that can hide them.

prefer to look modest. Clothing I can don and remove myself would be my preference."

Mme Olivier rolled her eyes at the thought of modesty and simplicity, but made no comment, turning instead to the topic of undergarments. "How will you support your bosom?" she demanded.

Katerina glanced down at the small swell in the front of her borrowed chemise. "It needs very little. Perhaps some stays will suffice?"

Mme Olivier circled around her and regarded the slender figure. "Yes. That will do nicely. A few extra pleats in the skirt will create the illusion of a more generous curve."

And make me look like a stuffed goose, I wager. "Very well."

* * *

Two hours later, Christopher returned for his wife. He had arranged to have Mackenzie move their meager possessions to their new home and posted an advertisement for a cook-maid, which was scheduled to run the next day. Soon, they would need to shop for more furniture, but today he had long since grown tired, and he was sure Katerina felt worse. By the time he settled the bill at the shop, their bed should be in their home and ready for a couple of newlyweds to retire in.

He entered the shop and found his wife standing on a stool while Mme Olivier adjusted the hem of a dress. The rich burgundy with black piping suited her dusky coloring, and the sleeves, rather than being heavily puffed to the wrist, were fitted to her slender arms. Lovely. Undergarments, nightgowns, and more dresses in sedate plaid and brown prints lay everywhere, ready to be purchased. A glorious gleaming-white party dress draped across the arm of an assistant, ready to be fitted to Katerina's delicate figure.

"She looks good in white," he commented idly from the doorway of the room.

"With her lovely coloring, she certainly does," the modiste replied.

"Well done. I see you haven't let her economize too much." He waved at the pile of garments.

The proprietress gave his wife a telling glance before turning to him with a smirk. "No, I know you are a man of excellent taste and want your wife to look her best."

"I do."

"I think this is excessive," Katerina said softly from her perch.

I knew she'd think that. "Hardly, love. I would say it's just enough."

She pondered this in silence for a moment, and then said simply, "Thank you." The words were accompanied by an intense look that promised more tangible thanks later.

"You are very welcome," he replied, risking the wrath of the modiste to lift his wife's hand to his lips before stepping back, letting the women finish their work.

Mme Oliver unlaced the wine-colored dress and pulled from Katerina's body, leaving her in a chemise and a set of short, waist-length stays, which supported her breasts without constricting her breathing. The assistant slipped the white gown over her head and quickly fitted for alterations. Finally finished, Katerina wriggled into a ready-made dress in a cream flowered print with a full skirt and heavy pleats in the bodice. The cut created the illusion of a full bosom above a tiny waist, done so skillfully that the ruse could not readily be detected.

Christopher paid for the dresses and led his wife out to a waiting hansom, which took them to their new home. As he had hoped, the bed had been placed in the largest bedroom, and the young couple retired for an afternoon nap which involved little sleep but proved wonderfully relaxing, nonetheless.

Chapter 11

ONDAY morning, Christopher headed to the cotton mill to meet with his father, Colonel Turner and some of the other employees. As he exited the hansom, he glanced at the tenements through a mist so heavy it was nearly rain.

What a shame people have to live like this. London has always been full of the poor and downtrodden, but recently, massive numbers of people swarmed into the city to work in factories. Most are poorly paid and end up living in places just like this. The failure of the potato crop in Ireland a few years before has only increased the crowding. Those squalid little apartments sometimes hold multiple families in their filthy depths. Disgusting. He hurried inside.

The heat and humidity inside the mill—necessary to keep the cotton strands supple—provided a welcome respite from the cold of the morning. Christopher met his father and the colonel at the door.

None of the men spoke. Over the earsplitting noise of the factory, there was no point. Colonel Turner extended a handful of masks. Christopher fitted his over his face.

From the door, he could see the long row of looms. At each one, a worker sat, also masked, working the shuttles as a rainbow of fabric emerged.

Men ran among the looms, gathering the products and transporting them. The place bustled with activity, each face set in serious lines as they communicated with one another using hand gestures.

The owners grabbed handfuls of raw cotton and fashioned them into earplugs before making their way among the weavers for their daily productivity check.

A new worker Christopher hadn't met before caught his eye. She sat at a weaving loom, a shuttle flying fast under her skilled manipulations. Something strange about her hand warranted a second look, and he felt ill upon noticing the ring finger on her right hand had been reduced to a raw, red stump. She seemed to sense his presence and looked up.

Seeing he was young and handsome, she winked at him above the mask.

She's a comely little wench, but my wife is more appealing. Then his eyes narrowed. She had a bruise around one eye.

Shaking his head, he followed his father and the foreman to the office, which was equipped with simple plain desks for father and son. The walls had been outfitted with the best sound-proofing which could be had in 1848; they were stuffed with newspaper. *Doesn't help too much,* Christopher thought, not for the first time, as his ears adjusted to the clanking and hissing of the factory.

"Well," Adrian asked as the men removed their masks, "how is everything, Turner?"

"Excellent," the bluff former soldier replied, smoothing out his silvered blond hair where the mask had rumpled it. "As you can see, we have a new girl, Miss Jones. She's quite accomplished on the loom."

"What happened to her?" Christopher asked, his voice dark.

Colonel Turner shot a look in Christopher's direction. "What, her finger? She lost it at her previous employment. Machine accident."

He shook his head. "I've seen that before. Who's beating her?"

"What?" The Colonel appeared thunderstruck.

"She has a black eye."

Turner lowered his eyebrows. "You know, I'm not sure. I'll see if I can get Mrs. Turner to talk to her and find out."

"That would be good." Christopher thought of his own sweet wife. *After our lovely weekend together, it was wrenching to leave her, she still seems so frightened and uncertain, but she has cook-maids to interview, and her lovely new pianoforte to keep her company.* He had finally left, and despite long good-bye kisses, he had almost been on time. *I suppose that means she's good for me too.*

The gentlemen settled into their desks upstairs while Colonel Turner returned to the floor. As usual, a mountain of paperwork awaited the father and son, and they settled into reading and signing.

Christopher filled out an order form for cerulean dye and for a new wheel for a loom that had turned cranky the previous week. *I'm looking forward to taking that bastard apart and putting it back together again,* he thought to himself, wondering what his old school chums would have thought. *Most of them didn't care a whit about working with their hands or repairing anything bigger than a faulty sentence. Not me. I've done every job in this factory from repairing the equipment—my specialty—to hauling bolts of fabric and bales of cotton with the men. Ah, well. Chacun à son goût, as the French say. I love my job.*

"So, son," Adrian asked, signing a document with a flourish and setting it aside to dry, "how is your marriage so far?"

"Quite good," Christopher replied, filling in an order form for dark brown dye. "We've settled into a little house and Katerina is interviewing cook-maids today. I bought her a pianoforte."

"Does she play?" His father queried, meeting his son's eyes across the room.

Christopher responded with a brief, enthusiastic nod. "Yes. She's incredibly talented. I'll ask her to play for you sometime. You'll be astonished. Mother didn't tell you this?"

"She may have," he admitted. "When she goes on about what her friends are up to, my mind sometimes wanders."

His mind wanders? If my wife wants to tell me something, I'll listen. Or if she wants to play or since for me again. She's incredible. Remembering his wife's skilled performance led to memories of the night he'd rescued her... and then to another distressing thought.

Adrian noticed immediately. "What are you not telling me, son? You look... upset all of a sudden."

Christopher shook his head. "It's nothing."

"Come on, Christopher," Adrian urged. "Let it out. Who else are you going to talk to? You've undertaken a massive and risky venture with this woman."

"Actually, she's doing better than I expected," he argued.

"Excellent. But?" Adrian waved his hand, urging his son to the point.

Christopher gave up prevaricating. "But she has a little... mannerism I dislike."

"And that is?"

"She flinches. A lot. Any time someone makes a sudden move near her, she shies away, covering her head." He made a face.

Adrian arched his eyebrow. "Does it surprise you?"

Christopher sighed. "No, not really. I just wish... she didn't do it to me, that she trusted me not to hit her. I suppose it's too soon."

"Does she shy away from every touch?" Adrian asked.

"Not at all, she's quite... affectionate." His cheeks warmed at the pleasant memories those words stirred. "Just easily spooked."

"Well then, she's not really reacting to you. It's the movement," Adrian reassured his son.

"Right. Of course." Christopher pondered. "Do you think she'll ever stop doing that?"

"Perhaps," Adrian allowed cautiously, "but even if she doesn't, is it really so bad? Many people have one or more annoying mannerisms, like nail biting or mustache twirling. I used to know a girl who chewed on her hair. It was revolting."

"Yes, it's bad." Christopher made a face. "Biting one's fingernails isn't very tidy, but it's hardly the same thing. *Do you really think I want a wife who recoils from every movement?*"

"It doesn't mean she mistrusts you," his father pointed out. "She can't help it."

Christopher looked out the window. The cold weather barely allowed for a dreary drizzle. A few degrees colder and ice would pelt the city. The bone-chilling droplets obscured the unlovely view of the tenement across the street. He debated whether to say more. *I shouldn't... she'd be embarrassed, but we're married. Everyone knows what that means, and I need advice about how to handle this.* At last, he blurted, "We were making love at the time. All I wanted was to caress her face."

* * *

"Sorry." Adrian grimaced. *How unpleasant that must have been at such an intimate moment.* "You know, son, in all marriages, there are things each spouse dislikes about the other. That's simply the nature of close relationships. You're not required to like everything about her in order to have a happy union, and I'm sure I don't have to tell you there will be things about you she does not prefer as well."

Christopher nodded.

"Listen," Adrian continued, "you're putting a great deal of pressure on yourself. Any marriage would have created this same period of adjustment. Allow yourself to dislike things about her—they don't imply you dislike *her*—and then remind yourself what is good about her. She's affectionate, she plays the pianoforte well, and she *is* quite lovely. I'm sure you can think of more positive qualities. Aren't all those things much better than a little nervous gesture she can't control?"

"Of course." Christopher scowled, affronted at the very suggestion.

"More will come, good and bad," Adrian reminded his son. "That's real life. That's your marriage becoming real. Does it help any to think of those things?"

"Some. I just wish she hadn't been so terribly hurt." Distress twisted Christopher's scowl into an expression of sad vulnerability.

"You know," Adrian said thoughtfully, "she may not be the only one with some grieving to do."

The unexpected comment seemed to jar Christopher from his contemplations. "What do you mean, Father?"

"Just this," Adrian replied. "You care about her. You've married her, and she belongs to you. That means her suffering affects you. She's not the only one who lost things she wanted. Weren't you cheated of a normal courtship, of the opportunity to take your time with her and let the relationship develop more naturally?"

"Yes." The bleakness in his son's voice rivaled the view through the office window.

"Doesn't it bother you?" Adrian insisted.

"Yes." Christopher ceased staring at the rain and focused on his desk. "You now have had to look at this woman—your wife—and see painful injuries on her body and know someone harmed her and you were powerless to prevent it." *I hate saying it, but he can't pretend it isn't an important aspect of their relationship.*

"I know. I hate that!" Christopher exclaimed, audibly grinding his molars.

"You should hate it. You should."

"My poor Katerina." Christopher's voice broke. He looked out the window again for a long moment. Then, eyes red, he turned back to his paperwork, ending the conversation.

Adrian regarded his son. *This is not going to be a rescue forever.* Christopher had progressed well down the road towards loving his wife, and as a deeply loving husband himself, his father recognized all the signs. *If his love means anything to Katerina, someday, Lord willing, they will have the kind of vital marriage they both claim to want.*

Father and son worked in silence for a long period of time, Adrian letting Christopher regain his composure, and then he spoke again. "You know, it might not be a bad idea for you two to take a little... trip together. A sort of wedding tour. You jumped back into everyday life three days after your marriage."

Christopher pondered the suggestion. "You know, you're right, but who will take care of... all of this," he indicated his desk, "if I went away?"

"Let your brother do it," Adrian suggested. "He needs a taste of the family business. I know how you run things, and I can guide him."

"Interesting thought," Christopher replied, smirking.

Adrian also smiled at the thought of his youngest child, a towering, flame-haired yet bookish adolescent, working in the family business he hated.

Then, Christopher spoke again. "Where should I take her? The south of France might be nice this time of year, and we both speak the language rather well."

Adrian sighed at the typical newlywed mistake. "Ask her where she wants to go. She might prefer Italy."

"Ah, good point." Christopher turned to face his father. "So, you would really be in favor of me taking an extended holiday on short notice?"

"I really would," Adrian assured him. "This is your family, son. Your marriage is for life. It's important."

"Well, all right then, Father. Thank you very much." His grin told Adrian how much Christopher liked the idea of spending time alone with his wife.

Adrian smiled also. He had been married a long time himself, but he could still remember the potent blend of desire and tenderness that accompanied the early days. Honestly, nothing much changed over the decades except those sizzling feelings deepened and strengthened. With luck, Christopher and Katerina's marriage would do the same.

* * *

"I think you'll do quite nicely," Katerina said, surprising herself with her calm, businesslike manner. *It's because this young woman is so personable. Something about her just makes me feel comfortable. She's not as experienced as the older lady who stopped by an hour ago, but that woman reminded me of my lady's maid Marietta.* A chill threated to run up her spine, but she suppressed it. *Judgmental and grumpy has no place in this household.*

"Why thank you, ma'am," Miss Katie Lawrence replied fervently. "I'll do my best and work ever so hard."

"No need," Katerina replied, waving her hand in the young brunette's direction. "There are only two of us, and while my husband is a bit... messy, I'm not. I'll never work your fingers to the bone. Only do your job to the best of your ability. That's all I ask."

"Thank you, ma'am." The girl's openhearted manner and country-bred accent made her all the more appealing.

If she gets over being nervous about needing a job, we might just become friends. "When will you be able to start? Is tomorrow too soon?"

"Not at all! I'll be here bright and early..."

"At nine," Katerina interrupted firmly. "After my husband leaves for work. That will give me time to help him find his socks and gloves and get him out the door so he's not late."

"I'll do just that," Katie vowed. "Thank you again, Mrs. Bennett."

"Excellent, Miss Lawrence. I'll see you then."

The young woman gathered up a flowered satchel in which she'd carried a stack of copies of her references and scooted out the door.

Flushed with success, Katerina decided to put off writing polite rejection letters to the other two applicants for a few minutes and wandered down the hall from her parlor to the music room. *I need to ask Christopher if he can secure me some fabric to make curtains. Surely, I can manage a simple straight hem or two. I hope he has a really vivid red. This room needs color and red looks so lovely with the black of a piano.*

She sank onto the bench and squinted at the sheet music in front of her. Changing her mind about serious practice, she instead translated her giddy, positive mood into a spritely bit of Mozart, and then chased it with "Fur Elise." The familiar pieces busied her fingers and allowed her mind to wander.

So far, I adore being married. My charming husband pleases me tremendously both in bed and out. The bishop made me think I would grieve and be miserable for a while and then begin to heal, but in fact, the two processes seem to be simultaneous. I still have those old feelings of fear and depression which have been my constant state for the last ten years of my life, but they're now interspersed with moments of radiant joy. I must allow myself to grieve when it rises; it has to be felt to be healed, but I'm far from miserable most of the time. How can I be when I have Christopher to hold and kiss and talk to me?

Grinning, music ringing in her heart, she had no trouble making her way to the kitchen for a cup of tea and then back down the hall to the parlor, where she hunted for paper and a pen. On the small table, Christopher had brought from his apartment, she located a folio filled with sheets of paper, which she opened in hopes of finding something blank.

Instead, each sheet had the logo of the Wilder printing company. The name Robert Browning capped several collections of raggedly uneven lines.

"These are poems," she realized aloud, setting her cup down and digging through the collection. "The conversation pieces Christopher mentioned, I'll wager."

She took a sip of her tea and regarded the first poem, her eyebrows drawing together at the title, "Porphyria's Lover."

Oh, it's a naughty poem, she thought. *Perhaps like Byron?* Feeling naughty herself, she rationalized, *Well, I'm a married woman, am I not? I have experienced passion. If this poem proves a little scandalous, I can handle it.*

So, she read, lips moving soundlessly as she stumbled over the ragged rhythm and hunted for the rhyme in the middle of multi-line phrases. *This poet writes with a bit of a lisp,* she thought.

"Oh, God!"

Katerina froze, backed up and read again. "He *killed* her? Dear Lord." She shook her head as her cheerful mood shattered. "He's a madman."

A sob crept up from her belly, choking her. "Not now!" she ordered herself sternly. Defiant tears welled up and streamed down her cheeks.

"Quickly. Something different." She flipped the poem over and examined the next one. " 'My Last Duchess.' Sounds harmless enough," she thought, her stomach jumping, and sure enough, the first few lines, with their description of the speaker's wealth, were almost boring. " 'I gave commands and all smiles stopped together.' " She closed the folio, so her tears would not stain the paper, and set it aside.

I came so close to being the subject of a story just like these. The only difference is that my lover saved me. If Christopher and his mother hadn't intervened, would I still be alive now to read poems and cry over them? Likely not.

Her tea forgotten, she buried her face in her arm on the table and gave vent to her emotions again, and that was where Christopher found her when he returned from work a few minutes later.

* * *

Oh, my poor darling, he thought, his mind still on the conversation he'd had with his father earlier. *He was right. We should get away. Go somewhere filled with sunshine and spend our days as newlyweds, just for a while.*

Without saying a word, he approached her from behind and wrapped his arms around her, intending to comfort her.

It was a terrible mistake.

She started violently, pulling away with a cry of terror and curling into a ball, protecting her head and belly from a perceived attack.

Cursing himself, he laid his hand on her shoulder. "Kat," he said softly, "I'm sorry I startled you."

"Christopher?" Her rigid body began to relax, and she straightened. They stared at one another for a breathless, unguarded moment, and then she launched herself into his arms. "I'm sorry," she murmured, her face hidden against his shoulder.

What's wrong with me? "You have nothing to apologize for, my love. It was my fault. Anyone would have been surprised to be grabbed from behind. I'm sorry." He slid his hand under her chin and raised her face. "Is everything all right?"

"Yes."

He regarded her in silence, waiting for the reason behind the tear stains on her cheeks.

At last, she added, "I read your poems."

"What, the Browning?" He squeezed her tighter.

She nodded.

"Oh, Lord. Terrible, aren't they? I *should have put them away. They're the last thing you need to read.*"

"They're real," she replied, and now that her fright had passed, the determination in her voice made him reconsider.

Might it be good for her to read them? They do show the evil of situations just like hers, and they show her she's not alone.

"They had to be terrible or they wouldn't be convincing. Isn't it interesting how both men blamed the women for their attacks on them?"

"Yes. But neither woman was at fault," Christopher pointed out, pulling back and looking down into her face. With his thumb, he wiped a tear from her cheek. "They didn't even know there was a problem. It wasn't your fault either."

"I know," she replied automatically.

"But do you believe it?" he asked.

She met his eyes with a haunting vulnerability, letting him see the pain that welled up from the depths of her soul. "God willing, someday."

She looked so sweet and pretty there in his arms, just where he wanted her to be, and he lavished on her a kiss that left her breathless and panting. "Is that any better?"

She snuggled against him. "Oh yes, lovely."

His body reacted instantly, but he pressed on with the conversation. *There will be time for that later.* "Now then, my darling bride, I have a question for you. My father recommended we take a wedding trip, and I think it's an excellent idea. What do you think?"

She blinked. "I have no idea. I've never traveled before."

"Would you like to try?"

A whirlwind of expressions twisted her face this way and that, but at last, she said, "I think so."

"Are you sure?" he asked. "Does the idea make you anxious?"

"A bit," she admitted, "but I still want to try."

"Good," he said. "I'd love to spend some time with you, just with you, far away from our everyday lives. I think it would be good for our marriage."

She nodded.

"Then we should think of a place to go. Nice is lovely this time of year. Warm," he suggested. "But there's also Italy. Do you have any family you might want to visit? Where are your parents from?"

"Florence," she replied. "I've always wanted to see it. I can still remember the wonderful tales Mama would tell me about her hometown and her family; her papa and mama and brother and all the many friends and relatives. It sounded like a dream of a place. I used to imagine running away there."

"Shall we?" he asked, glad she'd expressed an opinion.

"Would you like to?"

No, love, this is for you. "I would like to take you somewhere you want to go and see you excited and happy."

"That's easy, darling," she replied, stroking her hand down his cheek. "You only have to take me to bed."

He grinned. "And Florence?"

"If you would like it, I would."

Good girl. That's what I wanted to hear. "Shall we find out if your family is interested in a visit?"

"How? Wouldn't a message take almost as long as a voyage?" she asked.

"Yes, a letter would, but what about a telegram?" he reminded her.

"Ah, I forgot about that. Yes, let's."

"I'll go to the telegraph office tomorrow," he replied. "And now, you mentioned another little trip that would make you happy. Is there time before dinner?"

She glanced at the clock she had placed on the mantle. "It's 5:30. I made a stew, but I don't think it will be ready until around 7:00."

"Just barely enough. Let's go, love."

And he took her hand and led her to the bedroom for a brief voyage to Heaven.

Chapter 12

"I MUST say, Christopher," Colonel Turner began, shutting the office door and tugging his mask off his face, "well spotted last week. I had Mrs. Turner talk to Miss Jones. She said it was like pulling teeth but eventually she got the story out of her. The young lady's been courted by a man with a jealous streak. At first, she found it charming... until he turned violent. She didn't know what to do and was embarrassed to go to her family since they'd always told her he was no good."

"So, what happened?" Christopher asked, digging a wad of cotton out of one ear and sinking to a seat at his desk.

"Mrs. Turner and I took her to her father and explained the situation. I believe he had a talk with the young man, and her father's a butcher, so you can imagine how that went. At any rate, the courtship is done, and the young man is gone. Miss Jones seemed sad but relieved. I hope in time she will find someone better."

"That's good news," Christopher replied, tucking his mask into the desk drawer "Was her father angry with her?"

"Disappointed, but not truly angry. No man wants to see his child hurt," Turner said.

What a shame that isn't true, Christopher thought. *What must go wrong in a man's mind to blur the line between love and violence?*

It took Christopher a moment to realize Colonel Turner had gone on talking. He focused back on the conversation.

"The new dye is terrible. The samples faded before we could even get them onto the train. Some of the dyers said it looked weak in the vats, so let's not buy that one again."

"Agreed," Christopher said. "I suppose it was foolish to hope such an inexpensive product would have good quality."

"You get what you pay for," Adrian added quietly, glancing up from his own desk.

"Very well," Christopher said, pulling out an order form. "We'll go back to our usual vermillion dye. It's proven itself worth the money."

"The dyers will be glad."

"As will the customers," Adrian added, holding up a stack of invoices, all of them stamped with the name of Mme. Olivier's shop.

Colonel Turner nodded and replaced his mask, ducking out the door to return to the work floor while Christopher applied himself to ordering a new vermillion dye from the old supplier.

"Well, son, how are the travel plans going?" Adrian asked, interrupting Christopher's musings.

"Quite well." Christopher finished filling out an order form and set it aside to dry. "It's taking longer than I expected, but we should be ready to leave a week from Friday."

He glanced at his father and found him grinning. "Good. Did you settle on Italy or France?"

"Italy." Christopher dipped his pen and signed another document from his stack. *Oh good, the turn wheel for the broken loom should arrive before I leave. Devin will not have a clue how to fix it.* "Katerina's mother's family still lives there. We made contact with her grandfather, and he would like us to stay with him."

"How nice. Let's hope he's better than..." Adrian trailed off.

"Than her father?" Christopher shook his head. "Yes. I doubt he could be worse, and if it doesn't work out, Florence is a sizable city and we can certainly find a hotel, but we thought it best to start out this way, at least."

"No doubt you're right," Adrian agreed, dipping his own pen and signing a paper from his own pile.

* * *

The naked girl, her bound hands affixed to a hook in the ceiling whimpered under the lash and then moaned in pleasure, the sound muffled by the lush red velvet curtains on every wall.

Giovanni drew back his arm and whipped her again. *It's so much more difficult here, less satisfying.* He had to control his strokes, not just give vent to his rage. The fact that she was enjoying it reduced his pleasure tremendously. *What a disgusting whore.*

For me, this has never been sexual, he argued vigorously in his mind, *but with my daughter gone, there is no other choice. Of course, she turned out to be no better than the whore in front of me.* Only the other day he had looked in the parlor window of the townhouse his daughter shared with her bastard husband, only to see the couple embracing indiscreetly. *Vile.*

He brought the whip down again, harder, and the girl squealed in protest as her skin broke and a thin line of blood trickled down. "Sir, that's too much!"

"Silence, slut."

"No. You know the rules. Soften your strokes or I'll call the manager."

"*Merda,*" Giovanni muttered under his breath. *This is hopeless.* He had so wished to have Katerina back in his clutches today, but that damned burly footman had barred the door, threatening to summon the police. Now volcanic rage ripped at Giovanni, and this tepid, partial release would not suffice. *Somehow, I will get her back, and then she will pay like she has never paid before.*

* * *

The following Friday, Katerina clutched her husband's hand as he escorted her into his poetry party at the Wilder home. This time, she felt nervous but in good health. The bruises had been gone for days and the cuts on her back almost completely healed. She wore her stays, not a tight-laced corset, and thus she could breathe freely. No longer dizzy, she found herself able to take in the room and its occupants with greater attention than she'd paid before.

Mr. Wilder leaned against the fireplace, smoking a fat and acrid cigar. She noticed Christopher glance sharply at him and make a displeased face.

James Cary sat on a chaise, but this time he had the lovely Miss Carlisle perched beside him wearing another mint green gown that emphasized the green of her eyes. They were not touching, but stared at each other intensely, deep in a private conversation. Katerina could see the little blonde's lips pursed out slightly, though not precisely pouting this time. She held her eyes deliberately wide as she attempted to secure the handsome young vicar's interest. Her venture appeared quite successful.

Katerina looked away, granting them privacy. Christopher's thumb traced the side of her hand. It would have been more proper to hold his arm, but the allure of his strong fingers tempted her more than she could resist.

"Christopher," a young man with light brown hair and lines around his mouth and eyes that didn't fit his lack of years, approached them saying, "where on earth have you been? Mrs. Wilder says you disappeared from the party last time with Cary and Miss Valentino, never to be seen again. I've been to your rooms and you moved out without a word."

"Sorry, Colin," Christopher replied. "I was caught up in a situation that required immediate attention."

"Well, it must have been quite a situation for you to move and not let your best friend know where you'd gone. The most ridiculous rumors are circulating everywhere."

Christopher changed the subject. "I believe you've met Katerina before?"

"Yes. Miss Valentino." He nodded to her politely but without much attention.

"Good to see you again, Lord Gelroy."

He started violently at the sound of her soft voice. "She speaks. Good heavens! Will the sky fall next?"

"I think it's already fallen," Katerina replied, a hint of a smile on her lips.

"What rumors?" Christopher asked insouciantly.

"They say you've gone and married her, all on a whim." Colin waved carelessly in Katerina's direction.

"Humph. For once they've gotten it right, eh, love?" Christopher joked.

"It would appear so." Her smile widened.

Colin gawped at the two of them. "You're married?"

"Yes," Christopher said simply, slipping his arm around her waist. Katerina nodded.

"Why?"

The disbelief in his inflection caused Katerina's cheeks to color.

Christopher gave his wife a questioning look. *Must I give my oldest and closest friend the official story,* he seemed to be asking her silently, *or may I tell him the truth?*

Katerina looked back at her husband, feeling his conflict. She wanted to ease this moment for him. "I was in a... difficult situation. He came to my rescue. He's very much a hero." For emphasis, she rested her cheek on his shoulder in a warm embrace.

Colin looked at her, disbelieving.

"No, not that kind of situation," Christopher reassured his friend.

"What?" Katerina asked, her eyes skating from one man to another.

"Love, when a woman needs rescuing from a 'difficult situation,' she's often implying she's with child by someone irresponsible," Christopher explained.

"Oh. No, nothing like that. Lord Gelroy, my father, he was..." she looked at Christopher, cheeks burning.

"You don't mind if I tell him?"

Katerina's lips twisting, showing that, yes, she did mind, but she gave a curt nod. "He's your friend. He needs to know why you didn't tell him immediately." Her dark eyes met Colin's. "My Lord, I would prefer this not become public knowledge, please."

Colin nodded.

* * *

"He was beating her," Christopher said darkly. He returned his attention to Colin, taking in an expression of wide-mouthed shock. You can't imagine how badly. I couldn't leave her in that kind of danger." He gave Katerina an intense look, the kind of look he knew Colin had never seen on his face before. Though his wife blushed like a summer rose at the blunt words, Christopher took grim satisfaction in knowing that since that day, no further suffering had or would ever befall her. *The abuse might have spurred the hasty marriage, but I want to be with this woman. Maybe now that her shyness has abated somewhat, people will understand.*

Colin shook his head, "Married. Humph. Well, I suppose someone had to be first to take the plunge. Better you than me."

Christopher dodged the comment. "So, how did the meeting go?"

Colin sighed. "It went nowhere. No one will give extend me any credit because they know I will never be able to repay it. It's terrible. I'm responsible for repaying thousands of pounds not spent by me, because the *estate* owns them, but no one will do anything to ease the burden on me. The land gets more depleted every year—it wasn't good when I got it—but I can't *not* plant because of the debts and the taxes. It's a Gordian knot and I have no sword. I almost wish..." Colin swallowed hard. "I wish the tenants would move to the city for work and I could just abandon the entire enterprise... but I can't. I would still owe the same and have even less means to pay it."

"What are you going to do?" Christopher asked.

"Damned if I know, begging your pardon, Mrs. Bennett. I mean, I'm going to economize every way I can and work as hard as I can and hope to stave off disaster for a few more years. After tonight, I'm giving up my London lodgings and heading home. There's nothing more to be done here. I'll take stock of what I have left. Perhaps parts from the worst of the tenant houses can be used to improve the ones that still have some life left in them, and then, if we can extract another crop this year… I don't know. The land needs to rest for several years, but then no one will earn anything. It's an impossible mess."

"I'm sorry, Colin," Christopher told his friend. "Is there anything I can do?"

"Not unless you have about thirty thousand pounds you don't need and won't ask to have returned."

It was a staggering sum, and Christopher, though quite well-to-do, had nothing like that at his disposal. No one did.

Katerina laid her hand on Colin's arm. He looked at her. "I'm so terribly sorry, Lord Gelroy. May I… say a prayer for you?"

"You may," he replied, one corner of his mouth twisting into a grimace. "I think the Lord is the only one who can help me now."

"Then I shall do that," she said firmly.

"Thank you, Mrs. Bennett."

"Well, good evening, friends." Mrs. Wilder approached, ending the personal conversation.

"Good evening, Mrs. Wilder," Christopher greeted their hostess.

"Mr. Bennett, you are in disgrace tonight," she teased.

"Why is that?" he raised his eyebrows, alert for the opportunity to banter.

"You and Mr. Cary both left last time without a word, so early, and you took your poems with you. We had to improvise on the spot and found nothing to interest us."

"I apologize. I…" he considered his words. "I had an emergency."

"Yes, I know," Mrs. Wilder's teasing tone turned serious.

"You do?" *Oh dear. This can't be good.*

She raised one eyebrow. "Well, certain clues were left abandoned in my retiring room. They told a very interesting story. Would you like them back?"

* * *

Katerina blanched. In the sudden crisis, they had abandoned not only her wrap but also—horrors—her corset. Finding an undergarment left behind was certain to cause a scandal.

"Don't fret, dear," Mrs. Wilder assured her, patting her arm. "Fortunately, I found it first and hid it away. You may have it back if you would like, but there's quite a quantity of blood on it."

"I'm sure there is. I... we didn't..." she stammered, face burning.

Mrs. Wilder squeezed her hand soothingly. "I know what you did and did not do in my retiring room, dear. Scandalous behavior does not generally cause bleeding in the middle of one's back."

"Right." Katerina put her hand to her forehead.

"And Mr. Bennett is a gentleman," Mrs. Wilder added.

A sideways slant of her eyes revealed a telltale darkening along her husband's cheekbones. *Good. A shift in topic.* "Yes. He is. I'm the most fortunate of women."

"Are you truly married then?" their hostess asked, wide-eyed.

"Yes." Katerina leaned against Christopher in a gesture of pure affection.

Mrs. Wilder nodded. "Do you honestly want that thing back? If not, I can dispose of it."

Ugh. A memento of my last beating? I think not. "I would be very grateful if you would burn it."

Mrs. Wilder dipped her chin in acknowledgment of Katerina's request. "And your shawl?"

"Now that I would not mind having again," Katerina said. "It will be cold for many months to come."

"Indeed. Now then, Mrs. Bennett, do you think you might be prevailed upon to play for these gatherings from time to time?"

"Certainly, if everyone wishes it," Katerina agreed.

"Excellent. I think we may have begun a new tradition. We can meet in celebration of the arts, not just poetry." Mrs. Wilder beamed, tiny crinkles appearing around her eyes.

Katerina smiled shyly. "I shall have to begin researching and rehearsing new pieces, so I have something fresh to contribute as well."

"Friends," Mrs. Wilder addressed the room in a carrying voice, and all conversations ceased, "I have news. Our own Christopher Bennett has wisely not allowed his lovely pianist to escape but made her a permanent member of the group. From now on, Mrs. Bennett, and any other musician who has the skill, can aid with the before-dinner entertainment."

The words 'Mrs. Bennett' caused a shocked murmur to ripple through the group. Katerina, uncomfortable with all the stunned stares, clung to her husband's arm. He patted her fingers gently as she tried to make herself relax and smile.

"Excellent." The gentleman who had been so tipsy the last time, tonight sat sober on the settee with a lovely brown-haired woman of about thirty years. "My dear, you can't imagine the glorious concert we had last week. Well done, Bennett."

"Thank you, Reardon." Christopher gave his wife a subtle squeeze.

"Dinner!" a servant announced.

"No time to play tonight, I see," Christopher quipped. "Well, love, are you hungry?"

"Yes, very," she replied. *No point in denying the rumbling of my tummy.*

* * *

Sated and comfortably warm with the dinner and wine in her stomach, Katerina reclined against the velvet arm of the sofa in the Wilders' parlor, the friendly piano at her back, her fingers laced through her husband's once again.

Christopher opened the folio in his lap and lifted the less controversial and far subtler of the two poems, "My Last Duchess."

He reads so skillfully, Katerina thought, uncomfortable with the content of the poem. His voice sounded rigidly controlled but occasionally tinged with rage as he attempted to portray the mad Duke of Ferrara. Katerina shivered. *I hope I never to know what it was to receive such cold anger from my precious husband.*

143

" 'Which Claus of Innsbruck cast in bronze for me,' " he declared, finishing the poem with a manic flourish. Then, he closed the folio and set it on the table, laying his and Katerina's hands on his knee.

She looked at him silently, ignoring the puzzled conversation and focusing solely on Christopher. *Tomorrow we leave for our wedding tour, and I cannot wait. We depart by train for Southampton first thing in the morning, and then board a ship for Livorno. From there another train will take us to Florence, where Nonno will send a carriage to retrieve us.*

The idea of travel both terrified and excited her. She would never have done it without Christopher. *He makes me bigger and braver than I am. He's a creature I never expected to find... a good man.*

" 'Porphyria's Lover' " *Lord Gelroy announced, retrieving the folio and leaning against the wall near the fireplace.*

I do not want to listen to the other poem. It's too visceral, too graphic, and no number of re-readings have softened the blow. When Colin started to recite, she turned her attention to the hand she was holding.

Christopher might be the cotton mill's part-owner, but that hasn't stopped him from working with his hands. He told me he's operated every machine in the factory to test its safety, hauled cotton and bolts of fabric, and examined the looms and the dyeing vats. He has the strength of a laborer, the mind of an engineer, and the body of a god. He's glorious.

How could he be for me, for timid Katerina? It makes no sense. A reward this great must surely be for some colossal act of good, but I've done nothing, not one thing in my life to help others. I've been too isolated for that, living in self-centered terror.

She thought back over their marriage. It had only been a short time, but already she was learning him. She knew what he liked to eat for breakfast, and which newspaper he preferred to read, and that he would rather drink coffee than tea, and she knew his touch. *Ah, it's lovely, in his arms, in his bed.* As he had promised, the more they came together, the better it felt. He offered affection with the sex, and she took it greedily, never having realized a touch could heal and please, not merely harm and frighten.

She stroked his fingers, feeling calluses from both work and writing and scars from the wild things children did, like the time he had chased a bird and actually caught it. The beak mark would remain in his palm for life. Those were good scars, the marks of living a full and interesting life.

She too was permanently marred, but not with the marks of living. She bore the scars of the half-life of slaves and criminals. Fiercely, she reminded herself, *An unsmooth back is hardly the most horrible disfigurement a woman can endure. Vanity serves no purpose. Let it go. No one knows how badly I'm disfigured except my husband, and if there's a silver lining, it's that the sight of those wounds spurred him to marry me.*

Would I really trade my husband for smooth skin? No, I would not. Marriage was better, so much better. Every day was subtly better than the one before. Already she cried less, laughed more, not because she was trying to force herself, but because it just felt right to do so.

A sweet smile broke over her face. *I'm getting closer to understanding safe and even happy. Tonight, I will ask my husband to make me feel those good feelings again. I know he will be agreeable.* Her body tingled at the thought.

Colin finished the poem and tossed aside the folio as if in disgust of his own recitation, and the discussion broke out almost instantly, voices overlapping in such dizzying disarray she could not distinguish one speaker from another.

"What a dreadful thing."

"Is this a poem or a women's liberation propaganda piece?"

"Are you sure Robert wrote that and not his wife? It sounds like a woman's writing."

"Not really. No woman would write something so inelegant."

"I think it's horrible. I don't want to think about things like that."

Katerina, against her will, found her voice speaking into the din. "How convenient to be able not to think about it. Those who endure it do not have that option. The Duchess of Ferrara is fictional, and so is Porphyria, but real women and children are treated with violence in our city every day. Mr. Browning wants us to be aware, so we can help, be good Samaritans, not cross the road like the Pharisees."

The room fell silent at her unexpected comment.

"But, Mrs. Bennett, how can we help? The law says a man has a right to discipline his wife," Reardon demanded in a gentle, not sarcastic tone.

Mrs. Wilder snapped in response, "Is a woman a child in need of discipline? I think most wives are adults and can make their own choices about their behavior. If a husband has a complaint, he should try *saying* it. Being able to converse with your spouse is sensible, but so many men refuse just as the Duke of Ferrara did."

"Even if most husbands treat their wives gently, and most fathers discipline their children appropriately, not having a caveat in the law to deal with abuse leads to situations like these, where power-hungry men can torture their dependents and even kill them," Katerina said as she squeezed her husband's hand, thankful he was trustworthy.

He squeezed back and then slid his arm behind her.

"Well, I still think the poem is ugly," the girl who had been so prone to pouting last week said sulkily.

"Miss Carlisle," Cary told the girl, "given what he is trying to do, a pretty poem would make little sense."

"I suppose," the golden-haired girl sighed, "and I promise to give a tithe of my pin money this week to help... someone. Now, can we please read something prettier?"

"If you want something pretty, Miss Carlisle," Cary replied, his voice warm with attraction, his eyes urging her to notice him, "I have just the thing." He crossed to the bookshelf and scooped up a volume.

" 'The Lady of Shalott', by Alfred, Lord Tennyson. 'On either side the river lie/ long fields of barley and of rye...' "

From the first elegant lines, Miss Carlisle sighed with pleasure.

Katerina listened too. The sad, sweet beauty of the words washed over her, making her smile. *She* gave herself over to it, loving the skillful manipulation of words, the sound of James Cary's well-modulated voice as he attempted to woo Miss Carlisle, the shivery pleasure of her husband's hand on her, stroking.

Such a lovely poem provoked silence rather than conversation, and at its conclusion the guests began to drift away, drenched in images the lovely lady singing while she wove a tapestry.

"Ready to go, love?" Christopher asked as the scene faded from her imagination.

"Oh yes, let's." Katerina's smile grew wider. Rising they located their hostess. "Thank you for the lovely evening, Mrs. Wilder," Katerina said sweetly.

"Thank you for coming, Mrs. Bennett. Your apt comments were greatly appreciated."

"Mrs. Wilder, we will not be attending for several weeks," Christopher informed her. "We'll be taking a trip to Italy, starting in the morning."

Their host beamed at them. "Well, I hope you both enjoy yourselves. Some Italian sunshine in February sounds lovely."

"It does," Katerina agreed. "I'm looking forward to it."

With matching smiles, they took their leave and headed outside. Apparently, Katerina was not the only one who had been moved by the last poem. No sooner did the hansom driver hop into his seat behind them, then Christopher pulled her close, planting wet sweet kisses on her mouth, one after the other.

"Goodness, darling," she said as his lips trailed the delicate arch of her throat. "Is everything all right?"

"Oh yes," he pulled back and looked at her with glowing eyes. "I'm impressed you commented back there. You actually spoke up in front of everyone. You're doing so much better than I expected, love. Your courage is… very arousing."

"Well I'm glad you find it so," she said, batting her eyelashes flirtatiously at him. Then she turned serious. "I wasn't trying to be brave, you know. It just bothers me how people try to ignore things because the thoughts are unpleasant, while others are suffering and even dying around them. Bravo to Mr. Browning for making us look and think."

"That's how I feel too. Before I read the poems, I must confess, such things didn't occupy my mind as much as they do now." He told her more clearly what he meant by kissing her again. "Sweet love," he mumbled against her soft lips, "I'm so very glad I married you."

"Oh, so am I. You're a marvelous husband, Christopher."

"Thank you. It's so nice having a wife; someone I can talk to and kiss and make love to whenever we want." He nipped her lower lip.

She moaned softly. "It's all so good. Better than I ever expected."

He seemed to take her words as an invitation and tongued the edge of her teeth, eliciting another soft sound.

"Kat," he said, pulling away as though a sudden thought occurred to him.

Though the loss of his kiss made her want to pout, she focused on his words. "Yes?"

"Um, have you ever heard any of the other matrons talking about marriage?" He stroked one hand over her hip as he spoke, clearly trying to keep the mood on their intimacy.

I wonder where he's headed with this. "A bit, why?"

"Well there's kind of a ridiculous attitude about marital intimacy circling about these days, and I wanted to be sure you weren't confused by it."

"What would that be?" *Get to the point, love, so you can kiss me again.*

"Well..." he paused as though considering his words before continuing. "A small number of people are making everyone nervous by saying—or implying—that a decent woman ought not to enjoy making love at all, not even with her husband."

Katerina raised her eyebrows. "Is there any truth to it?"

He shook his head. "None that I know of. I mean, if men want to enjoy passionate relations with women, and adultery is a sin, what option does that leave?"

"Obviously the best one; a happy marriage." She trailed her fingers over his jaw, enjoying the prickle of the day's growth of whiskers. "And as you once reminded me, the scriptures are not shy about extolling the virtues of passionate, married love."

He smiled, teeth flashing in the darkness, and she could see she'd given the answer he wanted. "Exactly. I suspect some families, in an attempt to prevent their daughters from being seduced, teach them to fear intimacy altogether, or perhaps even be disgusted by it."

"That's possible," she said, pondering. "Also, having barely-willing wives gives dishonest men the excuse they want in order to be unfaithful."

His lips twisted. "Perhaps. Well, at any rate, it's not true, and I didn't want you to be swayed by it."

"You needn't worry about me, Christopher," she replied, touching her lips to his forehead. "Even if it were true, I care more for you than I do for the opinions of those who would best be served to mind their own business. I would rather sin with you—if it is a sin—than be virtuous."

"But it's no sin," he promised her, his silver eyes seeming to stare deep into her heart. "We're married, so you can rest assured that our lovemaking in no way damages your virtue."

"I know that." She returned his impassioned gaze. "I can feel it."

"And can you feel this?" He slipped her hand into his lap, below the cover, onto his straining erection.

She sighed with happiness. "Yes. How lovely!"

"And fortunately, here we are at home. Come along, love."

He had her through the icy cold to the door at record speed, and they hurried up into their cozy bedroom where they stripped off their clothing and stretched out on the bed, eager to be close again.

* * *

She's made such marvelous progress, Christopher thought as he stripped away Katerina's shift to reveal her slender curves—now noticeably fuller as she had learned to care for herself. *She desires more than ever to be touched and even bravely touches me in several ways. She's well on her way to becoming the kind of wife she wants to be.*

He had learned too, ways to approach her that minimized her defensive reactions.

"How beautiful you are, my darling," he told her as he leaned over her on their bed, attempting yet another seduction. He had complete confidence in their mutual success. "Look at this lovely face." He reached for her slowly, and instead of recoiling from his hand, she leaned her cheek into it. His other arm slid around her, pulling her against him. He stroked her back with one hand, her cheek with the other. She leaned forward and boldly pressed her lips to his, kissing him tenderly and letting her tongue snake out to taste his lips, then easing between.

Christopher let her explore, enjoying how comfortable she had become in bed with him. She nibbled his lower lip and then pulled back, looking deeply into his eyes. He caressed the uneven skin on her back.

"Don't do that, love," she said, grasping his hand and pinning it on her hip.

"Why not? I want to embrace you." He slipped his hand from beneath hers and headed for her back again.

"I'm not very nice back there," she insisted. "This skin is much smoother." She guided him to her front, planting his wandering fingers squarely on her breast.

"The scars don't bother me, you know. They're so much better now." But he stroked her willingly enough.

She hummed with pleasure. "They're about as better as they're going to get." Her voice had taken on a strained tone he recognized as the battle between her desire to state her opinion and her growing arousal.

"I know," he replied, admitting to himself that his own tone held a hint of the same feeling. "As long as they're not a danger to you, let them be. Don't worry, love. I'm not disgusted by any part of you. Those scars are a symbol of your strength."

"Hmmm," she hummed as he caressed her nipples, "taste me here."

Christopher allowed himself to be distracted by one of his favorite parts of her body, lowering his mouth and tugging one sweet peak and then the other.

* * *

Katerina squirmed and sighed as Christopher played with her breasts. *He's so good at this. I still feel like a hussy, but how can I complain?* She lay back, enjoying the surges of pleasure while running her hands up and down his arms, his shoulders and his back.

Her world narrowed down around her until only Christopher seemed real. Only his touch connected her to the world.

Parting her thighs for her husband, she let him know where she wanted to be touched. He stroked the dark curls and then gently opened them, easing his fingers into the dewy folds, and, having found the opening of her body, sliding deep.

"Ahhh," she sighed.

"You're very wet and eager tonight, aren't you, darling?" he asked, pulling back so he could push inward again.

"Oh yes," she moaned.

"Would you like a climax?"

"Only one?" she pouted.

He laughed. "Have I spoiled you so badly? Wonderful. What about two, one now, one later?"

"Perfect." She looped her arms around his neck while he slid his fingers gently in and out, building her pleasure higher. He found the swollen pearl of her clitoris and circled it with his thumb.

She arched eagerly into his caresses, wanting the release he had promised.

Christopher did not disappoint. He worked the little nub until Katerina wailed with pleasure and clamped hard on his encroaching fingers.

He kissed her sweetly as the peak faded.

"Well, love," he said, sliding his fingers out, "would you fancy a new position tonight?"

"Like what?" she gasped.

"I would like it if you would lie on your belly and let me enter you that way." He stroked her cheek, and the light in his eyes spoke volumes.

She turned away from him. "Oh, Christopher, I would rather not."

"Why not?"

She pinched her lips together. "It's my back. I'm just not comfortable with it."

"I told you it doesn't bother me," he reminded her.

With a sigh, she admitted, "It bothers me. From behind, I feel broken. I don't like that. There's no point in looking backward."

"Someday, love, you're going to have to integrate your past and your future," he pointed out.

She swallowed hard and broke eye contact. "I know, but not yet. It's too soon. Please?"

"Very well." Christopher rolled onto his back. "Let's put you on top then."

He reached for her. Katerina was still learning to believe in safety, but in bed at least, Christopher had never let her down. She gladly placed her hand in his and straddled his middle with her long, slender legs.

"Come on, love, take hold of me." He guided her hand to his erection and showed her how to stroke him. She blushed but complied. Together, they positioned him upright at the opening of her body. He grasped her hip and pressed, allowing gravity to get the job done.

Katerina closed her eyes. He pushed up on her hips, urging her to rise, and then released the pressure, letting her sink back down.

It only took a few tries for her to master the rhythm of this position, and then she took over the movement and began riding him. This freed his hands to caress her again, bring her the promised second peak. Her head fell back as ecstasy crashed over her, and her long hair tickled his legs. He grasped both her hips and pressed deep, so he could join her in fulfillment.

Long moments later, the lovers returned to awareness. Katerina lay on top of Christopher's chest. His hands rested on her back again, but this time the touch made her feel cherished. One hand slid up and he laced his fingers into her hair and brought her mouth to his for a long, tender kiss she could feel right to her soul.

What a man I found to marry me. I am the most fortunate of women.

Chapter 13

ATERINA had never been near a train before and looked doubtfully as the gigantic metal beast that puffed and snorted ominously at them through its bulbous smokestack. The black, soot-stained body of the massive vehicle gleamed dully even with the ribbed and vaulted roof of the station dimming the feeble sunshine. *How could such a large and heavy machine actually be faster than a horse?*

The steam whistle let out an earsplitting screech and she flinched. She wasn't the only one. Several of the milling passengers jumped at the noise. Christopher abandoned propriety and wrapped his arm around his wife. This earned them several sharp glances from stuffy-looking matrons, but they ignored them. He guided her up the stairs and found them a seat, quickly stowing their baggage on racks above their heads before joining her on the threadbare red fabric.

"How are you doing, love?" he asked, concern wreathing his face.

"Well enough," she replied as she settled back into the seat. "I had no idea trains were so loud."

"Oh, well anything run on steam is bound to be noisy," he explained. "It has to escape, you know? You should hear the cotton mill."

"May I?" she asked, curious about the work her husband enjoyed so much.

The question made him smile. "If you would like. I wouldn't mind showing it to you some time.

"I've heard... things about those places," she said, asking a silent question with pleading eyes.

"No doubt all are true," he replied grimly, acknowledging how sad factory work was for most employees, "but ours is not like that. Father and I ensure ours is one of the most congenial, best paid and safest. Our employees seem to appreciate it, but still, it's a messy, hot, noisy place to work." His eyes glowed as he spoke.

"You love it there, don't you?" she asked.

"Yes," he admitted easily. "I like to invent things, and a factory is a fine place to do it."

"Good. I think enjoying your work is good for you. People who hate what they do seem... grumpy."

"Well, love, work takes up a huge amount of a person's life. If you hate it, what's left? I don't want to live that way, and I don't want my employees to either. I wouldn't like to think they dread waking up in the morning and coming to the factory."

"With everything you and your mother have told me about the place," Katerina replied, "you've made it far better than you had to. Unless your employees hate the job itself, the environment shouldn't do it."

He grinned widely, teeth flashing, and she knew she'd said just the right thing. *Thinking of others is becoming easier, and I truly enjoy making someone else feel good.* This revelation set off her own grin.

Katerina turned to the window as the train departed the station. The crowded streets and cluttered buildings of the city give way to winter brown fields and naked trees. *Spring is still a long way off.*

Christopher also regarded the scenery. "This is so much nicer than traveling by carriage."

"It is?" she asked doubtfully, noticing the motion of the vehicle made her slightly nauseous.

"Oh yes. Imagine a weary mother and three children bouncing along a rutted road, the boredom and the whining... it was epic." He chuckled at the memory. "Sometimes Father would let me sit with him in the driver's seat outside. That was nicer."

"Where did you go?" she asked, trying to take her mind off her unsettled belly.

"To the seashore for a summer holiday. London gets a little… rancid in the heat."

"It does," Katerina agreed.

"Did you never go on holiday?" he asked.

"Not that I can recall," she replied. Watching the scenery speed past didn't help her belly. She turned her attention to Christopher. *That's better.*

"What a shame." He touched her hand, and she took the opportunity to lace their fingers together. "Going to the ocean was always a highlight of the year for us. Would you like to go this summer?"

"With your parents?" she asked.

"Yes," he replied, his expression distant as though he was already there, "and my brother, Devin. He's studying to become a solicitor. Can you imagine?" He shuddered. "He's said since early childhood that he wants to move to Brighton to live, not just go for holidays."

"That would be nice," Katerina replied. "I'd like to see the ocean, and I love spending time with your family."

He grinned at her and squeezed her hand. *New memories are being created every day.*

Katerina found, as they chugged through the countryside, that she had nothing to say. *Thank heaven Christopher is comfortable with silence.* She really didn't want to have to try to make small talk. Her fingers laced through his provided enough connection for the moment.

Shortly after noon, they reached Southampton and proceeded directly to the docks to board their clipper ship for Italy.

The ocean resembled nothing Katerina had ever experienced. Over the roar of the conversations, she could hear the screaming of gulls, the clanking and groaning of the ships in their moorings, the yells of sailors speaking dozens of languages. The myriad stimulations threatened to overwhelm her, but with the support of her husband's arm around her, she realized she felt quite safe. She drew in a deep breath, enjoying the brisk breeze after the close stuffiness of the train. The stink of unwashed bodies hung thick in the air and underneath it, the tang of the ocean, of salt and fish, freshness and decay. *Life and death mingling eternally together.*

They stepped out of the weak February sun into the shadow of the clipper, which rose high above them. Masses of billowing white sails attached to three tall masts topped with colorful pennants rolled and snapped in the breeze, like a toddler dancing and straining on the verge of some coveted adventure.

"Come on," the wind seemed to whisper through the ropes and lines as it set them humming. "Come on," it whispered through the rustling fabric of sails. "Life awaits us beyond the harbor. Let's go see what we can discover." The prompt tugged at Katerina's heart. She knew the journey would take over a week, perhaps closer to two depending on the cooperation of the winds. They would hug the coast of Europe, skimming France, Spain, and Portugal before passing the Rock of Gibraltar. From there it was a straight shot across the Mediterranean to Livorno.

Perhaps there I can understand how my story began, and why. Though she would never be able to put it into words, she had the strong sensation that knowing how she came to be would help her lay some of her ghosts to rest.

Joining an endless queue of passengers, they made their slow way up to the ship and then headed to their cabin. A bed extended below the small room's porthole, made up with a deep blue coverlet. Dark wainscoting on the lower walls contrasted with plain white painted plaster above. There was a small built-in table and the matching chair looked to be heavy, which no doubt prevented it from falling over in rough weather. Katerina dropped her bag on the floor inside the door and sank to a seat on the narrow bed.

"This is much smaller than we're used to," he said.

She shrugged. "I don't mind. Most of that space goes unused anyway."

He seemed to imagine them twined together, the way they normally slept, and the unspoken thoughts chasing across his face forced her to tug him closer, so they could share a hot, deep kiss, stroking each other with eager hands.

"Enough, love," Christopher told his wife eventually, his breathing uneven, "we should go above decks."

"Why?" she sulked, trying to draw his head back down.

He wriggled out of her grip. "Don't you want to see the ship leave the harbor?"

"Oh, I suppose." She sighed.

"We have many nights to spend in this cabin," he reminded her.

"True. One more kiss, and then we'll go up."

Christopher acquiesced, perhaps too willingly. By the time they emerged on deck, so many minutes had passed that all the spots along the rail were full. Thankfully Katerina was tall enough to look over the heads of a passel of red-haired children and see the departure.

The sunlight touched her face, a hint of warmth in the chill of deep winter. She took another deep breath. Though still cold, the sky looked less ominous, the gray lightening to almost a friendly silver, the shade of her husband's eyes.

Fat billows of clouds, pure white and clean, meandered slowly across the heavens, so unlike the smoggy haze that hung perpetually over London. This place was fresher, and in it, she felt cleaner and lighter. *I'm leaving England for the first time in my life, and there's no telling what this trip to Italy will bring.* She waved to strangers across the steely gray water for a long time, and then land disappeared from view and the vast ocean stretched before them. Behind them, a lone storm cloud floated ominously on the horizon.

* * *

They couldn't see him, but Giovanni Valentino stood on the docks, cursing vilely. He had attempted to snatch his daughter away in the crowd but had not managed it. A horde of urchins had rushed between him and his prey, hurrying to find a good position from which to watch the ship leave the harbor, and by the time the group had passed, she was out of reach.

This isn't over, puttana. I'll get you in the end, and when I do, you'll rue the day you deserted me.

Chapter 14

 HRISTOPHER strode into the cabin, two glasses in one hand, a bottle of wine in the other. Shouldering open the door, he stopped and sighed. "Sick again, love?"

Katerina, who had been perched on the edge of the bed, flopped onto her back, groaning.

Christopher set the bottle and glasses on the table and joined his wife, shifting her so her head lay on his shoulder. She nuzzled into his neck.

"In planning this trip, it seems we forgot to take the possibility of seasickness into account."

"I suppose so," she said in a thin, uncomfortable voice.

"Lie still, then. Doesn't that help?"

"It does." Already, she sounded stronger. "As long as I'm prone, I feel normal, but the second I get up…"

"Your belly begins churning?" he suggested.

He felt her nod against his body.

"What a shame there's nothing to be done about it."

"How long to Livorno?" she asked.

"A few more days," he replied. "We passed Gibraltar the day before yesterday, and the winds are favorable."

At the mention of wind, Katerina groaned and hid her face in his neck.

A sensation of moist softness suggested her lips on his skin.

"Love?"

"Hmmm?" her voice vibrated against his throat.

"Did you kiss me?"

"Hmmmm," she hummed again.

"I must say, your illness hasn't dimmed your ardor, has it?"

Katerina didn't respond. Confident at last that he treasured her passion, she touched her lips to him again, taking a flirtatious bite, one that might just leave a mark.

"Oho, is that how it's going to be?" he asked. *Who would have guessed her shattered heart could learn to trust at all, let alone so quickly? It humbles me.*

In response, she untied his cravat and opened his collar. Hardly averse to distracting her from her misery in the manner she'd requested, he quickly unbuttoned his shirt and trousers drawing away to struggle free of them while his wife wrestled off her shift.

"I want to do something new, love," she urged, lying back against the pillows, with her long dark hair spread across the white linens.

Christopher raised his eyebrows, considering his possibilities as he unlaced his boots. *I wonder... would she?* Growing up as isolated as she had, Katerina had never been exposed to anyone's attitudes about sex and completely lacked reservations. *If I tell her something is good, she believes me, and if it sounds appealing to her too, we try it.*

Naked at last, he stretched out beside her. "I do have one idea..." he suggested, suddenly feeling shy. "Now, love, if you don't want to do this, please, please tell me honestly. The last thing I want is to pressure you, but..."

"But?" she rose up on one elbow and looked into his eyes, eager and curious.

"You could...Um..." his face felt hot, but the eager straining of his sex urged him onward. "You could... You know when I've used my mouth and tongue on you... on your privates?"

"Hmmm. That feels so wonderful."

"You can do the same for me."

She raised her eyebrows. "Is that... allowed?"

"Only if you want to, but... it's not unheard of. Just an advanced technique."

She grinned and crouched over him. "Advanced. I like the sound of that. Show me."

He tangled his hands in her hair, gently guiding her down. She pressed a shy little kiss to the tip.

"Good, love. That's good," he groaned. "Just keep your teeth back. Other than that, be creative..."

She reared up a little. "This is very nice," she told him before opening and taking him in as deeply as she could.

Christopher's reply wasn't exactly formed of coherent words. He let her play with him, exploring and teasing until he hovered on the brink of exploding. It took every ounce of his willpower to slide past her warm clinging lips and urge her down onto the bed.

"Your turn," he said, but he'd waited too long. His body clamoring for release, he ran his hand down the center of her body. She opened her thighs and he touched her. *Thank God, she's drenched and ready.* He rammed his sex home in one hard stroke.

* * *

Katerina's eyes opened wide at the rough entry. *It didn't hurt exactly, but where is the tender lover who eases into me so sweetly night after night?*

He pulled back and drove deep again and this time she understood. *He's wild with desire... for me. He wants me so badly he's lost control.* She bit her lip to hold in a flattered smile. *This sophisticated, worldly man desires me this much. Me!* Though she wanted to deny the possibility, such ample evidence made the conclusion obvious.

She relaxed and lay passive against the passionate onslaught. The third hard thrust made her tingle. The fourth made her bite her lip and moan. The fifth sizzled like fire. One more was all it took, and Katerina screamed as a soul-deep orgasm crashed over her. It was fortunate she arrived so quickly because Christopher had only one more thrust in him. He slammed to the hilt inside her and exploded with a roar while she squirmed and clenched around him.

* * *

As Christopher's awareness slowly returned, he noticed Katerina's strong, nimble hands stroking up and down on his back. He opened his eyes, concerned. *She's still so new at lovemaking, so tight and innocent, and that was no way to take a lady. I hope I didn't hurt her.*

He needn't have worried. Her dark eyes glowed with satisfaction and amusement.

"Are you all right?" he asked, still not quite certain.

"Yes, darling. It was exquisite." She touched his face as though to reassure him.

"Really? I didn't hurt you?" he pressed.

"No. Well, I might be feeling this one tomorrow… or next week, but I'm not hurt. It was lovely." She giggled.

"What?" he asked, relieved to see her smile and hear her laugh.

"Now I know your secret," she teased.

If she's joking, she must be fine, he realized, shoulders sagging. "What secret?"

"Underneath the proper middle-class gentleman lurks a wild man just awaiting an invitation." She wrinkled her nose at him.

He kissed the tip. "Love, that's no secret. All men are like that. Gentlemanly behavior is learned, not innate."

"I see."

"I'm surprised you weren't frightened," he commented idly tracing his fingertips over the swell of her breast.

"Not at all. You weren't angry. You were loving me. It's a vast difference." She leaned into his touch.

"Ah, I see." He withdrew gently from her body, covered them both with the blankets and pulled her close for a long kiss that rewarded her sweetly for her courage and for her honest, uninhibited sexuality.

Being married is so much better than I expected, he reflected as her slender body relaxed in his arms. *She's so brave, so unutterably sweet.*

How she had escaped her childhood with her tenderness and affection and sense of humor intact baffled him. Day after day, as he tried to help her heal, he was rewarded with an outpouring of the best of a woman's heart. *It's close to love already. So close. I'm not sure if she'll recognize it in herself, but I do.*

As for Christopher, he had been hovering on the brink for days. Tonight had tipped the scales. *Any woman who could take a rough loving like that and emerge smiling is worth her weight in gold. I love her. I really do. I love my wife.* It felt wonderful.

He kissed her forehead and slowly drifted into a nap, amazed by the unexpected beauty of their relationship.

* * *

All told, the voyage took nine days. At last, they sailed smoothly into the port of Livorno, and within a short space of time, emerged down the gangplank over the glistening turquoise waters of the Mediterranean and onto solid ground.

"I quite understand why some travelers kiss the earth after a sea voyage," Katerina told her husband fervently. "The thought of doing this again makes me feel faint."

"It won't be soon," he reminded her. "We'll be here until the middle of March."

"Thank heaven. You know, it's only a little warmer here than in England." She snuggled deeper into her shawl.

"You're right," he agreed. "I suppose winter is winter."

"I suppose, and this is not the southernmost part of Italy either," she said. Though far from warm, the light that trickled down on them seemed stronger than anything she could recall, as though this more southerly climate lent it power. It kissed her face in a teasing way.

Her words might have sounded calm, but her insides fluttered at the sight of such un-English buildings, brightly colored and clustered close, one behind the other, to the top of a hill. Boats large and small bobbed in the harbor behind them, awaiting their next adventure on the Mediterranean.

"True," Christopher said, shaking her from her reverie. "Well, love, are you feeling courageous?"

"Perhaps. Why?"

"I don't speak Italian," Christopher reminded her. "If we're going to get anywhere, it will be up to you to handle the conversations."

"Oh, that's right." Shyness made her squirm, but she steeled herself against it. "I think I can manage."

Last month she would not have been able, she knew, but Christopher was like the Italian sun, all warmth and life-giving brightness, and in his arms, she felt herself blossoming like a spring flower. *It took no time at all for the affection and gratitude of our wedding day to deepen and strengthen. This… thing I feel will be good for our lifetime. I look forward to exploring it every day.*

He hailed a cab and she arranged for it to take them to the train station. The driver, a man on the verge between middle-aged and elderly, quickly loaded the baggage and the couple took a seat inside and then stared out the window at the sight of their first Italian town. *How different this is from London; colorful and sun-drenched, the winter sky a dazzling blue.*

Behind a marble counter, a young man with curly sideburns and a few pimples sprinkling his cheeks regarded her with a bored expression.

Katerina took a deep breath and requested in Italian, "Two tickets to Firenze, please."

He raised his eyebrows. "I thought you were English."

It wasn't his business, so Katerina ignored the comment. "When does the train leave?"

"Two hours," he replied, sulking that his nosiness had been rebuffed. He collected her money and sent her on her way.

Katerina regaled her husband with the account as they walked to a restaurant whose façade was covered in creamy plaster. They sat outside at a wrought-iron table, enjoying the scenery of the golden stone buildings with their bright red roofs. The aroma of roasted garlic washed over them. The bowls of soup they devoured perfectly countered the chill of the wind, though Christopher's puzzled expression showed he found the taste strange. He seemed to prefer the accompanying triangles of flatbread soaked in the best olive oil.

Katerina found the food comforting. Her parents' original cook, who had left after her mother's death, had come with them from Italy, and this tasty concoction of vegetables and white beans recalled a childhood that felt… better than her adolescence, though still tense and filled with uncertainty.

They made that simple lunch last a long time, busily examining the square.

"You look happy, love," Christopher told his wife.

"I think I am," she replied.

"Not sure?" He regarded her quizzically.

"Well, I have a good feeling," she said, trying to explain what she didn't understand fully herself. "If this is happy, then yes. I am. Something about this place speaks to me, even though I've never been here before. I'm so glad to be exploring it, and having you here makes it best of all."

"How sweet." He captured her hand and kissed the knuckles. "Thank you, love. This is quite an adventure for a staunch British sort like me."

"Ha," she replied. "In a bygone generation, you would have gone to sea as a privateer."

Christopher's eyebrows drew together. "Why do you say so?"

"I don't exactly know," she replied, smoothing an errant strand of dark brown hair from his face. "You wear the trappings of a middle-class gentleman, but there's a wild romantic adventurer in your soul. I mean, just look at what you did for me."

His lips turned up in a half-smile and he shrugged his shoulders. "Perhaps. At any rate, I'm glad to be here with you as well." He stroked her fingers. She trailed them over his cheek. "Well, sweet girl, shall we go back to the station and await our train?"

"Yes, I think so."

* * *

The train ride to Florence took a little longer than their previous one, and by the time they arrived at the station, the sun hung low in the sky. When the couple emerged, an Italian gentleman immediately approached them. He appeared about sixty years of age, but in robust health, with gleaming white hair that contrasted with his bushy black eyebrows.

"Katerina?" He bore down on her with the lumbering gait of a water buffalo.

"Sì." She gave her husband a worried glance. He laced his fingers through hers.

A conversation in lilting Italian followed, of which Christopher could understand nothing. His years studying French provided little help because the sounds of the languages were so different.

Then, the gentleman dragged his wife into a tight embrace, squashing her. She beamed. "Christopher, this is my nonno, my grandfather."

Christopher reached out and shook hands with the other man. Katerina's nonno had a powerful grip. *Here is another man who works with his hands.* Christopher squeezed back, not to challenge the old lion, but to prove he was no dandy.

The bushy black eyebrows shot up and then an unrestrained grin broke across the tanned and rugged face.

"Nonno, this is my husband, Christopher Bennett," Katerina said as they released each other, seemingly unaware of the silent assessment passing between the men.

"Pleased to meet you, signore, I am Alessandro Bianchi. Katerina's mother was my daughter." Despite his heavy accent, Christopher could understand him easily enough.

"A pleasure, sir. I've been looking forward to meeting the rest of my wife's family. I admit I wasn't impressed with her father." He compressed his lips in contempt.

"Bastardo," Alessandro muttered under his breath, the meaning obvious even to Christopher.

Katerina blushed and giggled.

"Step into my carriage, and let's head home. It's quite a drive and there is a lovely hot dinner waiting for us."

"Sounds wonderful," Christopher assented. "We've had nothing since a bowl of soup in Livorno, and I don't know about my wife, but to me, a hot meal sounds very promising."

"Yes, I agree," she seconded. "Thank you, Nonno."

He nodded in acknowledgment and sent them up into the carriage. Once everyone was comfortably seated, Alessandro took up the conversation again. "So, Signor Bennett, what do you do?"

"My father owns a cotton mill. We make fabric," Christopher replied, slipping his arm behind his wife's back.

"Cotton mill?" The bushy eyebrows came together in an unmistakable expression of disapproval.

"No, Nonno, not that kind of mill," Katerina defended her husband. "Christopher and his father run a progressive mill. They have safeguards for the employees and pay decent wages. They do everything they can to make their mill a pleasant place to work. They're so generous that some social reformers won't buy fabric from anyone else."

The bushy brows returned to their normal position. "Ah, I see. Well then, Mr. Bennett, I suppose you know where I can get good quality cotton fabric?"

"I'll see what I can arrange," he agreed. *Exporting to Italy. Now that would be new. I wonder what Father would think of the opportunity.*

"Do you offer a family discount?" Alessandro asked with a sly smirk.

Christopher grinned. "Perhaps. I'll have to talk to my father, but it seems likely."

"Buono," Alessandro replied, leaning back against blue velvet upholstery.

"And you, sir?" Christopher asked to continue the conversation.

"Our family has owned a large olive grove for generations. We export oil all over the world. We also have a small vineyard. It's not as expansive as the orchard, but we make a charming red wine for our family to use. The people of Firenze buy a bit for restaurants as well. Would you be interested in a glass with your dinner?"

"That sounds wonderful, Nonno," Katerina assured him.

Christopher nodded in agreement. *After so much travel, a nice glass of wine would be very soothing.*

* * *

The three lapsed into silence. Katerina's eye flitted to the scenery passing outside the window of the carriage where dense city thinned to open countryside. A strange sensation gradually grew within her, and she turned to see Alessandro regarding her with a considering expression.

"Cara," he said to her finally in Italian, "How did your mother die?"

She looked at him, feeling haunted. "She had a fever," Katerina replied at last, in the same language, quite forgetting her husband did not understand.

"So, it was a natural disease?" he pressed.

She bit her lip. "Are you sure you want me to answer that question?"

"Sì."

Katerina closed her eyes against a sting. "The fever undoubtedly killed her, but the source of the fever was not natural disease."

"Did that figlio di puttana cause it?" Alessandro snarled.

"Sì." Pain welled up in her soul.

Christopher took his wife's hand. *He has no idea what we're talking about, and yet he knows I need comforting.* She gave him a sad smile.

Alessandro continued his interrogation. "And you, cara? Were you in danger too?"

"Sì." She looked down at her lap, smoothing the fabric of her skirt with nervous fingers.

"Did he hurt you?"

She raised her eyes to meet his. "Sì."

Alessandro growled.

Katerina quickly added, "But Christopher rescued me."

"By marrying you?"

She nodded. "He is my hero."

"Then I'm glad to know him."

She inhaled through her nose, trying to calm herself. Christopher's thumb stroked over her fingers. Another question rose up in Katerina's mind. "Nonno, why did Mother marry my father?"

He thought for a moment. "She insisted. We didn't want her to. No matter the scandal, we would have stood by her. Understand, Katerina, your mother was a good girl, but very young. Your father... manipulated her."

Poor thing. "Was she... incinta?"

"Sì."

"With me?"

"Sí."

"So, I'm responsible." She closed her eyes against the wave of agony.

Alessandro reached across the seat and grasped her free hand. "No, no one thinks that. You were just a baby. *He* was the one."

She smiled sadly. "Right. Nonno, I would rather have been born a bastard."

His eyebrows drew together, and his mouth turned down. The loss of his shiny smile made him look old and sad. "I'm sure, but you're safe now, and you have a kind husband to look after you."

"I do." She snuggled up against Christopher and laid her cheek against his shoulder.

"I'm so glad." He looked away for a long moment.

"What was that all about?" Christopher asked his wife quietly.

"He wanted to be sure I was safe. He knew about my father's behavior."

* * *

Seeing Alessandro's attention wander away, Christopher hugged his wife gently. She leaned into his embrace. They turned together to watch the hills outside the carriage window. A river ran parallel to the road. The Arno, their research had told them. On the other side, a massive olive grove shivered its myriad branches in the evening breeze.

After a little time passed, Alessandro returned his attention to his guests, catching them snuggled together. He raised his eyebrows, but both looked back steadily at him, unwilling to release each other.

"Well, this brings up another question," Alessandro addressed them both in English. "In the past, when I have had visitors from England, husbands and wives have demanded separate rooms."

"One will do," Katerina told her grandfather firmly.

"I suspected as much." He winked at them. "That will be fine. Well, children, here we are. Come along."

They climbed down into the chilly evening air and walked quickly to a gracious, tile-roofed home constructed of golden stones. Full dark had fallen, concealing the olive trees from view, but the golden glow of lanterns illuminated the house and complimented the warm sunshine yellow of the stones and the thick creamy mortar between.

It was an irregularly-shaped construction, charming in its eccentricity; a two-story rectangle, with a sharply protruding exterior wall to the right, and a recessed area in the center. All the wings had sloping roofs that appeared, like the buildings in Livorno, to be of bumpy red tile, although in the dark, the detail was hard to discern.

As they approached the front entrance with its huge, arched double door, Katerina noticed that to the left, what appeared to be a square stone tower rose two stories above the normal roofline of the house.

The chill had turned biting, so they hurried through the door and down a hallway lined with cream plaster walls. An ancient wood floor gleamed in the dim light of lamps fueled by olive oil.

They entered the dining room and sat at a rough-hewn table. There, as promised, a hot meal waited. It seemed to be a kind of stew or casserole made of beans and sausage, piled on thick yellow plates.

The three ate eagerly. The rich red table wine tasted as delicious as Alessandro had promised. As they devoured the repast, Katerina asked her grandfather a question. "Nonno, where is my grandmother?"

Alessandro's eyes turned sad. "She passed away about six years ago."

Her hand fluttered around her mouth. "Oh, I never knew. I'm sorry."

"Thank you, dear." He reached across the table and grasped her hand. "I miss her still."

"What was her name?" Katerina asked.

"Caterina, just like you, but with a C," he replied.

"It's not normal to use the K, is it?" Christopher asked before taking a hearty bite of hot homemade bread.

I wonder if he finds it odd that the bread has no salt, or if he realizes the fierce seasoning of the stew compensates for its blandness, she wondered idly, trying to distract herself from the intensity of the conversation.

"No. That was your mother's idea. Since the child—you, cara—was born in England, the K seemed easier for the locals to understand," Alessandro explained.

"I see," she replied.

"Oh, and, cara, Signor Bennett, I have organized a party in honor of your visit."

Katerina shifted in nervous discomfort.

"Please, we're family. Christopher will do," her husband urged, drawing attention away from his wife's nervous squirming.

"Buono. Then you must call me Alessandro," her grandfather replied, seeming not to notice her reaction.

"Certainly," Christopher replied with an easy grin.

They get along so well already, these two open-hearted people. I still want to hide like a rabbit.

Now is the time I have to choose. Choose to accept what I'm not sure I want to please someone else. Nonno wants so badly for me to be fine, so he can feel better about everything else. Therefore, I have to be better than I actually am.

"What's wrong, cara?" Alessandro asked.

"Nothing," she said quickly.

Christopher spoke for her. "She doesn't care for parties. She's very shy, but if you have a pianoforte, that will help immensely."

Oh, Christopher, did you have to? She realized he was trying to protect her, but without the chance to talk privately, she had no way to tell him.

"Of course, I have a pianoforte." An odd light flared in the older man's eyes. "I also have a musician."

"Yes?" Katerina asked, eyebrows raised in question.

"Her name is Aimée St. Jean. She's a French soprano, and I've hired her to entertain at our little *festa*."

"How nice. Isn't that nice, Katerina?" Christopher pressed, squeezing her hand.

She gave him a sharp look. *I'm not stupid. She squeezed his hand in a gesture that lacked their usual affection.*

He made an apologetic face, seeming to realize he'd been talking to her like a simpleton.

She crooked an eyebrow at him in rebuke before turning to address Alessandro. "Oh yes, very nice. Thank you, Grandfather. I'm looking forward to hearing her."

"Well," Alessandro said abruptly, changing the subject, "I can see you're both finished. Your bags should be unpacked in your room by now, and I imagine you are both tired from your travels. Would you care to retire?"

"Yes, thank you, Nonno. That's just what I was hoping for." Katerina yawned.

"In the morning, I will give you a tour of the house and estate. The *festa* is next week."

"Perfect. Grazie." She smiled, hoping to dispel any shadows their conversation had raised.

"Yes, thank you," Christopher echoed in English.

Chapter 15

ORNING dawned, brightly sunny but with a winter chill that could be detected even through the walls of the house. They ate a quick breakfast of hot sweet rolls and powerful coffee before meeting Alessandro in the parlor of his spacious manor.

It was a gorgeous room, boasting delicate blue walls and several floor-to-ceiling windows decorated with ornately cream-colored wood frames and moldings. The wood floor was covered with a mostly-red rug accented in a blue that complemented the walls.

Cream and dark wood furniture stood in several seating areas, and in the open space between the furnishings, a small crowd of people in uniforms stood stiffly at attention.

Alessandro rose from one of the dark armchairs at their approach. "Everyone," he boomed in a hearty, carrying voice, "my long-lost granddaughter and her husband have finally come home. May I present Katerina and Christopher Bennett!"

The staff applauded, their eyes curious and happy. One particularly round barrel of a woman approached Katerina, chattering rapidly in Italian. She kissed her on both cheeks and lumbered away, wiping her eyes with a plump hand.

"Who on earth was that?" Christopher asked.

"Oh, she's the cook," Alessandro replied, eyes alight with laughter. "She knew your mother growing up. They were... friendly, I suppose.

"She thought I was too skinny and is currently planning to cook something decadent to fatten me up." Katerina grinned. "She might just succeed."

"Do you think you might share?" he asked, regarding her with teasing silver eyes.

"It depends," she teased him back.

"All right you two," Alessandro growled, "don't shock my servants." He dismissed the staff with a word and led the couple on a tour of the house. On the first floor, they left the spacious parlor, passed the dining room and peeked into Alessandro's study, housed in a cavernous library with books stacked floor to ceiling on oiled wooden shelves.

Next, they arrived in the kitchen. The ceiling of rough-hewn and weathered gray boards drew the eye upward, where gleaming copper pans dangled. The size of the space caused Katerina to draw in a deep breath, filling herself with the aroma of garlic and olive oil. The cook grinned at them and handed them each a pastry. The sweet treat made Katerina's eyes roll back in her head. *It won't be hard to gain weight in this place.*

Last, they explored the music room. Compared to the tiny space in the Bennetts' London townhouse, the Bianchi music room was huge. It contained a beautifully carved pianoforte and a harpsichord along with various other instruments displayed on tables and hung on the wall. In particular, a small instrument that resembled a guitar snared Katerina's eye. Clearly Spanish in origin, it bore ornate decorations in inlaid wood. She looked at it for a moment before being drawn by the magnetic pull of the pianoforte.

Sliding onto the bench she played a series of lightning-fast scales and smiled. *Lovely tone.* Then, her fingers itching to play, she added a spritely Chopin melody.

"Very nice," Alessandro told her when she finished, "you're quite accomplished."

"Thank you, Nonno. I love music." She switched to Handel and played the slow opening chords of "I Know that My Redeemer Liveth." Then she sang.

* * *

Christopher remembered her telling him she could sing rather well, and he had teased her about opera, but after their rapid and traumatic wedding, he had forgotten the conversation. *Truly she is no operatic soprano, he realized. She's better.*

Katerina's voice, delicate and soft, rang like chimes. She hit each note with pinpoint precision, and her clever fingers never faltered on the keyboard. Just as she climbed the scale to a high note, which she touched with the lightness of a butterfly's wing, her impromptu concert was interrupted.

"Brava," a strange woman said, her voice slightly unpleasant as she eyed the pianoforte with a proprietary air. "Signor Bianchi, who is this ingénue? Are you replacing me?"

Alessandro's suntanned skin darkened. "Of course not, Madame St. Jean. This is my granddaughter, Katerina Bennett. Remember, we're having a *festa* in her honor?"

"Oh, that's right. How sweet. And the gentleman?" She ran hungry eyes over Christopher's frame.

"Her husband, Signor Christopher Bennett."

Katerina felt a twinge of anxiety. *This singer is much showier and more beautiful than I. Her golden hair gleamed, and her rosebud lips curbed into a flirtatious smile as she regarded the young man.* Her low-cut morning dress displayed her voluptuous figure almost to the point of indecency, and she fluttered her shoulders in a way that might have been a simple fidget… but wasn't. *She knows how to attract male attention, this one.*

Katerina glanced at her grandfather. He was watching the curvy beauty watch his grandson-in-law, and a look of anger crossed his craggy face.

Hoping to break the uncomfortable silence, Katerina rose from the piano bench and took her husband's arm. He patted her reassuringly. "Pleased to meet you, Madame St. Jean. I'm looking forward to hearing you sing. I'm sure you'd like the music room to yourself, so you can practice. Grandfather, I would *love* to see your olive grove now, if you have time."

Alessandro shook his head as though to clear it. "Yes, in a moment. Can you two go back to the parlor and wait for me? I have something I have to do. You do remember the way, do you not?"

"We do," Christopher assured him, and escorted his wife from the room.

Once the door was closed behind them, Katerina sighed... and then giggled.

"What, love?" he asked as they made their way down the hallway.

"I believe Madame Aimée St. Jean was chosen for more than just her musical ability," she said, feeling naughty for even suggesting such a thing.

"Oh?"

"If I'm not very much mistaken, she appears to be his mistress." Katerina's cheeks warmed.

Christopher chuckled. "Yes, I did get that impression. Does it bother you?"

She laughed. "Of course not. He's been widowed a long time, and she's quite lovely and very young. I doubt she's seen forty years. Good for him."

"Yes, well, she has a wandering eye. I'm not sure how he figures on keeping her."

"Perhaps he doesn't," she replied, unperturbed. "He might just be enjoying the moment. However, I don't like how her eye wandered to you."

"No worries, love. I have all I need right here." He swept her into the parlor and kissed her.

* * *

Christopher had known the sight of the flirtatious blond would unsettle Katerina, but honestly, he had been completely unmoved by her. *Mme St. Jean has a certain blatant sex appeal, and once upon a time such things tempted me, but no more. I love my wife. I need to tell her, but I want to find just the right moment. Every other part of our relationship has been done in a panic-stricken rush, but this is too important.* In the meanwhile, he assured her with long, tender kisses, cradling her in his arms like the priceless treasure she was.

As always, she eagerly returned his affection.

"Ahem." the clearing of a throat interrupted the embrace. Katerina's grandfather was eyeing them with an amused look on his face.

"Oh, hello, Nonno," Katerina said, trying for nonchalance, but not quite managing it.

She's so adorable when she's flustered. Christopher smoothed a strand of hair back into his wife's coiffure.

"Hello, lovebirds."

Katerina blushed and giggled at his comment.

"Shall we tour my estate?"

"Oh, yes please," she agreed eagerly, and Christopher assented with a nod.

"Better cover up," Alessandro suggested. "It's chilly this morning, though I must say, you two look warm enough."

Chapter 16

 HE days of the visit passed pleasantly, filled with delicious food and superb conversation. Christopher and Katerina both enjoyed getting to know Alessandro, who proved to be a kind and amusing gentleman with a gruff manner that belied a tender heart.

Slowly they because aware he was also dangerously enamored of his little French musician, and she played with him, keeping him on his toes. In fact, only Aimée made the visit difficult. She teased and flirted with Christopher, which made Katerina wild with jealousy, and Alessandro furious.

She also had a skill for knowing when Katerina wanted to play the pianoforte or the harpsichord in the music room and chasing her out. Katerina's first impulse was to avoid the music room altogether and spare herself the endless harassment, but after careful consideration, she decided it should not be necessary to do so. Katerina wanted to play, and she sought out the room at random moments, searching for a time when she would be able to do so unmolested.

About two days before the party, she was seated at the piano bench at six in the morning, working on a piece of sheet music she had found.

"You again?" Aimée stormed into the music room, stopping as close to Katerina as she could get and hovering over where she sat. "Get out of here. I need to practice."

"Since when do you practice at six in the morning?" Katerina asked in a calm voice that belied the pounding of her heart.

"The party is the day after tomorrow. I need to be ready." The woman made shooing motions with her hands.

"I understand the importance of that," Katerina replied, not budging from the bench. "If you could let me know when you're going to practice, I can work around you."

"No." Aimée stuck her nose in the air. "I will work when I want to. I do not owe you a schedule. I am the professional. You're only a guest. My need is greater than yours."

"I'm not disagreeing with you," Katerina said, forcing her voice to calmness, "but, Madame St. Jean, you don't practice all day. Mightn't I be here when you're not?"

"No." The blond crossed her arms over her ample bosom and glared.

So, you're not willing to make even a token attempt to be reasonable? A thread of anger sparked above Katerina's nervousness. "Why not?"

"Because I don't have to be. I will have exclusive rights to this pianoforte, and your grandfather will let me. There's nothing he would deny me." Aimée smirked.

"No doubt that's true," Katerina said sarcastically, "but you're not the only musician in the house."

"Yes, I am," Aimée sneered. "You're nothing but a dilettante. Go away."

"I won't. I have as much right to be here as you do." She surprised herself by saying it, and she drew in a startled breath.

Her rival blinked, rosebud lip drooping, but she recovered quickly. "You'd better tend to your own business, Mrs. Bennett. If you're occupied at the pianoforte, I might just decide to amuse myself by spending time with your husband. He's very handsome."

"Aren't you a bit old for him?" Katerina shot back.

Aimée's eyes narrowed at the unkind comment. "It makes no difference. Besides, you're such a mouse, I could take him from you in an instant. He would be glad to go."

Katerina struggled to maintain her confident manner, but the threat hit her in a weak place. "Unlikely. He doesn't believe in adultery."

"Maybe, but I could make him wish he did."

Does she have to say that? What if she's right? Katerina rose from the bench, for once taking advantage of her height to try to intimidate her rival. "You stay away from my husband."

Aimée refused to back down. "Nervous, are you? You should be. Choose wisely, Mrs. Bennett. Your husband or the pianoforte."

Katerina's fear disappeared under a wave of pure anger. "My God, you're disgusting. What's wrong with you?"

"Nothing," the woman crowed. "I know what I want, and I take it. I don't hide in the shadows, mouse."

"Oh, be quiet," Katerina said with a flamboyant hand gesture.

"*Non*," the singer sneered.

"Madame St. Jean?" Katerina demanded, "I haven't done a thing to you. I'm not asking anything from you. All I want is to play *my grandfather's* piano when you are not using it. What problem could that possibly pose you? What do you want?"

"I want you to go away. I don't like you," Aimée said brutally.

Katerina shrugged. "You don't have to like me. You have Grandfather. Isn't that enough?"

A flash of something... softer appeared for a moment behind the singer's eyes.

She does *care for him, in her way*, Katerina realized, though she didn't quite understand how to integrate that knowledge with Mme St. Jean's threats towards Christopher.

Aimée's expression hardened. "I don't want you in my space. This room is mine. I belong here. You're intruding. You're not a real musician."

"I disagree." Katerina met Aimée's eyes with a squinty glare.

"You think you're better than me?" Aimée challenged, puffing up in indignation.

"I have no way of knowing," Katerina snapped, growing even more annoyed by the woman's continuing rudeness. "I've never heard you perform. Besides, it's not a competition. I just want to share this space from time to time. I can't imagine why you have such a problem with that."

"Competition?" The French woman's sea-blue eyes turned considering. "Yes, very good. A competition. I challenge you, Mrs. Bennett, to a musical competition. It can take place during the party. Each of us will sing three songs and then everyone will choose who is the better musician, you or me. The winner gets exclusive rights to the music room for the remainder of your visit."

"I would rather play than sing," Katerina requested, swept along by the emotion of the conversation and agreeing to something she hadn't taken the time to consider.

"*Non.* A singing competition. It won't be fair if we are not on the same instrument."

Katerina felt trapped. *How can I refuse? Maybe on the piano, but singing?* On voice, she felt very much like the dilettante she'd been named. Casting about for any logical objection, she blurted, "Who will accompany?"

"We accompany ourselves."

If I can play as well, I might have a chance. Heart pounding, she took a deep breath and released it in a wave of nausea that almost rivaled the worst of her seasickness. She swallowed down a gag. "Very well. I accept your challenge, on two conditions."

"Yes?" One blonde eyebrow shot upward.

"You *have* to let me practice," Katerina replied with all the firmness she had left in her.

"I suppose." Mme St. Jean rolled her eyes. "You get one hour in the morning, six to seven, and one in the evening."

Katerina nodded. *I hope it's enough.* "And you stay away from Christopher."

The woman's smile turned feral. "Worried, are you? How do you know I will keep my word?"

Katerina didn't reply and Aimée didn't promise. Instead, she stalked from the room.

Katerina turned back to the pianoforte and began to practice for all she was worth. *What in the world have I done? Gotten caught up in a silly quarrel over a musical instrument? Let myself get so angry I made a foolish decision? What's wrong with me? The piano isn't that important, but Christopher is. I cannot allow that little tramp to seduce my precious husband.* It was a feeling the likes of which Katerina had never imagined; sharp, painful and disconcerting. *Christopher is mine, and no brassy French tart will threaten what we have.*

* * *

In the master suite, Alessandro woke to the pleasurable sensation of Aimée's luscious naked curves pressed against him. He had met her over a year ago when he was planning his son's thirty-fifth birthday party. Entranced by her golden beauty and her flirtatious manner, he had boldly invited her to share his bed and had been shocked when she agreed. In the years since his wife's death, he'd been rather chaste, but Aimée drove all such thoughts from his mind.

Their affair had progressed from occasional encounters when he hired her to sing, until now when she very nearly lived with him. He harbored no illusions that he would be able to keep her. She was young, not quite forty, and he had celebrated his sixtieth birthday only a month ago. She should marry, have a baby, and leave her wild days behind. Alessandro could hardly offer her those things, but he would enjoy her while she was willing.

I never thought I would fall in love with her, and now, a handsome young man has captured her attention. Though he had expected this, it hurt more than he had realized it would. Not to mention the man she had chosen was married to his granddaughter, a girl he was quickly coming to adore. Not that he was worried. Christopher seemed not to care about—or even notice—Aimée's blatant flirtation. The youth adored his wife, but the point was she had been swayed by someone else, which surely meant their affair was almost done. *Dannazione! I'm not ready to let her go.*

Well, I don't have to right now. He began to caress her lovely, round body, pleased that he still had enough animal spirits to make love to a pretty woman and satisfy them both.

Long moments later, Madame St. Jean stretched in her lover's arms and snuggled up against him. "Cheri," she said, "I've just made the most exciting plan for the music at your little party."

"What's that?" he asked, feeling indulgent in his satiation.

"A friendly competition between Madame Bennett and me. We're both going to sing and play for the guests to see who the better musician is." She said this insouciantly, as though it were a lark.

"She agreed to this?" Alessandro asked, surprised. *Katerina seems very shy and meek, not one who would compete with a professional musician in a public venue.*

"She did." Aimée's studied innocence aroused his suspicions further.

"Sounds interesting. What are the rules?" he asked, trying to get to the bottom of the story.

"You know, I don't know," she replied, waving one hand in the air. "We didn't get to that part, except we each do three songs. You're going to be the judge, of course, so maybe you should make the rules."

"Hmmm. Let me think on this. I'll let you both know a little later."

"Wonderful. Won't this be fun?"

She's trying too hard. There's more to this story. "I hope it is." He still had his doubts about Katerina's willingness, but he would talk to her and see what it was all about.

* * *

Two days later, as the early sunset turned the Tuscan horizon scarlet, a large group of Italian locals converged on the Bianchi estate, eager to meet the respected landowner's long-lost granddaughter.

Katerina painted on a false cheerful smile and greeted each new arrival warmly as she clung to Christopher's arm, trembling with nerves. *This could all go very badly.*

"Ladies and Gentlemen," Alessandro said loudly in Italian, "thank you for coming tonight. I am so pleased to introduce all of you to my granddaughter, Katerina Bennett and her husband Christopher, finally come to visit us. For our entertainment this evening, Katerina has agreed to sing and play the pianoforte."

This caused a murmur that demonstrated Alessandro's affair with his musician was hardly a secret.

"She and Madame St. Jean will be competing for the title of musical expert. We are all going to be judges. Here are the rules. Each lady will sing three songs, accompanying herself on pianoforte or harpsichord. One song will be in Italian, one in English, and the third will be of the lady's choice. Then we will decide who the better musician is. Madame St. Jean, are you ready?"

Going last gives me a slight advantage, Katerina thought. Still, her heart pounded so hard she feared she might be sick.

"Yes, I am ready," Aimée replied in French-accented Italian. Curtsying to the crowd, she seated herself at the harpsichord and announced, "I would like to begin with 'Greensleeves.'"

She played a few simple chords on the keyboard, setting the key, and then took a deep quiet breath and began to sing.

Instantly, Katerina knew she was in deep trouble. The years separating the two singers made a huge difference. A true professional, Aimée's voice was flexible, rich, and captivating even though she didn't play the harpsichord particularly well. Her accompaniment consisted of a series of simple chords to help her keep in tune. Her English pronunciation was also rather bad, but it made no difference. The maturity of her tone would turn this competition into one between a pipe organ and a piccolo. Then, to increase the difficulty, she stopped playing and sang *a capella* during the middle verse. When she played again on the third verse, she was still perfectly in tune. The guests murmured in appreciation of the trick. She ended plaintively, "who but my lady, Greensleeves?'"

The audience applauded. She rose and flounced to her seat. The opening gauntlet had been well tossed. *It is not a performance I want to follow,* Katerina admitted to herself as she shuffled, her knees weak, to the harpsichord bench. Swallowing hard, she looked at the instrument for a long moment, pleading silently with it to help her.

" 'Scarborough Fair,' " she said at last. Then she placed her fingers on the keys and began a complicated run of notes. She had never been so aware of the people staring at her back. She felt vulnerable, exposed, and she glanced up.

Warm gray eyes met hers encouragingly. *Christopher. Christopher will support me.* Soothed by his sweet look, she turned her attention inward and began to sing. " 'Are you going to Scarborough Fair/ Parsley, sage, rosemary and thyme/ Remember me to one who lives there. /She once was a true love of mine.' "

She sang the nonsensical lyrics lightly. She couldn't match Aimée for depth and richness, so she didn't try. Instead, she focused on the feather lightness of her nineteen-year-old voice, singing sweetly and prettily, accompanied by flashy notes on the harpsichord. *It's the best I can manage. I pray it's enough for a pleasing performance.*

As the end of the song neared, she had a flash of insight about its message. *True love can overcome insurmountable odds, perform impossible tasks. Haven't Christopher and I done that?*

We have. We've done the impossible. It means something.

Understanding dawned at the end of the last verse.

It means I love him. Truly love him. At the staggering realization, her voice faltered and grew husky. She played a fancy interlude to cover the mistake, and when she began to sing again, it was for her husband's ears alone.

" 'When at last he has finished his work/ Parsley, sage, rosemary, and thyme/ He'll come to claim his cambric shirt/ And ever be a true love of mine.' "

She finished with a flourish of fingers and took a deep breath, only to jump in alarm as applause thundered around her. Feeling unsteady, Katerina remained seated at the harpsichord.

Aimée moved to the pianoforte and began immediately. Not surprisingly, the other woman's second was in French, another folk song, called "Jeune Fillette." This teasingly flirtatious number described falling in love in the springtime, with pointed references to fickle lovers, male and female.

It was a clear invitation, and she gave her rival's husband a pointed look as she tripped lightly over the coloratura notes, demonstrating that a mature voice did not need to be heavy or slow. She could beat Katerina at her own game, and in her own marriage, her blatant glare seemed to claim.

Again, the tension rose. *How can I meet this challenge?* Not in her rival's own language, to be sure. Katerina had intended to sing in French also, but abandoned the plan, making a last-minute substitution. *I can't out-flirt Mme St. Jean, but perhaps I can offer something more poignant.*

Remaining at the harpsichord, she played a few simple chords and then began with "Drink to Me Only with Thine Eyes," a plaintive love song. Again, it was a message to Christopher, as though no one else were in the room. The couple could have been in their row house for all the attention she paid to any other member of the audience. She could see from his intense expression that he understood she was singing to him... and liked it.

Last was each woman's Italian song. Aimée had practiced hard to master the complicated accompaniment, so she could play it by muscle memory and turned her full attention towards Christopher as she began to sing "Se Tu m'Ami" by Paolo Antonio Rolli. Everyone in the room but him knew Italian and understood what this woman was doing. The song sent a blatant message; a girl of easy virtue offering herself to a man, but making it clear he should expect no fidelity.

From her seat on the harpsichord bench, Katerina could see that Christopher remained oblivious, but Alessandro did not. Neither did most of his guests. *What a sad blow to be dealt in such a public venue,* Katerina thought, regarding her grandfather in sympathy.

Unaware, focused on undermining her rival's confidence, Aimée continued to flirt with Christopher through song, naughtily promising everything but her heart. Though she performed with superior skill, the audience applauded tepidly.

They didn't like her manner, Katerina realized. *They found it inappropriate.* The realization mattered less to her than how her husband would react. He didn't. His lovely silver eyes remained fixed on her, and it warmed her to her core. She smiled at him.

At last, it was time for Katerina's final song. She walked slowly from the harpsichord to the pianoforte. Once again, she chose to give her husband her unveiled heart: "Per la Gloria d'Adorarvi" by Bononcini from the opera Griselda.

She pleaded with him in song to ignore her rival and give his attention to his wife, to her heart, which she was offering without reservation. Her emotion, her adoration vibrated palpably in the room. Unfortunately, he had no idea... *or maybe it is fortunate. I would be embarrassed if he understood.*

After a delicately shimmering high note, the song ended, and the room erupted with applause, startling her again. Red-faced and trembling, she slunk back to her seat beside Christopher. He took her hand and held it indiscreetly.

Alessandro rose from his seat, his face red but his voice falsely cheerful. "Thank you, ladies, for those lovely performances. We will give our verdict after dinner. And now, friends, shall we adjourn to the dining room?"

There was a general exodus, and it wasn't until later that the guests noticed their host had not joined them.

* * *

As Aimée moved towards the door, Alessandro caught her arm in a hard grip, pulling her back. "What exactly was that?" he asked her, his expression thunderous.

"Music, cheri," she answered in her usual flirtatious lightness.

He shook her. "No. You know what I mean. Why were you throwing yourself at my granddaughter's husband?"

"I was only playing. I don't care in the slightest about Mr. Bennett." She twined her arms around Alessandro's neck, trying to distract him from his anger.

"Then why the hell were you flirting with him?" His grip on her arm tightened to bruising force, and he yanked her away from him. "You embarrassed me. Everyone knows I'm your protector, Aimée."

She attempted to placate him by stroking his cheek. "No, don't be angry, cheri. I didn't mean anything by it."

"If you aren't attempting to seduce him, what were you trying to accomplish? Were you hoping to upset Katerina by undermining her relationship with her husband?" He removed her arms from him.

"No, it was a joke," she whined, her voice pleading.

"Well, I, for one, am not amused. I'm sure Katerina isn't either. You know, I think I've had about enough of you. Go pack up your possessions and leave. I don't want to see you again. Goodbye, Aimée."

He turned and left.

The beautiful soprano stared after him in shock. She had not stopped to consider the consequences of her actions, determined as she had been to see her perceived rival humiliated. She hadn't given a moment's thought to how her behavior would reflect on Alessandro. And now he was furious... and he was gone.

She had gone too far, she realized, and she deserved his anger. No part of her behavior had been acceptable. She had been cruel to Katerina, and ridiculous towards the girl's husband. *How stupid.*

Tears streaming down her face, she walked slowly to the room she'd been sharing with Alessandro. She wasn't ready to leave him. Perhaps she never would be, but it would be a miracle if he would forgive her now.

* * *

At the table, Katerina sat between Christopher and an Italian gentleman in his late thirties, whose name she could not remember.

"Excellent performance," he told her, his dark eyes shining.

"Thank you," she replied. After the stressful and uncomfortable performance, a simple conversation could no longer make her blush. "I'm sorry, sir, but what was your name?"

"Me? I'm Carlo Bianchi," he replied.

"A relative?" She raised her eyebrows. "*I've met so many tonight, I can't remember who is who.*"

"Your uncle. Your mother was my twin sister."

"Oh." Her face burned. "Sorry."

He smiled at her. "Not to worry, my dear."

She smiled, glad he wasn't angry.

"You remind me of her. She loved music, though she didn't have your... skill." Carlo's eyes turned sad. "I've missed her terribly. We were very close. Did she ever... mention me?"

Katerina looked down at her plate. "Sorry. Our life was not one to encourage idle conversation."

"I suppose not." He growled. "I hated that she married him. Did he ever... soften?"

"No," Katerina replied without prevarication.

Carlo closed his eyes. "Did he kill her?"

"More or less," she admitted sadly.

Carlo cursed softly. "My fault."

"How?"

Sorrow crumpled his expression, making him look older than his years. "He took her away because of me. I saw her after the wedding, so thin, so distressed, and covered in bruises. We were only sixteen, you know. I went to him and showed him what it felt like to be beaten. He left the next day."

Katerina shook her head. "It's a tragedy. I'm so sorry."

"Was she a good mother?" he asked.

Katerina nodded. "The best. I miss her so terribly, but she's at peace now, Uncle Carlo. She's finally free of him."

His gaze turned even more intense. "And you, Katerina? Are you also free of him?"

"I am, thanks to my husband." She glanced at Christopher and smiled.

"He seems like a good man," Carlo commented.

"Yes," she replied, "I owe him my life."

"Don't think that way, cara," her uncle urged. "You owe him your heart."

"He has it," she replied simply.

"Buono. You have his too."

She smiled. *It's a pleasing sentiment even though there's no way it can be true.*

* * *

After dinner, the guests returned to the parlor. Alessandro remained, looking out the window onto his estate, his expression sad. Aimée was nowhere to be seen. Several of the guests approached the master and talked to him privately. At last, he shook them all off and sought out his granddaughter. "Cara, why did you agree to that competition?" he demanded.

"What do you mean, Nonno?" Katerina replied, not wanting to cause trouble.

"You didn't want it. I could tell." His mouth twisted into a wry expression.

"No," she agreed.

"Then why?"

She considered, and then admitted the truth with a sigh. "It was the pianoforte. I wanted to play it. She refused to let me. She said the winner of the competition could have the rights to the music room. I didn't want it all to myself, I just wanted to use it sometimes."

"Dio mio!" Alessandro threw his hands into the air. "You mean all this was over the piano?"

"Sì."

He hugged her gently. "You should have talked to me. It's my piano. Of course, you can use it."

She gave him a pleading look. "I wasn't sure. I can see she has some influence over you."

"So do you," he reminded her.

Katerina smiled.

"She's been tormenting you, hasn't she?"

Katerina bowed her head in lieu of an answer.

"Well don't worry. She won't be here anymore. After her scandalous behavior tonight, I've sent her away."

"Oh, don't do that," Katerina pleaded.

"Why not?" his expression turned thunderstruck.

She touched his sleeve. "I know you care for her. Don't make her leave on my account."

"I'm not. She made me look like a fool," he growled.

"Oh." *That she did, and what a mess. I almost feel sorry for her.* "Well, maybe it was a mistake. You know, things got a little out of hand. I would hate to see you unhappy."

"She tried to steal your husband," he reminded her.

"She couldn't. I don't think he even noticed her. Even if he had, he's a man who honors his vows."

"Doesn't it matter that she tried?"

"I don't know if she was really trying," Katerina objected, biting her lip. "More likely, she was only attempting to upset me."

"What a bully." Alessandro gestured with the fingers of his upraised hand. "I'm sorry you ever had to meet her."

"It's true," Katerina admitted at last, "but still… she is important to you. I only wish we could have been friendly."

He shook his head. "Well, that's between Aimée and me. As for you, you may use my instruments any time you like," he vowed, hand on his heart.

"Thank you, Nonno."

He hugged her again. She slid her arms around his neck. *I love my grandfather. I'm so glad Christopher suggested coming here.*

He released her and turned, addressing the room again. "I've heard from many of you, and I believe we are all in agreement. Choosing between two such superior musicians would be impossible. One has more training and experience, the other more sweetness and passion. Therefore, I declare the competition to be a draw. No one loses, and we all win because we all had the privilege of hearing such a fine concert."

Heads nodded in approval, and a round of applause set Katerina's cheeks glowing. Then, her uncle claimed her arm and took her to meet his wife and their children.

* * *

Alessandro approached Christopher, who was conversing sedately with a middle-aged British couple.

"Signor, signora," he addressed the couple, "may I borrow my grandson-in-law for a moment?"

The couple acquiesced and Alessandro escorted Christopher to a quiet corner.

"Is everything all right?" the young man asked.

"Yes. I just wanted to thank you."

"For what?"

"For Katerina," Alessandro explained. "For rescuing her, keeping her safe. I often wished to do the same. I feared for her, especially after her mother's passing."

"You had cause," Christopher said grimly.

"It must be very gratifying that what began as a good deed turned into such a deep love," Alessandro commented.

"It is," he replied, unembarrassed to lay his heart clearly on his sleeve. "Perhaps someday she will heal enough to love me back. I look forward to that day."

"No. She already does," the older man insisted.

"What?" Christopher gaped. "Why do you say so?"

"Because of her last song. Could you understand any of it?"

"No, what did it say?"

"Ask her. I could tell she meant every word." Alessandro winked.

Christopher nodded. "Yes, she seemed very sincere."

"Definitely. You're a lucky man, Christopher Bennett."

"I know it. Thank you." *And now I need to find out what my wife was singing to me.*

* * *

Despite her concerns, Katerina actually enjoyed the party once she found her husband and took his arm. Being close to Christopher made anything seem possible, even conversing comfortably with strangers in a foreign country. She stood as near to him as she was able, until she could feel the heat from his body, and she smiled sweetly at the people around her. *I am not a mouse, not a rabbit. I stood up to a bully, challenged her, and won. Not the contest. I never cared about winning that. I won the battle of wills. I'm braver than ever before. Aimée will never bother my husband again, and if she does, I will give her a piece of my mind she'll not soon forget.*

The hours went by, neither flying nor dragging, just passing until at last the appointed ending time arrived. The guests who lived nearby returned home, and those from farther away retired to guest rooms. Finally, Katerina pleaded exhaustion, kissed her grandfather goodnight, and led her husband to their room.

* * *

Alessandro waited for the last lingering attendees to depart before finally heading off to bed. Ending his liaison with Aimée had left him unhappy. *Her behavior was unconscionable, and I'm still angry, but damn it, I love the wench.*

He undressed and slid between the sheets, knowing full well sleep would be difficult. He drew an unsteady breath. The bed felt cold and empty without his warm, vital woman filling it.

The mattress sagged. Familiar arms slipped around him.

"Alessandro, my love," the sweetly accented voice washed over him, "I'm so sorry. So very sorry. It was so bad of me. Please, please forgive me. Please don't throw me out. I never meant to hurt or embarrass you."

"Aimée," he shook her off, "why was claiming my piano so important to you that you put my granddaughter through all of that?"

"Why do you think?" she demanded, fiery as always. "You have so little for me. The music room is one place where I have always been able to please you, where you've always been proud of me. Without that, I'm just the *putain* you're sleeping with. If she replaces me, what am I but a whore?"

"You're an artist, not a whore," he protested.

"I know. I also know what you and everyone else thinks of me. Do you honestly believe I lay with you because I have no morals? Do you know how many other men I've had in my bed?" she demanded.

He rolled to face her, taking in her expression. "How many?"

"Only one. Only my husband."

He raised his eyebrows. "So there really was a Monsieur St. Jean?"

She nodded, her hand lifting as though to touch his face, but she hesitated and let her fingers slip back to the bed. "There really was. We married young, and he died young, but he left me a little money, and I used it to study music."

"I never knew," Alessandro said.

"You never asked," she retorted.

"But if that's true, then why me?" he asked. "I'm old enough to be your father. Why are you here, Aimée?"

"I don't exactly know," she replied, speaking slowly while she considered. "When we started, you were so... comforting, so safe. Life is hard and frightening, and in order to survive alone, a woman has to be strong. With you, I could be soft again, be a woman. I wanted you, and then, after we came together, and you still cared for and respected me, I never wanted to leave. I'm afraid, Alessandro."

"Of what?" he asked.

"Of what comes next. If we separate, my heart will be broken, but if we don't... I've already buried one husband..."

"And I've already buried one wife. No matter what, life is hard, Aimée. Tell me what you want."

"What I can't have. You. All to myself, always. I would..." She broke off, her plump cheeks pink, her blue eyes averted.

"You would what?" Alessandro put one finger under her chin and lifted her face, so she could look at him.

Whatever she saw in his eyes must have strengthened her resolve. "I would marry you if you would have me. I wish we could. It would be so much better."

"Better for whom? As you've said, there's a real impediment to us being together."

She nodded slowly. "There is, but I think I would still choose you, even knowing what's coming. I would rather have you while I can." An odd note in her voice gave him pause.

"What are you not telling me, cara?" he asked, seeking answers in a face whose expression he'd never seen before.

"You've given me more than a piano, Alessandro." She looked at him intently, urging him to understand.

Understanding warred with disbelief. "Dio mio, are you joking?"

"No."

"But..." he sputtered. "Is this some kind of ploy to force me to forgive you?"

"Not at all. Look at me and see for yourself."

He pulled back the covers and regarded her nude body. Her curves looked rounder than ever, her breasts massively swollen, her belly full.

"How long?" *And why didn't you notice, man?*

"Nearly five months, I think," she replied.

"Why didn't you say anything?" he demanded.

"I was waiting for the right moment. I thought I had time."

"Then why tell me now?"

"Because I made such a terrible mistake. I don't want to lose you. Despite my bad behavior, I want you, only you. I love you, Alessandro. Can't you please forgive me?"

"Perhaps, but I'm not going to make it easy on you. First, you're going to have to do something for me."

"Anything," she vowed.

"Apologize to Katerina and her husband. You made their visit uncomfortable." He scowled at her. *Don't get cocky, wench. You have a ways to go.*

Her expression turned contrite. "Yes. I'll do it first thing."

"And no more flirting," he roared. "*That hurt me more than you can imagine.* We look odd enough together. If you appear dissatisfied, I look like an old fool."

"You're right. I didn't think." Her eyes skated away from his, and the shame on her face told him what he needed to know.

"You're a very bad girl, Aimée," he said, unable to remain angry with her.

"Are you going to punish me?" she asked, wide-eyed.

"Yes, I think so."

"How?" The wench looked worried.

Good. "Let's see how loudly I can make you scream."

Very loudly, it turned out. She had to put the pillow over her face to muffle the noise of her orgasm.

Chapter 17

IMÉE and Alessandro weren't the only couple making love that night. In the guest bedroom, Christopher tenderly undressed his wife in preparation for a thorough bedding.

She participated willingly, eagerly opening his buttons. Despite contending with complicated party clothing and its multiple layers, they stripped each other nude in no time. Katerina stepped close to Christopher, pulling his head down for an endless kiss. His arms encircled her lower back, pressing their bodies together.

"Love, what did the last song say?" he mumbled against her lips.

She pulled back a fraction. "The Italian one?"

"Yes."

She blushed, not wanting to answer.

"Tell me, Kat," he urged. "You know you can trust me. You do know that, don't you?"

She met his eyes with a tender look. "I've never wanted to trust anyone before."

"And now?"

She burrowed closer to him. "This is the safest place on earth, here in your arms. Yes, Christopher. I trust you."

He pulled the pins from her hair. "I'm so glad. Please, love, tell me what the song said."

She glanced away and took a deep, shuddering breath. Then she raised her eyes to his face. "It speaks of one who is so wonderful, so perfect, that he is worth loving even though there is no hope of reciprocation. With him, even the pain of unrequited adoration is a kind of glory."

"Were you... singing to me? It looked as though you were."

"Yes." Her cheeks grew even pinker, but her voice remained sincere and steady.

He nodded and lowered his mouth to hers again, stroking his fingers over the uneven flesh along her spine. She squirmed, trying to pull away, but he held her fast. "Do you really think, foolish girl, that your love is unrequited? It's not. I love you, Katerina. I love your beautiful face, your tender heart and your lovely body. I even love your scars."

She didn't reply at all as the long moments passed. A tear trailed down her cheek, and then another. Her breathing grew ragged.

He placed his hands on her arms and turned her, sweeping her long dark hair over her shoulder and giving himself an unobstructed view of the ruined flesh. Now that all the injuries had healed, he was able to see the jigsaw puzzle effect of overlapping whip marks cut indelibly into her skin from her shoulder blades to her knees. "My God, Kat. How did you survive?"

"I don't know," she choked. "I'm very glad I did."

"So am I. Poor darling."

The quality of her voice changed, sharpening. "Don't pity me, Christopher. Please don't."

He shook his head. "No. I admire you. You're so strong, so brave."

"You make me brave," she replied.

"You chose courage, so you could come away with me and be my wife," he told her, tracing one scar across her back from side to side. "I'm honored."

"You chose me to rescue out of the sea of battered women," she replied. "I'm the one who's blessed."

"Did you know the French word for wounded is blessée?" he asked, his voice too nonchalant.

"Yes. I've always found that ironic."

"It fits." His tone wavered.

"Yes, I suppose it does," she conceded, wondering what he was up to.

"Come here, love." He led her over to the bedside table and urged her forward, so her hands rested on the wood.

She gasped and went utterly still.

Christopher had no way of knowing how deeply ingrained this posture was for her, how many times she had been bent over a solid surface in preparation for a brutal beating. Nearly every mark on her body had been received in such a position. The only way to keep the onslaught from turning even more violent was to submit in silence to each blow. The instant her hands touched the table, Italy faded, Christopher faded, and Katerina was back in her father's home, trembling as she waited for the whip to fall.

Something hot and wet touched one deep, thick line, tracing it gently. The delicate touch to her flesh, arousing despite the muting effect of the scars, confused her. *What is this?*

Hands slid up her torso and cupped her breasts while kisses rained onto her back, touching one scar after the other. Her breasts tingled with familiar pleasure, and her breath caught, held, before releasing in a gasp. He plucked the tender peaks as his lips slid lower down her back, dropping kiss after kiss on her ruined flesh. Her body relaxed and moistened, but her mind remained confused, trapped between the past and the present; the fear of pain and the pleasure of the caresses.

Hands worked her nipples as the lips kissed down to her bottom and knelt behind her. Gently hands widened her stance. A tongue teased her succulent folds.

She sucked air through her teeth in an audible hiss. The touch of lips and tongue on her intimate places tightened down her belly. Pleasurable tension coiled in her deepest recesses, awaiting the touch that would release it.

He slid his hands to her sides. One he braced on her hip. The other snaked around her bottom and between her legs. Long blunt fingers slid deep into her, tickling the secret places only he knew how to touch, and she exploded. The beauty of the orgasm broke through her terror and awakened her on a new level. At last, Katerina came fully alive, on fire with pleasure that wrung ragged cries from her throat.

Christopher rose behind her, covering her body with his so he could surge in deep.

The fear is gone, she realized. *He's behind me, and I'm not afraid.* She bent forward, letting him thrust and pull back as she enjoyed being taken.

"Say it, Katerina," he growled as he filled her.

"Oh, Christopher," she moaned.

"Tell me," he urged.

"I love you. Oh God, I love you, I love you. Oh yes." Her head fell forward as her pleasure peaked again. He came with her in a rush, groaning as he shoved in deep and released.

He slid free and scooped her into his arms, carrying her to the bed and joining her so he could pull her close. He kissed her lips gently. "Did you mean it, Kat?" he asked, suddenly sounding vulnerable.

"Yes. Did you?" She twined her arms around his neck.

"Of course." His lips touched her forehead.

"Good. Then all is as it should be."

"It is." He traced her lower lip with the tip of his thumb before leaning close and kissing her mouth again. "Good night, sweet girl."

"Good night, my darling."

* * *

In the morning, Christopher woke early. His lovely wife lay sound asleep on her side in his arms, her back to him. He studied the ravaging scars in the light of dawn. *She's my phoenix, my firebird, forged in hell and yet capable of carrying me to heaven.* Suddenly shy of his intense feelings, he slipped from the bed and dressed. Scrawling her a brief, affectionate note, he headed out for a walk.

A hint of warmth in the winter air carried a sensation of coming spring. He walked through the olive grove and further out in the morning mist, over the tree-studded hill that separated the Bianchi family property from the unclaimed land beyond.

The sun broke the horizon, coloring the landscape gold and scarlet and sparkling on the waters of the Arno. Christopher felt a dawning hope. Oh, he had hoped before, hoped against hope, but now he dared to believe. *Maybe she really will be all right. Not just survive but thrive, be happy, live the kind of life she always dreamed of. She's so strong.* He loved her with a fierce passion, and she loved him. She had said it, and sung it, and meant it. He believed her.

A gust of wind cut through Christopher's coat and made him shiver.

"Blast." The breeze carried with it a nearby voice, as well as a crumpled paper covered in messy handwriting and scratched-out errors. Christopher picked it up. Nearby, another sheet tumbled past, and then another. He began collecting them, following the trail of papers back to the source. On the other end, he found a gentleman, a bit older than himself, with a full and bushy chestnut beard, but no mustache at all. The man was frantically scooping up scattered sheets as he went. Silently Christopher bent to help, and eventually returned a large pile to the stranger.

"Is that all of them?" the bearded man asked in perfect, unaccented English.

"I believe so, sir," Christopher replied.

"Excellent. Thank you for your help." He gathered the papers into a folio and set it down, holding it shut against the wind with a rock. Then he extended his hand.

"You're welcome." They shook. "I'm Christopher Bennett, by the way."

"Welcome to Florence. Are you relocating?" the stranger asked.

"No, I'm here on my honeymoon. My wife's family owns the estate nearby," Christopher explained.

"The Bianchis?" At Christopher's nod, the man commented, "They're good folk."

"They are," he agreed. "And your name, sir?"

The man grinned, seeming to realize he'd forgotten his manners. "Oh, my name is Robert Browning."

Christopher's jaw dropped. "The *poet* Robert Browning?"

"You've heard of me?" The man's eyes widened in shock.

"Yes," Christopher replied fervently. "I've read your poems. My goodness, I had no idea you lived here."

"Well," Browning said in a gruff voice, "my wife's father isn't keen on me. We thought it best to live far away."

Christopher grinned. "I can relate to that. It's an honor to meet you."

"Thank you. Most people know my wife better."

How awkward it must be, to be less well known in your own field than your wife. "I'm sure, but my friends and I, we discovered your poems. You really made us think."

"Good. That was the goal. It's a shame no one else cares. I'm tempted to give it up. I probably would except… the muse is a terrible mistress."

"I'm glad to hear you're persevering," Christopher said. "It's difficult to fight for an unpopular cause, especially in the absence of recognition, but it really is worth it. You know, my father owns a cotton mill."

Browning crooked one eyebrow.

"It's a progressive mill. We would get more profits if we exploited our workers, but we won't. We've always tried to be aware of our workers' needs. From time to time we hear we've made a difference for someone. It always helps."

Browning looked lost. "Why are you telling me this, Mr. Bennett?"

"Because if something my father and I have done has made a difference, I like to know," Christopher explained. "Reminds me of the reasons we do what we do. So, I wanted you to know that… you made a difference."

"What do you mean?"

"Well, I was aware of violence against women before I read 'Porphyria's Lover,' but I never really thought much about it. Perhaps it was Providence, but the day after I read it, I met a young woman in a dangerous situation. I couldn't bear the thought of her ending up like poor Porphyria, so I married her. I would never have given her a second thought, and certainly not done what I did, except the murder in that poem was so fresh on my mind. You made me aware. That poem saved her life."

Browning smiled. "Ah, well, thank you for telling me. Your marriage?"

Christopher beamed. "It's very good. We're happy."

Browning nodded. "I'm glad for you then and glad to know I helped. She's like a grain of sand though."

"I know. *It's sadly true. There are too many innocent victims,* but until the laws are changed, we can only do what we can do. I can't save them all, but I saved this one. That matters. Your role in it matters. Thank you, Mr. Browning, for having the courage to write what you did."

The man's mouth turned down. "Everyone hates it."

"Guilt," Christopher suggested.

"Perhaps."

"And perhaps the time is still not right for the larger society to embrace it, but I know your poetry will continue to make a difference. I intend to keep sharing it and to keep speaking out. *Please, don't give up. Your work is so important.*"

"I won't. It's hard as hell to swim upstream, but I will persevere. I must."

Christopher grinned. "Good luck to you then."

"Thank you, Mr. Bennett."

"Thank *you*, Mr. Browning."

The men shook hands and then Christopher hurried home. His bride was waiting for him, and suddenly he wanted to see her.

* * *

Inside the Bianchi manor, Katerina sat in the breakfast room, sipping a cup of coffee and wincing at its strength. She became aware of a movement behind her, but for once, did not jump in nervous anxiety. She simply turned to see. *How refreshing. Another sign of the progress I've made.* Her pleasure faded to a scowl at the sight of Aimée St. Jean. "What do *you* want?" she asked the other woman coldly.

Before Aimée could even open her mouth, Katerina continued. "You may have the damned piano' you may have Grandfather, but you will stay away from my husband, is that clear? He's mine, and he doesn't want you anyway. Leave him alone."

"Yes, of course, I will. You're right. I never wanted him either. As you said, he's too young for me." Her chastened tone made Katerina even more suspicious.

"Then what were you doing?" Katerina demanded, eyes narrowed. She spat the words like little flames from a bonfire.

"Trying to unnerve you," Aimée replied, looking appropriately stung.

"Why?"

"Petty jealousy. I was jealous of your talent and of your grandfather's attention. It was mean-spirited, and I apologize." Aimée sounded disarmingly sincere.

"Why?" Katerina demanded again, giving no quarter.

"Because I'm woman enough to admit when I'm wrong," Aimée replied. "I should never have treated you this way."

"You needn't be jealous of my talent," Katerina commented, giving the tiniest inch of leeway. "Yours is greater."

"No. My experience is greater, but I think you have more natural musical ability."

Katerina rolled her eyes. "Is it still a competition, Madame?"

Aimée ventured a timid smile. "No. It's not."

Katerina continued, gesturing with one hand. "I mean, you're a talented artist. So am I. Why can we not commiserate, since we share so many things in common?"

"I don't know. I've been feeling very… off lately, you see…" she leaned over and whispered in her ear.

Katerina's mouth fell open.

"It's no excuse," Aimée continued, "but I was so worried he was losing interest in me because of you."

Katerina shook her head. "There's no comparison. You're the woman he loves. I'm his granddaughter. There's no competition there either."

"You're right," Aimée conceded, "but I'm not thinking clearly these days."

Katerina pursed her lips. "I can see that. Well, I suppose you two had better get married. How odd to think your child will have a niece from the first moment of life, a niece twenty years his senior."

"That is amusing," Aimée chuckled. "So, Mrs. Bennett, can we start over, please? I mean you're going to be my step-granddaughter."

"Am I?" Katerina raised one eyebrow.

"Oh yes," Aimée replied, her head bobbing so her golden hair bounced. "We worked it out last night."

"Very good. When?"

"Soon," the woman explained. "Probably before you leave. Will you come?"

Katerina pressed her advantage. "On one condition."

"What's that?" Aimée asked, a hint of suspicion in her face.

"Let me play at the wedding," Katerina replied.

The two women regarded each other, each taking the measure of the other's will.

Aimée tilted her chin at last in concession. "Of course. Will you also sing?"

Katerina smiled, knowing she'd won. "If you like."

"Do you know the Schubert 'Ave Maria?' "

"I do."

"Please?"

"Of course."

The women grinned at each other, and moments later, Christopher arrived.

Unconcerned with Aimée's presence, he scooped his wife into his arms for a long and coffee-flavored kiss.

"I love you," he told her softly.

"How sweet you are, Christopher. I love you too." She gazed up at her husband, letting her adoration show in her eyes.

"Good. It's beautiful outside. Would you like to go for a walk?"

"That would be most pleasant," she concurred.

"Let's go then. Madame St. Jean." He bowed, and they left her.

Chapter 18

HE rest of the visit became exceedingly enjoyable, but vacations don't last forever, and in the middle of March, Alessandro drove them back to Livorno, foregoing the train in favor of a few more hours spent together.

Too soon, the travelers arrived at the docks. Alessandro hugged and kissed Katerina and then Christopher before the newlyweds boarded the ship for their return to England.

The return trip seemed to be a repeat of their previous voyage, with Katerina being terribly seasick. If anything, it was worse this time. Her poor stomach could hardly hold food, and every dip of every wave caused a corresponding dip in her belly. She suppressed this as best she could, not wanting to alarm her husband, but she still retched often and miserably.

As they sailed past Gibraltar into the Atlantic, the captain issued an invitation for all first-class passengers to join him for a special dinner and socializing hour. Glad of a distraction from Katerina's discomfort, the Bennetts readily agreed.

After dinner, Katerina clung to her husband's arm for balance as they mingled in the ship's dining room, beneath a white-painted ceiling divided into squares with strips of golden wood. They wandered among rows of chairs with cream upholstery around small round tables set with white cloths and chatted, accompanied by a string trio.

"How do you like the music, love?" he asked as they paused in their circuit of the room near a support pillar.

"It's quite good," she responded, smiling though her belly cramped and roiled.

"I agree," a man said, approaching with a glass of champagne in one hand. His accent sounded American. "Dr. Peter James." He stuck out his free hand, from which a compact black bag dangled, and Christopher grasped his hand firmly.

"Christopher Bennett, manufacturing. This is my wife."

"Pleased to meet you, Doctor," Katerina said. "Where in America are you from?"

"Good ear," the doctor said. "New York. State, not city. I've come to Europe in search of traditional medical techniques that could be adapted for modern use."

"Interesting," Christopher replied. "I have heard a rumor in my mill that one of our dyes has the ability to reduce pain. Would you like me to show you?"

"Surely," the doctor said.

The ship dipped and Katerina tilted, bumping her shoulder into the pillar. Christopher tightened his hold.

When the motion eased, Katerina suddenly became aware that she felt... strange. Not nauseous, but dizzy. She tried to ignore it, to focus her attention on the conversation, but it grew worse, more insistent, and black spots began floating in her field of vision.

"Christopher," her numb lips could scarcely form his name.

His face swam before her, distorted. "What is it, love? Are you ill again?"

"I..." and then unconsciousness rushed upon her and she sank into a faint.

* * *

Christopher caught her before she could fall and carried her to a seat, cradling her against his chest.

For the most part, the conversations continued unabated. It was not at all unusual for young ladies to pass out.

The doctor approached cautiously as Christopher patted his wife's face gently, trying to rouse her. "Is she all right?"

"I have no idea," Christopher replied. "She hasn't fainted in ages."

"How tightly is she laced?" the man asked, suddenly every inch a professional.

"She isn't. She has no laces at all. She doesn't need them." *Surely, it's no problem to admit such a private detail. The man's a doctor after all.*

"Well if she's not tight-laced, and you say she's not prone to fainting, I wonder what's going on. Is she ill?" the doctor asked.

"She's seasick," Christopher replied.

"Perhaps she's become dehydrated," the doctor postulated. "That can happen when one is nauseated. Does she show signs of dehydration?"

"How should I know? You're the doctor."

"Would you like me to look her over?"

"Yes, I think so."

"Let's take her back to your cabin."

They left the party and headed to the Bennetts' room, where Christopher laid his wife gently on the bed. He gave the doctor a hard look. *I will under no circumstances be leaving the room.*

Dr. James didn't even ask. "Can you loosen her dress a bit for me?"

Christopher opened the gown, demonstrating that there was, in fact, no corset underneath. Only the short stays that supported her naturally slender figure without squashing it.

The doctor checked Katerina's pulse and breathing. "I don't detect any immediate threat," he said, pulling some smelling salts from his bag. Waving it under her nose, it roused her with the potent aroma.

"Ugh," she moaned, waving the pungent mixture away. "What's happening?"

"You fainted, love," Christopher informed her.

"I did?"

"Yes."

"Now I remember. I became dizzy. It was so unpleasant. Oh, Doctor James, why are you here?" She looked from one man to the other, blinking.

"He was concerned about you," Christopher replied. "He offered to help us understand why you became faint, in case your seasickness has made you dehydrated."

The doctor lifted Katerina's face and looked into her eyes. Then, he pulled down her lower lip. "She doesn't have the look. I don't suspect dehydration. You've just come from dinner. I saw you eating, so it wasn't hunger that caused your faint. You've been seasick?"

"Yes," she admitted, her voice a faint groan.

"Vomiting frequently?"

"Yes. Is that why?"

"I doubt it. Vomiting can be a mechanism for malnourishment or lack of fluids, which can cause fainting, but in itself is unlikely to do so. Hmmm. May I ask you a very personal question?"

"Yes, I suppose so," Katerina replied.

"How long since your last menstruation?"

She blushed furiously and then began to think…and think…and think. Her lips parted in surprise. "New Year's."

The doctor raised his eyebrows.

"What?" Christopher demanded, not following the conversation.

Dr. James ignored him. "When did you marry?"

"Mid-January."

"Well that answers the question then, doesn't it?"

"Oh, it can't be!" Katerina cried. "I'm not ready."

"What's happening?" Christopher asked, more insistently. The doctor's rapid, expressionless questions and his wife's increasingly panicky answers made him nervous.

"Your wife is with child, Mr. Bennett," the doctor said mildly.

Christopher looked at Katerina, startled. "Is that true?"

"It must be," she replied, and the corners of her eyes tightened. "Oh, Lord, almost three months, really?"

"Yes, really." The doctor replied.

"But... how?" Christopher asked.

"Mr. Bennett," the doctor said dryly, "I assume you understand how the process works?"

Christopher's cheeks warmed. "Of course."

"Well then you know what happened," Dr. James replied, talking as though to a simpleton. "You married this lady, you took her to bed, and now she's pregnant. That's how this works. That's the purpose behind marriage."

"Oh, Lord."

Seeming to sense their distress, the doctor dropped his lecturing tone and attempted to reassure them. "It's no cause for concern. Married ladies are supposed to become with child."

"I know," Christopher replied, "but it seems too soon."

"As long as the conception took place *after* the wedding, there's no such thing as too soon," Dr. James pointed out.

"So perhaps my wife's seasickness..."

"Was exacerbated by the nausea of early pregnancy."

"But I've not felt sick any other times. Only on the ship coming to Italy, and now, heading home," Katerina interjected, still seeming not to believe it.

"Well, if you only feel sick when at sea, your early pregnancy is going better than some. Of course, as far along as you are, you are likely almost done with the unpleasant part anyway," Dr. James informed her. "Around the fourth month, most women begin to feel better. Now that I'm convinced you're healthy, I'll leave you in privacy. Be sure you keep eating and drinking normally. And congratulations."

"Thank you, Dr. James," Christopher said woodenly as the doctor let himself out of their cabin.

Katerina looked at her husband in stunned horror. He looked back, his expression mirroring hers. They leaned forward and hugged each other in fierce silence. There was nothing to say, so they just held on tight while the whole world shifted and changed around them.

Chapter 19

HE voyage progressed more slowly this time, with less cooperative winds, and the ship did not sail into Southampton until the end of the first week of April.

After so many days traveling, walking into the house felt like a dream come true.

Home, Katerina thought, admiring how it suddenly looked and felt perfect. In their absence, the furniture they'd ordered had arrived, and their employees had placed it. The music room now contained two comfortable armchairs and a table. Paintings hung from the walls, warming the space. Katerina smiled and sank onto the piano bench, warming up her rusty fingers on an instrument belonging to her alone.

Welcome home, the instrument's smiling curve seemed to say, *I'm here for you.*

She closed her eyes and played the Moonlight Sonata without a second thought. The notes seemed to express her own confused feelings, which ranged from mournful to frantic.

* * *

Christopher approached carefully, making sure to stay in her line of sight, and embraced her, urging her away from the piano and up the stairs. "Let's rest, love, in our own home. In our own bed."

She nodded, allowing him to lead her up the stairs. Between their bedroom and the furnished guestroom down the hall, a third remained empty.

Katerina looked at the blank walls and bare floors for a long, silent moment.

Christopher slid his arm around her waist. He didn't say it would be an ideal nursery. He didn't have to; it was obvious. He could sense her discomfort, and it didn't surprise him. *This is a heavy burden for a woman still so unsure of herself.*

* * *

In the morning, Christopher headed off to work, late as usual.

Katerina, after a long bath and a hearty breakfast, scrawled a brief note to her mother-in-law, letting her know they were home and sent it by messenger. Julia arrived for a visit two hours later.

"Oh, how lovely this house is," she exclaimed, claiming a spot on the sofa while Katerina rang for tea.

"Thank you," Katerina replied, her tone subdued.

"And how was Italy?" As usual, Julia bubbled with enthusiasm. She seemed not to notice Katerina's lack of excitement.

Rather than spoil the visit with her gloomy mood, Katerina pasted on a false smile and gushed, "Wonderful. We met my grandfather. He's been widowed for several years, but he recently remarried a lovely singer from France."

Julia smiled. "I'm glad to hear it. It's not good to be alone."

"No. I suppose not. Um, Mother?"

Her tone must not have been as neutral as she'd intended because Julia suddenly focused on her. "Yes, love?"

Katerina swallowed. "I wanted to ask a favor of you."

Her mother-in-law leaned forward with an encouraging nod. "What do you need?"

"Well," Katerina said slowly. "I remember you were talking about having a party for us, for our wedding..."

"Yes. I did want to do that."

"Well," she chewed her lip and thought another moment, "my birthday is coming up at the end of April, and I was wondering if you would..."

Julia seemed to understand her reluctance and didn't force her to complete the question. "Yes. Of course. Just tell me how you want it to be: how big, whom we should invite. I don't want to overwhelm you."

"Thank you," Katerina said, relaxing. "I appreciate it."

"You seem... better," Julia commented.

"Oh, I am. So much better." She smiled.

"And also troubled."

Drat, she noticed. "Well, yes, that also."

"Care to talk about it?" Julia asked, her eyes kind.

"If you'd like," Katerina replied. *But how on earth will I be able to express myself this time?*

"Of course I will listen to anything you care to share, my dear. First, tell me what's good."

That part, at least, was easy. "I love Christopher. He loves me too. We figured it out in Italy."

"Excellent!" Julia exclaimed, her wide smile showing slightly gapped front teeth. "And the troubling part?"

A sharp pain drew Katerina's attention to the fact that she had nibbled her fingernail to the quick. "I'm... expecting."

"Expecting?" Julia gave her a quizzical glance.

"Yes. Expecting a baby."

"Oh dear. That happened fast, didn't it?"

She does understand. Thank the Lord. "It did. I'm... not ready. I don't know how I'm going to handle this."

Julia patted her hand. "Well, fortunately, babies are born with simple needs. It allows mothers a chance to grow into caring for them. When is the baby due?"

"Late September or early October, according to a doctor we met on the boat."

Julia considered for a moment. "So, this must have happened right away?"

"It would seem so." Her cheeks burned. The evidence of her hungry sexuality being baldly presented this way embarrassed her.

Julia gave her an indulgent smile but thankfully remained focused on the topic at hand. "Let me reassure you that every new mother is nervous at first. It's overwhelming. You're hardly the first to be upset by it."

"But this is different," Katerina said, her voice nearly a whine.

"How so?" Julia asked.

Her eyes stung. "You know what I come from. What if I pass it on? What if I hurt my baby?"

Julia shook her head slowly from side to side. "You won't."

"How can you be sure?"

"Do you want to?"

Katerina frowned. "Of course not."

Julia patted her again. "Then you won't. Don't worry, Katerina. Everyone will help you. You won't be left to deal with this alone."

"I don't want to deal with it at all. I don't want to be pregnant. I don't want a baby." She hadn't meant to say it aloud. She glanced at Julia, expecting to see anger or disapproval in her mother-in-law's expression.

She saw none of those things.

"That's quite normal, my dear," Julia said softly in a neutral sounding voice. "Don't be angry with yourself for feeling this way. I was no different the first time, and like you, I conceived very quickly after the wedding. It passes. Even if you're never fully comfortable with motherhood, it's not impossible to do the best you can for the child you have, and then not have any more."

"Is that what you did?" she blurted without thinking, and then she cringed. *What a terrible thing to ask.*

Julia took no offense. Her face and tone remained kind. "No. Some of my friends did. After a time, towards the middle of the pregnancy, my feelings changed. I grew glad, but neither way is wrong. You feel what you feel. It's the actions that count."

Katerina steadied herself with a deep breath. "That's good to know."

"How's Christopher?" Julia asked, shifting the topic.

"Excited and happy. I haven't been able to tell him how upsetting this is."

"Perhaps it's best if you don't," her mother-in-law suggested. "He won't know what to do about it, and it's possible your feelings will change down the road, once you adjust a little."

"I hope so," Katerina admitted. "Right now, I'm just terrified."

"It's not a bad thing, dear. It means you are thinking about your responsibilities. A child could do much worse than having a thoughtful mother."

"As a comfort, I'm afraid it falls a little short."

"I'm sure." Julia hugged her. The warm, motherly arms soothed her more than any words. "Try not to panic, Katerina. You're not alone. You have many people who love you and want you to be a successful mother."

"Thank you," she choked, undone by the outpouring of support. *I love my husband, but his family makes the whole thing perfect.*

"Do you know what you need, dear?" Julia asked, pulling back to look into her face.

"What?"

"You need to talk to Mrs. Turner about this. She was trained as a midwife before her first marriage, and she delivered all of my children. She's also someone who knows what it is to suffer from difficult relationships. Will you talk to her?"

Oh good, more help. "Yes, I would like that. I think it would be very reassuring."

"Well then let's plan on it. She has young children, so most likely you will need to go to her."

"That's not a problem," Katerina assured her.

"Good. Let's make a plan to visit her this week."

"Yes, let's do it."

* * *

A few days later, Katerina found herself seated in a comfortable parlor on a chocolate-colored sofa with a cup of tea and a sugar biscuit, a little girl playing near her feet. It amazed her that even though the two women were the same age, Julia's sons were both adults; Christopher twenty-four years old, his younger brother Devin still at university, but close to completing his course of legal studies. Elizabeth Turner was also the mother of an adult child; however, her second marriage had begun when she was over thirty, and in addition to Colin, she had three much younger children.

She was such a relaxed and comfortable matron that Katerina instantly felt better in her company. She always had, ever since the colonel's wife and Katerina's own mother-in-law had taken the shy musician under their collective wings over a year before.

"Now that you're settled with tea and sweets, Julia said you wanted to talk to me. What is it, dear?" Mrs. Turner asked.

Katerina swallowed a mouthful of biscuit, which suddenly felt dry in her throat. "Well, I'm... *enceinte*. I didn't expect this so soon and I'm terribly nervous about it."

"That's a perfectly normal reaction," Mrs. Turner replied.

"Do you know about my... history?" Katerina asked, for once glad the secret wasn't such a secret. She had no desire to explain.

"I do. Is that part of why you feel nervous?" the midwife asked.

"Yes. I would hate to perpetuate the legacy of violence."

Mrs. Turner met her eyes and nodded. "It's a legitimate concern. One key to successful parenting is to know yourself. You've received abuse, and you have those seeds inside you. Honestly, dear, everyone does. Anyone can snap at a child in frustration. That's why you must be honest with yourself about getting help when you need it. Do not allow yourself to become excessively aggravated."

"My father required no frustration to become violent," Katerina said darkly.

"I'm sorry, dear. Some people are just evil," Mrs. Turner replied.

"How do I know I'm not? I'm his daughter." Katerina swallowed. *I don't think I'm evil... but Father doesn't think he is either. What does evil feel like?*

"Have you harmed others?" Mrs. Turner asked, cutting off Katerina's spiraling thoughts.

She shook her head. "No. I've had no opportunity, but I didn't hesitate to take advantage of Christopher's offer, even though I knew I wouldn't be good for him."

"Katerina, stop," Julia said gently. "You were in desperate need of help, and I disagree with the idea you've been bad to him. Don't you love him?"

"Yes," Katerina replied firmly. *But that doesn't mean I'm good for him.*

"And he loves you. He's not stupid. He wouldn't love you if you were a violent, evil monster."

Put that way, Julia's point made perfect sense. Katerina smiled a little. "Perhaps not."

Mrs. Turner took over the conversation again. "Rest assured, despite your difficult circumstances, you are capable of being a good mother if you decide you want to be. How far along are you?"

"The doctor on the ship estimated about three months. I think closer to four now."

"How are you feeling?" she asked, turning professional.

"Pardon?" Katerina replied, not exactly sure what she was asking.

"Nausea? Fatigue? Soreness?"

Oh, that. "The nausea has finally passed, thank the Lord. Fatigue, definitely. It's hard to get up in the morning. I'm only sore in... two places."

"I know what you mean," Mrs. Turner said, taking in Katerina's pink cheeks. "That's normal. Don't let it worry you. Oh, and here's one other thing that shouldn't concern you. You may be... close to your husband as often as you would like. There's no harm in it."

"Good to know." Katerina put her hands on her burning face.

The midwife chuckled. "Unfortunately, there's no modesty allowed for expectant mothers, Katerina. You'll cope. Do you understand the delivery process?"

"Um, no. I didn't even understand the conception process until Christopher explained it to me on our wedding night."

Mrs. Turner made a sound that resembled a laugh choked down.

She must have been imagining how that conversation went. I think I might have to hide under the sofa.

Even if Katerina's ignorance amused her, all the midwife said was, "Ah. Well, there are some things you should know about what's coming. Oh, and I'll be happy to deliver your baby if you would like. Doctors are becoming more popular, and if you prefer, I can recommend a good one, but most of the time they're not necessary."

"Oh, no. I would rather have you. It's better. *The last thing I want is a strange man looking at me at such an intimate moment.* Childbearing is women's business."

"Yes. That's how I felt too." Julia agreed.

"Well we're all in agreement then," Mrs. Turner said, smiling. "And I'll be happy to answer any questions you have in the meanwhile. Just come and see me or send a note anytime."

"I'll do that. Thank you."

* * *

The visit proved to be a turning point for Katerina. Although the idea of motherhood still terrified her, she was willing to trust her friends to help her through it. In the privacy of her mind, she admitted to herself she would rather not be doing this, but it was too late. Now she just had to do the best she could for her little one.

By the end of April, her lower belly had a visible curve. As she watched her body change, the reality of the little person inside her dawned more clearly every day. She also began to experience strange sensations in her innards. Curious what it might mean, she invited Mrs. Turner over for tea.

"Well, look at you, dear," the midwife said. "You're starting to show nicely."

"I'm supposed to have a birthday party next month," Katerina fretted. "I hope I'm not too big. I don't want to be uncouth, putting my belly on display."

"I think, with the right dress, you might just be able to get away with it," Mrs. Turner replied." I'm not sure why pregnancy is considered rude. A woman with child is a beautiful thing."

"*So Christopher keeps telling me* I'll have to talk to Mme Olivier about it. She's a genius. She'll be able to create something suitable, I'm sure."

"No doubt," Mrs. Turner agreed. "Now then, I can see you have something on your mind. What's worrying you?"

"I have a funny feeling in my belly," Katerina said. "I hope it doesn't mean anything is wrong."

"What does it feel like?" The midwife asked.

"It's hard to describe. It tickles."

"Does it feel like bubbles?"

"It did for a while. Now it's more like soft thumping, as though someone were tapping a finger. Oh, there it goes again."

"Where?" She placed her hand on Katerina's belly. Katerina guided her to the spot where a rhythmic little impact was repeating.

The midwife giggled. "Oh, how lovely."

"What is it?" Katerina asked.

"Your baby has hiccoughs!" she exclaimed.

Katerina gasped. "What? That's the baby?"

"Yes, dear. You're well into your fourth month. It's not surprising you can feel it."

Katerina placed her hand on the spot. "Goodness."

She was still in awe when Mrs. Turner left. Alone in her parlor, she experienced a growing awareness of a sensation she hadn't expected this time a month ago. It was a feeling of... excitement. *The little bump in my belly is my child, mine and Christopher's. Soon, only a few months from now, I will deliver this little person and it will be ours, our son, or our daughter. I will experience the joy of watching Christopher be a father. He'll be wonderful at it.*

As though her thoughts had summoned him, Christopher arrived, his dark hair rumpled by the spring breeze. "Hello, love," he said, kissing her forehead.

She wrapped her arms around him and pulled him close for a much longer kiss, mashing her lips to his and squeezing him tight.

"Well, well," he said, "it seems you're feeling all right."

"Yes, wonderful. Here, give me your hand." She pressed his fingers to her belly.

"What, Kat?"

"Hush. Just wait."

He waited. Long moments later, a little squirming sensation fluttered under his fingers. His eyes widened. "What was that?"

"Our baby."

"Oh, Lord."

"I know. Isn't it amazing?"

His smile grew huge and beautiful. "Yes. I can't believe it. Oh, love, you should see yourself. So happy. Are you happy, Katerina?"

"Yes. I think I finally am. There's a baby here." She pressed her hand over his. "A baby who is part of you and part of me."

"Yes. I love that." He lowered his lips to her forehead.

"Has there ever been such love?"

"Not that I know of," he replied. "Well, every couple probably feels this way, but it's special because it's us."

"Yes."

He cupped her cheek with the fingers of his free hand and lowered his mouth to hers, kissing her again. "I love you so much, Kat."

"And I love you, Christopher."

"And you're not so worried anymore?" he asked.

She looked away. "You knew about that? I didn't think you noticed."

He cupped her chin and drew her back into his gaze. "Do you think there's anything about you I don't notice?"

"Weren't you upset?" She bit her lip.

"No. I understood. I'm just glad you're accepting it now."

She smiled. "You know, I think I am."

Chapter 20

HE evening of Katerina's twentieth birthday party began as she dressed in front of the mirror. The special dress she had ordered for the event fit like a glove from the rib cage up and floated away from the swell of her belly below, disguising the fact that she was past halfway through her pregnancy.

After this party, I'll have no choice but to enter confinement, and not attend any other public events until I recover from the delivery. It sounds rather boring, all in all, though Mother's promised to keep me company.

She ran a brush through her hair and began twisting it into a heavy coil at the back of her head.

I hope some of the young matrons will do the same. In particular, she had become close to Eliza Cary, née Carlisle, the pouting girl who liked pretty poetry. She and James had wed during the Bennetts' honeymoon. *Eliza still teases her husband mercilessly, but the gleam in his eyes tells me he doesn't mind one bit. Now she only uses the pout for effect.*

They had been invited to the party tonight, which was held at the elder Bennetts' home, rather than Katerina and Christopher's little townhouse. Also invited were Christopher's younger brother Devin, down for a visit from the university, Colin and his mother and stepfather, the Wilders, and the Reardons.

"Are you ready, love?" she called to Christopher, who was in the bathroom, shaving. "I'd rather not be late to my own party."

"Almost," he replied.

Katerina sighed in resignation.

* * *

Two hours later, after dinner, they proceeded to games, beginning with a rousing round of charades.

The Carys won handily, earning them the right to choose the next game.

"Let's play hide and seek," Eliza proposed. "The birthday girl should be it."

"Very well," Katerina agreed, feigning disappointment.

"I think I'll sit this one out," Julia said, subsiding onto a chase with a cup of tea. Her husband joined her, as did the Turners.

Katerina covered her eyes and began counting to one hundred. Fabric swished as her guests hurried out of the room. *I'm… having fun, she realized as she worked her way through the sixties. It would have seemed impossible six months ago.*

She flashed the elders a quick smile before heading out of the parlor to search for her guests. *Perhaps I can find my husband first, in some dark corner where I can let him steal a kiss before I continue stalking our friends.* It felt wonderful to be able to relax and be ridiculous.

With that thought in mind, she entered the front hallway, where a wide staircase in dark wood with a scarlet runner led to the second floor. *I'll begin here.*

"Katerina." A commanding voice spoke in a lilting Italian accent.

She froze like a small prey animal, poised between one step and the next. *No, I won't cower. I am not a rabbit. I am a woman and a wife, surrounded by friends. No one can hurt me now.* With slow deliberation, she straightened her spine and turned. "Father," she replied coolly in Italian, "what are you doing here?"

"Obviously there was some mistake," he drawled, gesturing with his hands. "I heard you were having a party, but my invitation didn't arrive."

She quirked an eyebrow. "There was no mistake. You were not invited. I do not want you here."

"I am your father, Katerina. That will never change," he said darkly.

"More's the pity," she replied, sarcasm dripping from her tone, "but no matter. I don't need a father."

Giovanni narrowed his eyes into a disapproving glare.

Katerina's stomach clenched, and her heart began to pound, but she refused to back down. She met his stern look with one of her own.

He pressed harder, trying to gain the upper hand. "I can't believe you ran away with that... cotton weaver. Have you no pride, girl?"

She snorted with derisive laughter. "I can't believe you would be surprised I did. Honestly, Father, I would have run away with a Gypsy if one had appeared at the right moment. How fortunate I was to find Christopher. He's very good to me, though I doubt you're concerned with *that*." Her hand fluttered around her belly in a telling though unconscious gesture.

He noticed. "Are you *incinta*? Already? What a whore. You're just like your mother."

She shook her head. "No, Father. Not a whore, a wife. It's my duty to provide children for my husband." Then she shook her head. "Do you know something? I really don't wish to talk to you anymore. This is not your home and you were not invited. I hate you. Get out." She dismissed him with a flamboyant hand gesture.

"Puttana," he yelled.

"Bastardo!" Katerina shot back.

There was no worse thing she could have said to her father. Sensitive to the fact that he was descended from an illegitimate line, royal though it might be, any question to his legitimacy made him wild. If she had slapped his face, it would have been no less effective.

Turning, she stalked up the stairs away from him, confident she was finally safe from him.

She was wrong.

With a cry of rage, Giovanni leaped into the room pounded up the stairs.

Out of the habit of protecting herself, Katerina took too long to react to the sudden movement, giving him time to grab the heavy coil of hair at the back of her head and pull hard.

She shrieked as she fell, thudding down three steps and landing on the wooden floor of the entryway. Her head slammed down hard. A crunching noise reverberated inside her skull, and stars bloomed in her field of vision. Unconsciousness threatened.

Hold on. Don't succumb. If you pass out, you're dead! Rolling painfully onto her side she curled into a ball, protecting her baby with her arms and legs and back.

A heavy boot connected with her spine.

She whimpered, and he kicked her again. The thick scars protected her somewhat from the blows, but she was getting badly bruised. More kicks rained out, colliding with her back, her arms. Stubbornly she clung to her protective posture... and to consciousness.

A hand coiled in her hair again, pulling her head back, and a meaty fist connected solidly with her nose. Blood sprayed and again blackness threatened. He dropped her, and her wounded skull collided with the floor.

This time, there was no escape. Her last sight as consciousness faded was a boot descending inexorably towards her unprotected belly...

* * *

Christopher stepped into the shadow near the stairs. *I'd like to be found quickly.* It was silly, but the potential for more fun pulling his wife into the corner with him proved irresistible. *Not that I need more, of course. We kissed for ages before leaving home. With Katerina, there's no such thing as too much.*

He heard her soft voice floating up from the parlor. "Ninety-eight, ninety-nine, one hundred."

Good, she's coming soon. He readied himself to pull her into the shadowy angle of the stairwell. *It's a risk, grabbing her without warning*, he thought. *I believe she's better enough to try it. Where is she? She should be up here by now.*

A low male voice filtered up to him, but he couldn't make out the words. *It doesn't sound like Father... perhaps Colonel Turner?*

Katerina answered, her voice hard and cold.

She would never talk to the colonel in such a sarcastic tone. I still can't make out the words... wait... The familiar rolling rhythm of Italian rose.

Oh God, no!

Only one person in all of London could speak Italian to his wife and receive such a harsh reply. Christopher hurried to the top of the stairs, horrified by a roar of masculine fury, a feminine shriek, and then a loud thud. Looking down, he could see his wife falling to the floor, her body tightly curled as her father kicked her over and over with his heavy boots.

"Help!" he shouted but had no idea whether anyone else could hear him. Despite descending the stairs at reckless speed but was unable to reach them before his father-in-law pulled back Katerina's head to deliver a massive blow to her unprotected face. As she lost consciousness, he stretched her out, preparing to stomp on her abdomen, on their baby.

"No!" Christopher roared, shoving the older man in the chest and knocking him backwards onto the floor.

"Christopher, what on earth?" Julia poked her face out of the parlor.

"Mother, get help, quickly!" he shouted.

"Oh, God." Julia fled.

Drawn by the noise, the guests poured into the room.

Giovanni rose to his feet, his rugged face a mask of pure rage. He approached Katerina again, but this time Christopher was ready for him. Stepping over his wife's prone body, he positioned himself between her and her father. Cold anger filled him until his blood flowed like ice in his veins. He moved forward. From the corner of his eye, he saw Mrs. Turner, guarded by her husband, picking her way across the room.

Christopher stepped forward again, closing the distance between him and Giovanni so he could draw the other man away from Katerina. "Get the hell away from my wife!" he bellowed.

"She is mine," the dark-haired man roared.

"She's not," Christopher snarled through his teeth.

"You stole her from me," Giovanni accused, pointing a finger into Christopher's chest.

"I saved her from you," Christopher corrected, crowding even closer to his adversary. He could hear his blood pounding in his head.

"Why?" Giovanni sneered.

"Because I love her, you miserable bastard! You could have killed her!" He dared a glance back towards his wife and his stomach clenched. *Don't lose control, Christopher. You can't help her if you're not thinking straight. Embrace the cold.*

"I am not a bastard!" Giovanni shrieked. "And she is mine. My child. My property. Mine she to discipline."

"Not anymore. Now she's mine to defend. You hurt my wife. My God, you could have hurt our baby." Christopher closed in on his adversary again. He didn't say another word. Instead, he drove a furious fist into Giovanni's jaw, quickly followed by another blow, this time to the gut.

Giovanni doubled over.

"Your wife's brother fought you when he was sixteen and won. He was a child, you fool, strong, but surely untrained and inexperienced. Let's see how you fare now."

An experienced fighter from his school days on, Christopher had studied pugilism for sport. He brought every one of those skills to bear now and inflicted on his father-in-law the thrashing of a lifetime. He kept hitting the older man long after he fell to the floor in surrender, submitting in terror to a shower of blows from which he could not escape.

Christopher's cold rage flared into heat, a fire that sought to consume his enemy until his lifeblood drained across the floor. He would undoubtedly have beaten Giovanni to death had not James and Colin finally pulled him back.

"That's enough, Chris," Colin said softly, "you'll kill him."

"He deserves it," Christopher snarled, wrenching his arms against his friends' grip.

"I know, but you need to stop," James urged.

"He hurt her!"

"He did," Colin agreed. "It's terrible. It should never have happened, but don't kill him. Don't become a murderer. Come, you need to see to your wife."

"What about this piece of shit?" Christopher poked at his father-in-law with his toe.

"I'll take care of him," James volunteered. "Go on, Chris. Katerina needs you."

"Listen now, Valentino." Standing menacingly over his father-in-law's twitching body, Christopher spoke in a voice cold enough to freeze a steam boiler. "If I *ever* see your sorry arse again, even by accident, you will die."

He let his friend lead him away.

* * *

James looked down at the beaten man and shook his head. He realized he had blood on his trousers. *Disgusting.*

"Well, Mister Valentine," he said sarcastically, intentionally mispronouncing his name, "you're certainly in a world of trouble now. I've never seen him this angry. You'd better get the hell out of England while you can and pray to God Katerina and the baby both come through, or I'm quite sure he will hunt you down to the ends of the earth and disembowel you alive. You know... there's a ship leaving for America in the morning. Maybe you should plan to be on it. Because I'm certain of one thing—he was not exaggerating. He *will* kill you if he gets the chance, and London isn't so big people can't meet by accident."

He hoisted the battered man to his feet. Blood poured from Giovanni's nose and mouth, and he spat a tooth onto the floor. He stared at James in silence.

"I would offer to pray for your soul," the young vicar said, "but I wouldn't be able to do it. I saw what you did to her too. Now get out."

James wrenched the door open and shoved Giovanni hard, sending him stumbling down the stairs to land in a crumpled heap on the sidewalk below.

He slammed the door and then hurried into the parlor, where a piteous tableau awaited. Katerina lay unconscious on the sofa. Christopher knelt beside her, clutching her hand to his cheek. Colonel Turner gingerly touched Katerina's head with one fingertip. "I hated to move her, not knowing how badly she's injured."

"I know, but it wasn't safe there, not with that fight going on," his wife replied, though she looked just as alarmed as her husband. She laid a hand on Katerina's belly, her focus shifting away from the conversation.

"Has anyone called for a doctor?" James asked.

"Yes. Your wife just went to send the housekeeper to fetch him," Mr. Bennett said.

"Good," Colonel Turner said. "I'm worried about her head injury."

Christopher looked up, tears streaming down his cheeks. "Why won't she wake up?"

"I'm afraid she's got a skull fracture," the colonel said, his face twisted with concern.

Christopher's face went ashen, which darkened the bruises on his cheek and jaw from the two blows Giovanni had managed to connect. "Oh my God. Will she live?"

"It depends on how bad it is," Turner replied grimly. "I've seen many of these in the cavalry... people thrown from horses or kicked. Some survived, but not all. Did you see how far she fell? Just from standing?"

"She was on the stairs," Christopher said. "She must have fallen three, maybe four steps before she hit the floor."

"Then we have another problem," Mrs. Turner said. "Falls in pregnancy can cause premature delivery. At only five months, if the baby is delivered now, there's no way it will survive. Did he do anything else to her?"

"He kicked her all over." Christopher's voice cracked and shattered.

"Her belly?" she queried.

"No. I stopped him before he could do that."

"Good. Listen, Christopher," she took his free hand and made him look up at her. "Katerina and the baby may both pull through this. It's in God's hands now. I suggest you pray like you've never prayed before. It's serious, but not hopeless."

"It was my job to protect her. I failed." He lowered his face again, as though unable to look away from his wife.

"How could you have known he would come here?" Adrian demanded, trying to break through Christopher's fixation.

"I should have guessed," Christopher snarled. "I instructed our servants at home to turn him away at all costs, but I didn't tell anyone here. I thought he had given up, that she was finally safe."

"Well, she's safe now," James said from the doorway.

All heads turned in his direction "How do you know?" Christopher demanded.

"After the drubbing you gave him? He's not stupid. I suggested he take the next ship to America. I'll check in the morning to be sure he's on it."

"What?" Christopher demanded, appalled. "You didn't call for the police?"

"Think, Christopher. You beat him to a bloody pulp. If the police came, whom would they be arresting? Not only him. Don't call for them. I think he's going to respect you now, and just go away."

"Or put a bullet in your back," Colin commented darkly.

Christopher didn't say a word. He leaned over and pressed his lips to his wife's face. Her blood smeared on his lips.

If her nose isn't broken, it would be a miracle, James thought.

No one spoke. They just stood by, supporting the couple as best they could. James put one hand on Christopher's shoulder. With the other, he pulled his wife close. Eliza wept softly into his shirt.

* * *

About half an hour later the doctor arrived. Christopher could barely take in the details of a small, dark-haired man in a black suit, but the white fingers compressing his wife's head remained emblazoned in his memory forever. "Fractured skull," he said at last, and Julia let out a low moan. The doctor sighed. "It's a significant break, but not necessarily fatal. The bone is cracked but not shattered and there's no depression."

"Will she live?" Christopher demanded.

"It's possible," the doctor allowed, "but I can't guarantee it. You see, it's not so much the break that presents a danger. Her brain hit her skull, not once but twice, from what you've told me. It's sure to swell. If it swells a little and then subsides, she'll live. If it swells more, she'll die." Though the words might have seemed brutal, he spoke them with sympathetic kindness.

Christopher ground his teeth.

"How much time has passed since the attack?" the doctor asked.

"About three-quarters of an hour," Colonel Turner replied, surprising Christopher. Between the battle rage and the utter fear, time had changed its course in Christopher's mind. *I thought it was less... or more. I'm not sure.* Confused, he blinked as the men kept talking.

"Her best outcome will result from moving her as little as possible. The last thing we want is to exacerbate the swelling," the doctor informed them.

"Well, she can certainly stay here as long as she needs," Julia volunteered, and her husband concurred with a nod.

The doctor acknowledged their offer with a dip of his chin. "Wait a while. At least an hour. Then, if nothing has changed, move her slowly to the bedroom. Can anyone assess her condition?"

"I can," Colonel Turner replied. "I became a sort of a de facto medic when I was in the infantry, though I certainly didn't expect to assess war wounds in London... on a woman."

The comment incited grim silence. Christopher gulped. *It was a war. I won, but that doesn't matter. None of it matters if Katerina...* his mind veered off, unwilling to finish the terrible thought.

"I'll come back tomorrow and check on her," the doctor said. "If something happens, call for me, though—I'm sorry to say this—if she takes a turn for the worse, there's really nothing I can do for her. It's in God's hands now."

Eliza Cary sobbed, and Julia sniffled.

The doctor rose, patted Christopher hard on the shoulder, and removed himself from the room.

Gloomy silence entombed the formerly cheerful partygoers again.

"Let's pray," James suggested. As one they moved to form a circle, surrounding Christopher and his wife and grasped hands. "Lord..." he began, but his sonorous preaching voice wavered, and when he continued, it was in a quieter, more subdued tone. "Lord, heal Katerina, protect the baby and strengthen Christopher." He made a choking sound. "Amen." After a shaky breath, he added, "Sorry, Christopher. I just... I didn't know what else to say. Some vicar I am."

"It's enough that you're here," Christopher replied, speaking without reflection, directly from the heart. "You've been here through so much, helped so much. Thank you, my friend."

The reply James made sounded something like a mixture of grunt, sob and sigh. As the circle broke up, he made his way to Christopher and clasped his shoulder. "I'll keep praying."

Christopher responded with a dip of his head; his voice had finally failed him.

As before, the hour passed in agonizing slow motion, and yet when the clock chimed, it startled him.

Colonel Turner approached and knelt before the unconscious woman, checking her breathing, her eyes and her pulse. "She seems the same," he said, sighing with relief.

Christopher nodded. "I'll take her upstairs. What bedroom, Mother?"

"Take her to your old room," Julia replied.

For reasons he couldn't fathom, the suggestion twisted Christopher's heart. "I... uh... all right."

"We'll just go now," Cary said. "There's nothing more we can do here. I'll keep praying, Christopher. I swear it."

"I know," he replied. "Go on. Thank you for... for everything." He bowed his head as agony closed in on him again.

James paused as though uncertain how to continue. Then he dragged his friend to his feet and crushed him in a hard hug.

Through swimming eyes, Christopher regarded his friend. *He's gone beyond anything I ever expected,* he realized. *I underestimated him.*

As James and his wife trailed out, the sound of her soft crying echoing down the hallway, Christopher eased Katerina into his arms.

"I'll come up and check on her shortly," Mrs. Turner told him, her voice calmly compassionate.

He acknowledged her with a glance before making his slow way into the hall. To reach the stairs, he had to pass the entryway, and the blood on the floor raised a gag in his throat. *Dear Lord, how could this have happened?*

Never have stairs been climbed as slowly and carefully as Christopher did carrying his injured wife. It seemed to take a year before he reached the top. He progressed across polished floorboards, past the place where, only a short time before, he'd lain in wait to capture his wife with naughty kisses. *Will I ever kiss her again, and feel her shy, eager response?*

He turned right down a long hallway of bedrooms, hardly noticing the gleaming wainscoting on the walls, the cream-colored plaster, the painted portraits of the family hung in gilded frames. His whole attention remained riveted on the door at the far end. *She's never seen my room.* The thought struck him as odd. This woman, who now reigned as queen over his heart, had never seen the bedroom where he'd spent his childhood. He opened the door and stepped in.

Christopher tenderly laid his wife on the bed and collected water and a cloth to bathe her face. Her nose had stopped bleeding, and she looked better, though bruised, once cleaned up. He stood slowly and looked down at her.

I promised her, damn it. Promised she was safe, trained her to be safe, and in so doing I left her vulnerable to another attack. His breath caught in a harsh sob. A little sizzle of pain shot through his hand and he frowned to see his sore, oozing and split-open knuckles. He had damaged them... all over his father-in-law's face. *Shouldn't I feel something about that? Regret? Pride? Something?* Only numbness sank heavy over his heart, in contrast to the stinging of his torn skin.

"You need to clean that," his mother said matter-of-factly, as though she were not looking over the hand that had just beaten a man bloody.

"What am I going to do, Mother?" he asked, his voice breaking again.

"Endure. Pray." She hugged him tight, stroking his back.

"Do you think she'll live?" *Katerina, please pull through, my darling.*

"I hope so, son. I hope so."

By the time Mrs. Turner arrived, Christopher's knuckles had been bathed, and he had changed his wife into a loose cotton nightgown. He lay beside her, holding her hand and murmuring in her ear.

Mrs. Turner sat on the bed beside Katerina and pulled the covers down. She lifted the nightgown. "I don't see any blood or amniotic fluid on Katerina's thighs or privates," she informed him. "Her cervix is tightly shut." Then the midwife settled her hand on the swell of her client's belly. "The child is moving," she added, "and there are no contractions."

"Well?" Christopher demanded, "what does that mean?"

"I can't tell you about her head injury, but at this point, I see no signs of impending miscarriage. If she survives, the child should be fine," the midwife informed him.

"Thank God." He touched his lips to his wife's temple.

"I'm so very sorry, Christopher." She patted his hand. "The poor girl. No one deserves that."

"I'm such an ass. I was so proud of myself, proud of my sacrifice. I saved her. That's what I told everyone. But I was the one who put her in danger." His unsteady voice broke several times.

"No. You rescued her from danger," Julia insisted. "It's not your fault it followed her."

"I couldn't get there in time." He ground his teeth.

"I know." Mrs. Turner laid a soothing hand on his arm.

"Why did this happen?" he exclaimed, and his angry shout caused Katerina to twitch, though she made no further sign of waking up. "Hasn't she suffered enough?"

"She has, son," said a deep voice from the doorway.

"Father?"

Adrian crushed his son in a tight hug. "Remember, Christopher, she suffered for years. With you, she was happy. You gave her the best months of her life, and, God willing, you will again."

"Are you still sorry I married her?" he asked in a tentative plea for his father's approval.

"No. Why would I be? My concern was that she was too damaged to love you. Clearly, that wasn't the case."

"No. She loved me, Father. She truly did." He met his father's eyes and saw that tears shone there.

"I know," Adrian said softly.

Christopher's vision blurred. Hot tears clogged his throat. "I love her so much," he said raggedly.

Adrian gripped his shoulder. "I know you do, and she knows it too. If anything can pull her through this, it will be your love."

Christopher's crumbling composure cracked. He sank onto a chair beside his bed, taking his wife's hand. His mother gripped one shoulder, his father the other, while his grief poured from him, unchecked and unstoppable.

* * *

In the morning, Katerina still breathed but remained unconscious. The doctor checked her and found no change for good or ill. Mrs. Turner examined her also and found her pregnancy still holding, the baby still moving appropriately in its mother's body. There was nothing to do but wait. And so, they waited. In the early afternoon, she finally stirred, eyelids fluttering.

"Kat, can you hear me, love?"

A soft exhalation of breath escaped her.

"Kat?"

Her dark eyes opened.

"Oh God, no!" Christopher exclaimed. Katerina was alive, awake, but that spark, that warmth that made her the woman he loved, the awareness, the sentience was gone.

Katerina was gone.

Chapter 21

HE was gone, the family soon realized, deep inside herself. Her eyes didn't focus. She didn't react to speech or stimulation. She would swallow water dribbled into her mouth, but not food. She took no nourishment, and she gave no sign whatsoever of awareness.

Three days crept past and she remained in this suspended state. On the afternoon of the third day, the doctor examined her thoroughly.

"Can you do anything?" Christopher pleaded.

"No. I'm sorry."

"Is this the fracture?" Christopher asked.

"No. She's withdrawn," the doctor explained. "The fact she's awake at all means the fracture likely isn't going to kill her. Not this many days later. That would have happened much sooner. The broken bone will heal in the next six to eight weeks. However, if she doesn't wake up and begin eating soon, healing won't matter. She'll just... fade. And only she can change it."

"So, this is a mental break?" Christopher gulped.

"Yes."

"Do you think she'll come out of it?" he asked. *Please, please let her come out of it.*

"Hard to say," the doctor replied. "It's up to her at this point. I'll just go now. She can hear you if she decides to listen. I think talking to her might be her best hope. Keep trying. Don't give up."

So, they talked, and talked, and talked, trying to break through, trying to get her to listen and engage. By the end of the fifth day after the attack, their hope began to fade.

Adrian dragged his son to the guest room and forced him to lie down and rest. Julia remained with her daughter-in-law.

"Katerina," she said softly, "that's enough, love. You need to come back to us. You need to wake up. Your baby needs you. Your husband needs you. We all love you. Can't you wake up?"

The girl stirred.

Julia held her breath. *How I love this girl. I chose her for my son, and not just because of the danger. I wanted Katerina for myself, to be my own daughter, and now, there's a real chance that both she and the baby she's carrying will die. Lord, why? You took my daughter when she was six. Will you really take this one too? Must you? Please let her live, let them both live.*

Katerina rolled to her side and closed her eyes.

Exhausted, strained to the breaking point, Julia's temper flared. "You selfish girl. You can't do this. You can't just give up. If you die, your baby dies with you. Stop this. Wake up and fight to live, Kat. Your life is not over."

"Mother, stop," Christopher said from the doorway where he leaned against the doorjamb.

"I was trying to break through, to wake her up," Julia said, trying to defend her harsh words.

"I know," he replied, "but maybe it's too much to ask. She's been so hurt for so long. Perhaps she finally reached her limit. Who are we to say she's being selfish? She's already endured more than anyone should have to. It might be asking more than she has to give."

"Do you want her to 'fade' Christopher?" his mother demanded, fresh anger flaring.

"Of course not," he replied, "but I can't choose for her."

"Do you understand, son, that if she dies, your child dies with her?"

"Yes, Mother. I understand. I would lose them both." His breath shuddered in his throat.

"And then we would lose you, wouldn't we, son?"

Christopher didn't answer.

"Damn you, Katerina, wake up." Julia shook the girl's arm sharply.

"Enough, Mother. Enough. Please, just go."

Unable to think of anything else to say or do, Julia walked unsteadily down to the parlor where she cuddled up with her husband and wept.

* * *

Christopher crawled into the bed beside Katerina and slid his arm under her, cradling her. He turned her towards him.

With his free hand, he traced the curve of her cheek, the fullness of her lip, the line of her nose. *She's so beautiful, like an angel. I love her with every fiber of my being, and I will lose her. I'm already losing her. How can I live without this woman who warmed my life, my body, and my heart?* The future stretched before him, cold and empty.

"Don't go away, love," he begged her. "Don't go where I can't find you. Come back."

Tears fell and splashed on her face.

* * *

Katerina had been wrapped in a silver mist for the longest time. She burrowed into it like a comforting blanket and hid. If she emerged from the shadows, something so horrible, so excruciating awaited her that she would die in agony.

Better just to let go slowly. Nothing hurts here, in the mist, in the darkness. Hunger didn't bite at her and pain didn't assault her. She was numb and content to remain so until numbness dissolved into death. *Yes. That's the way to go. Just slowly release life. Release.* It was easy to die. Simple. She was vaguely aware of people talking around her, trying to encourage her to engage, but she could ignore them as easily as a housefly buzzing against a windowpane. *What does their struggle have to do with me? Nothing.*

Something wet hit her cheek. She had been bathed enough times and could ignore it, but this was not bathing. Another drop splashed on her skin. *It's like warm rain. What is this?* Curiosity awakened within the mist. She wanted to know what was happening. The darkness would still be there if she roused herself for a second, just to understand. Another drop. Another rained on her.

She struggled to engage, to move up through the numbness back into her body and into awareness. *There are arms holding me. I know these arms, but how? They mean something. They've held me before, and it was always good.*

She emerged more fully into reality and saw the face. Handsome, chiseled face, scruffy, unshaven, eyes tightly shut, tears dripping from beneath the lids onto her.

He was crying. Crying on her. The hot rain of his tears fell, streaking across her skin and burning her. They forced her to increasing awareness. *I know this man, know his body, his heart and soul*

The darkness beckoned, receding. If she wanted to withdraw with it, she needed to do it now, because life was taking hold of her again. She could feel it. It would hurt. She didn't want to hurt. She wanted peace.

But why is he crying? What made this beautiful man so sad?

She retreated, or she tried, but his voice tempted her back as he sobbed one word over and over. "Katerina, Katerina."

That's my name. Is he really crying over me?

Despite her desire for oblivion, she couldn't leave him in such pain. She tried to think of a word that would help. *What is it?*

"Christopher?" her voice sounded rusty and harsh. The darkness retreated further. She tried to hold onto it, but it slipped away from her.

Silver eyes opened and seemed to sink into her soul, snaring her and anchoring her to reality. "Kat?"

She had to choose. The darkness would soon be gone, leaving her stranded here where everything hurt. But here also was Christopher, hurting and crying. *How can I leave him in such pain?*

The beautiful face drew close to her. Soft full lips touched hers, and that touch was pure light, obliterating the last of the darkness.

She flared to life again, at last fully present.

He crushed her to him, sobbing in relief.

She cuddled in his arms, liking the connection to this man. *My hero. My husband. The father of my child.*

At last, she remembered the terror that stalked her. "Chris..." Her breath caught as agonized horror broke over her.

"Yes, love?" Pure tenderness poured from his tone.

"The baby. Did the baby survive? No, it's not possible. I'm sorry. I tried to stay awake and protect the baby, but Father hit me so hard. I couldn't stay awake, I..."

"No," Christopher protested, interrupting her. "The baby is fine."

She swallowed hard, forcing down her tears. "What? How? He... he stomped..."

"I stopped him," Christopher explained. "I was just at the top of the stairs. I'm sorry I didn't get there in time to stop him from hitting you, but he never got to the baby. You've been checked several times and there's no sign of problems." He placed her hand on her belly, so she could feel the little movements.

Her mouth opened. "Fine?"

"Yes."

"Oh, thank the Lord. Thank you, Christopher. I was so afraid... I said I didn't want a baby... But now I do... I couldn't bear the thought that..." she stammered.

"No. That didn't happen."

She nodded, exhaling in relief. "Father?"

"Gone. On a boat to America. We're safe from him."

"Good."

He cupped her cheek. "Oh, Kat, are you really back with me?"

"I think so." Now that her fears were relieved, the pain in her head and muscles and the empty ache in her stomach blossomed to life.

"Thank God. I was so worried." He kissed her lips again.

She tried to pull him closer.

"Easy, love. You have to be still."

Sharp pain speared through her. "My head hurts."

"No doubt. You have a fractured skull, but it's healing."

"That explains why I'm so dizzy."

"It might also be hunger. You haven't eaten in days. Can you stand to eat, love?"

"I think so, but you'll have to help me. I... I can't sit up."

"Of course. Kat?"

"Hmmm?"

"I love you." He rose and rang for a maid, his eyes remaining fixed on his wife as he waited. She gazed back, feeding her fragile soul with the pure love flowing between them.

A middle-aged woman in a dressing gown poked her head in the door and beamed to see the young woman finally awake.

"Could you get my wife some broth and some tea, please," Christopher asked.

The woman nodded and hurried from the room. Her boots clattered on the wooden floorboards in the hallway.

She tried to swallow, but her dry throat turned it into a cough. Christopher poured a glass of cool water from a pitcher on the table by the bed. Then he sank back onto the mattress beside her and helped her sit partially upright against a pile of pillows behind her back, so he could raise it to her lips.

She took a deep sip. "Can you forgive me, love?" she asked, finally fully awake.

"For what?" he asked.

"The attack. It was my fault." She closed her eyes as a tear slipped down her cheek.

"How?" he asked, puzzled.

"I didn't hide. I told him... I didn't want to see him. I told him to go away."

"But that's good, love," he assured her, stroking her hair. "It means you're finally getting strong."

"It made him so angry."

"And I wasn't there to protect you." Now Christopher looked ashamed.

"Yes, you were. You stopped him. You're my hero again." She touched his cheek with one delicate hand.

"I'm no hero," he protested. "Just a husband who adores his wife. You're the brave one."

"But I'm not brave. Not without you." She stroked her thumb over the scruff on his cheeks.

He covered her hand with his. "Then be with me."

How could I have ever wanted anything else? "Oh yes. I'm here now. I'm sorry I went away."

He smoothed an errant lock from the tangled mass of her hair and looked tenderly into her eyes. "You came back. That's what matters."

"I love you, Christopher. There's no place I would rather be than here."

"I'm so very glad."

He brushed his lips against hers in a kiss of such aching tenderness that she was finally able to release the terror in a flood of wracking sobs that shook her slender frame, but she was not alone. She was part of something bigger than herself. She was part of Christopher, and he was part of her, and both of them were part of the child she carried.

Now, at last, she could finally finish healing and make herself into the woman she had always wanted to be, and he would be here with her.

She was finally safe.

Afterward

Dear Reader,

I hope you have enjoyed the time you have spent with the Bennetts. If you did, I would appreciate it if you would head over to Amazon and leave me a review. I also love to hear from readers. If you have any questions, comments, or issues, or if you just want to get in touch, you can email me at simonebeaudelaireauthor@hotmail.com.

Keeping Katerina is intended to be part of a three-book series. Book 2, Devin's Dilemma, is also available. Turn the page to read an excerpt from chapter 1. Book 3, Colin's Conundrum, is written and should be released in early 2020.

You can also check out my website http://simonebeaudelaire.com to see my upcoming writing projects and works by other notable authors.

Historical Note

The Victorian era was a time of dawning awareness of the rights of the poor and disenfranchised, as evidenced by Robert Browning's poems, as well as by the passage of several laws intended to improve the lives of the working poor, particularly children. And after all, socially conscious middle-class families like the Bennetts could hardly be expected to own anything else, right?

Robert Browning, who is one of my all-time favorite poets, is famous for his marriage to the poetess Elizabeth Barrett, who during her lifetime was far more famous than her husband. Her father, like Giovanni Valentino, did not want his daughters to marry. However, it is not generally believed he was abusive. Just possessive. When Robert and Elizabeth married in secret, they returned to their separate homes after the wedding and later ran away to Florence, where they lived happily together for several years, and had a son. While living in Italy, Robert encountered many works of art and wrote about the artists: Fra Lippo Lippi and Andrea del Sarto, for instance. And Browning's poetry *was* hated at first. It was only later that people began to appreciate his vision.

The cotton mills of the Victorian period were well known to be horrible places: hot, dangerous, and prone to employing small children, who often died or were maimed. No precautions were taken to protect these small and vulnerable workers. There was no health or life insurance. Of course, a progressive family like the Bennetts would not allow such things. This wasn't unheard of at the time, but it was rare.

Bullying is quite a buzzword these days and thus might seem like a modern term. However, the concept is not new. People have been bullied forever, and the term first appeared in print in the 1500s.

Child abuse has been a scourge of society for a very long time, but in the early Victorian period, people were becoming increasingly aware that such things happened and were debating how to deal with it. I wish I could say the problem has been effectively dealt with, but that would be too great a piece of fiction.

Excerpt from Devin's Dilemma (The Victorians Book 2)

Simone Beaudelaire

Chapter 1

"Harry! Harry, please come here. I need you."

With a sigh, Harry put her book aside and rose to stand. Her feet ached in her cousin's too-large boots and her second-hand petticoats drooped to the floor. *I have to make time to alter this monstrosity.* But she knew better. The petticoat had been tripping her for months, and yet, when she had a chance, it was a novel, not a needle, that drew her attention.

"Harry, please hurry!"

Harry hurried down the hall from her small bedroom under the eaves to her cousin's larger room on the second floor, careful to keep her noisy boots confined to the soft black and red runner, lest they boom like thunder on the floorboards. A racket like that would certainly draw Uncle Malcolm's attention... again. *That's the last thing I want.*

She wrestled the cranky crystal knob on her cousin's bedroom door until the catch conceded to release and slipped into the room.

"What is it, Fanny?" she asked. But even as she spoke, Harry knew the answer. Her cousin, Fanny, stood in the center of her room in her underwear, muttering under her breath as she laced her corset to the carved mahogany bedpost. Her pale forehead shone with sweat and her black hair clung to it.

"Fanny, stop," Harry urged. "We tightened that thing already, remember? You don't need to do that."

"It's not enough," Fanny whined, her rosebud lip poking out into a pout.

"Why not?" Harry crossed the floor and smoothed Fanny's hair back. "It's not necessary to turn yourself inside out, you know. You have an enviable figure. Why tight-lace?"

Fanny looked down at her generous bosom, her tiny waist, artificially narrowed by years of tight-lacing, and her perfect, round hips. "Once William proposes to me, then I'll loosen my laces, but until then... I can't let my guard down. What if I have to make another match?"

Harry closed her eyes and took a deep breath. Her own, much looser-fitting garment restricted her, but not to the point of dizziness. "You won't," she insisted. "William adores you. He has your father's permission to court you. You'll be his bride before you know it, but what happens if you pass out tonight? You'll miss all the fun, and they'll have to loosen your laces anyway."

Fanny's pout in no way diminished. "That's easy enough for you to say. You don't have to worry about finding a worthy husband."

Harry bit her lip. "You're right." *And how kind of you to remind me I've gone from a poor relation with few prospects to a domestic with none.* Then she sighed. Fanny's comment had not been made from cruelty. "At any rate, I still think you'll be fine with it the way we had it. And you won't need to worry. Heaven forbid if something were to happen to William, you'd have a line of suitors waiting to claim you whether you tight-lace or not."

"Do you really think so?" Fanny's huge blue eyes widened until they seemed to swallow up all of her pale, heart-shaped face.

"I know so," Harry replied, patting her cousin's shoulder. "Now, why not bathe your face in some cool water and let's get you dressed. You have a big night tonight."

Fanny beamed, no doubt thinking of her beloved William, and Harry relaxed. Her cousin's obsession with her looks bothered the bookish young woman, but she had to admit, they were more likely to win her a comfortable existence than any tome ever written. *It's not like you would have been popular anyway, Harry Fletcher. Not with your...* she let the dangerous thought trail off. Taking slow, deliberate steps, carefully placing her boots on the floorboards so as to avoid stomping, she approached an ornately-carved wooden wardrobe. Red-paneled doors gave way to rows of hanging dresses, each one worth far more than she earned in a year. Harry pulled out the midnight blue and lace ball gown her cousin had commissioned for tonight's dinner.

"It's dreadfully hot," Fanny commented as she splashed cold water on her face.

"It is," Harry agreed, carefully removing the dress from the wardrobe and laying it out on the gold brocade bedclothes. "Did your father say when we're leaving?"

"To Brighton?" Fanny turned away from the ewer on her mirrored commode and approached the window, parting the curtains a crack to peer out onto the loud and dusty street. "He said it depends on me. If I can bring William up to scratch in the next week or so, we'll have to wait until all the arrangements are made. Otherwise, we'll leave next week, and he'll have to catch up with us there... or wait until next season."

Harry grimaced. Fanny certainly would not like either of those options. *I suspect there's to be a great deal of pouting in my future.*

Fanny turned from the window and Harry carried the corset to her, settling it around Fanny's perfect figure and beginning the laborious fastening process. *Thank goodness she didn't tighten it more. That can't be healthy.* But Fanny didn't worry about her health, only about her beauty, so Harry had no choice but to accommodate her.

* * *

Devin tossed the document onto his desk with a sigh, then threw his hands into the air, upsetting a cup of tea, which spilled over his paperwork.

"Damnation," he growled, flinging himself to his feet and sweeping away as much of the tepid beverage as he could before it stained the wood. The will he'd been drafting was ruined and he'd have to start over. "I love my job. I love my job. I LOVE my job!" he reminded himself. "Anything is better than that noisy, sweaty factory with Father and Chris telling me what to do."

Taking a deep breath, Devin screwed up the paper and tossed it into the bin. *At least you didn't upset the inkwell, dolt.* Too aggravated with himself to restart the document that had taken him several hours to prepare, Devin rose carefully, managing for once to avoid hitting his head on one of the low rafters and ducked into the out-of-doors in search of a cup of tea that didn't endanger his paperwork.

Exiting his place of business—little more than a box hung with brown brocade curtains—Devin blinked in the sparkling June sunlight and rambled down a street lined cheek by jowl on one side with a row of brightly colored but narrow homes.

On the opposite side, adjacent to the building in which his office formed a small portion of the first floor, other shops and businesses competed with each other by decorating picture windows with gaudy displays of lace, hats, toys, cigarettes, and other goods and services, just waiting for the first influx of holidaymakers from London.

Après moi, le déluge, Devin thought irreverently. Not that he was going anywhere. His business remained fairly steady regardless of the socialites who tended to flood Brighton after Midsummer's Eve.

Only a week to go now. A week and the lovely solitude of the coast, which refreshed him after long hours hunched over his too-small desk in the semi-darkness, would be crowded with pretty and expensive-looking young ladies, trying desperately to be noticed by a gentleman who was titled, wealthy, young, handsome and kind. In short, a phantasm.

Devin sighed again, the cool ocean breeze insufficient to lift his melancholy. *Only a week until that damned Sir Fletcher will arrive and demand his will… which I just ruined. If he likes it, all's well and I can draw up a marriage contract for his daughter. If not, I'll lose the most lucrative client I've ever had.* Recalling the pressure that cramped his back and hands until he felt as though he'd tripled his twenty-five years, Devin's comforting sunlit walk began to feel like a dangerous indulgence. *Must get back to the will.* Ducking into his favorite tea house, he took a seat and awaited the arrival of the owner, his favorite lusty widow, Mrs. Murphy. As he waited, he scanned the stuffy interior. Suffocating pink striped fabrics billowed from the tables and clustered around the windows, as though trying to smother the diners with their alaire

Chaptggressive cheer.

Sure enough, Margaret Murphy arrived at his side in a moment, with two cups of steaming tea and a plate of scones.

"Hullo, Mr. Bennett," she said in the impartial, businesslike voice that always startled him as she took a seat by his side. *How can such a passionate person feign coolness so well?*

"Mrs. Murphy," he replied in a parody of blandness.

Her emerald eyes twinkled with humor at their discreet exchange.

"How goes the legal world?" she trilled in her captivating brogue.

"Well enough," he replied, not wanting to talk shop, "and the world of business?"

"Slow." She sighed. "I'm looking forward to next week, even if I do have to work like a dog when they come."

"I understand," he replied. His eyes dropped to the hint… well, more than a hint… of cleavage revealed by her replica of a fashionable dress, and then returned to her eyes. He drank his tea and nibbled the scone while their gazes spoke words that could not be uttered in public.

"Will you be needing any help with the pavers in your garden tonight?" he asked at last, in an undertone, though the only other patron in the shop was an old woman so deaf, even shouting failed to capture her attention.

"Yes, I think so," Mrs. Murphy replied, biting her lip to contain a laugh. "An old widow like me should count herself blessed to have such a tall, strong young friend to help me with my gardening."

Gardening? Is that what we're calling it now? Devin grinned. *No seeds will be sown, to be sure, but no matter. It's as good a metaphor as any.*

"I'd better get back to work," he said, setting aside his cup. The scone, though flaky and tender as always, had seemed to stick in his throat, and lay half-eaten on the plate.

Mrs. Murphy nodded, frowning at the abandoned pastry.

"I'll see you at seven."

He winked at her, restoring her grin, and left the shop. *Finish that will, Bennett, and you'll earn a relaxing turn in the sheets with your favorite redhead.* Grinning, he ambled back down the sunny street and into his office, where his now-dry desk awaited. *I will finish this time.*

Books by Simone Beaudelaire

When the Music Ends (The Hearts in Winter Chronicles Book 1)
When the Words are Spoken (The Hearts in Winter Chronicles Book 2)
When the Heart Heals (The Hearts in Winter Chronicles Book 3)
Caroline's Choice (The Hearts in Winter Chronicles Book 4)
The Naphil's Kiss
Blood Fever
Polar Heat
Xaman (with Edwin Stark)
Darkness Waits (with Edwin Stark)
Watching Over the Watcher
Baylee Breaking
Amor Maldito: Romantic Tragedies from Tejano Folklore
Keeping Katerina (The Victorians Book 1)
Devin's Dilemma (The Victorians Book 2)
Colin's Conundrum (The Victorians Book 3)
High Plains Holiday (Love on the High Plains Book 1)
High Plains Promise (Love on the High Plains Book 2)
High Plains Heartbreak (Love on the High Plains Book 3)
High Plains Passion (Love on the High Plains Book 4)
Devilfire (American Hauntings Book 1)
Saving Sam (The Wounded Warriors Book 1 with J.M. Northup)
Justifying Jack (The Wounded Warriors Book 2 with J.M. Northup)

Making Mike (The Wounded Warriors Book 3 with J.M Northup)

The story continues in:
Devin's Dilemma by Simone Beaudelaire

To read the first chapter for free, head to:
https://www.nextchapter.pub/books/devins-dilemma-regency-romance

Printed in Great Britain
by Amazon

39097696R00156